The Magical Diaries of Char

Copyright © [2023] by [G.S. Tabberner]

All rights reserved.

No part of this publication may be reproduced, distributed, or transmitted in any form or by any means, including photocopying, recording, or other electronic or mechanical methods, without the prior written permission of the publisher, except as permitted by U.S. copyright law. For permission requests, contact [include publisher/author contact info].

The story, all names, characters, and incidents portrayed in this production are fictitious. No identification with actual persons (living or deceased), places, buildings, and products is intended or should be inferred.

First edition [2023]

Dedication

To my wife, Jenn, first and foremost, for letting me be myself. And to my daughter, Kim, for being herself. I would also like to express my sincere gratitude to author Jerri Schlenker for her invaluable insights and proficiency. Thank you.

The Magical Diaries of Charles Lester Seymour
Chapter One

She melted away into the early evening with the child swaddled and crying beneath her hooded cloak. Leaving the large house behind, she left the gravel drive and kept to the shadows of the trees that ran alongside. She would have preferred to wait until dark, but Beattie insisted. He reminded her of the child's mother and her dying words. There was no time for hesitation. If she were to leave, it would have to be now. She grabbed what she could carry while Beattie gathered the child and some blankets. Within minutes, she was gone, with no plan or providence, just a desperate need to escape. Beattie had pushed an envelope into her pocket as he hugged her tenderly and then ushered her away without a word. Grief and worry lined his already furrowed features. She hurried between the house and the gated entrance, not stopping to glance behind her. Emerging from the trees, she hastened through the gates and turned left toward the village. From there, she could find transportation to somewhere safe.

She feared using the road. It would be safer to stay in the shadows of the outlining trees, keeping the road in sight. When she felt she was at a safe distance, she stopped to gather her wits. Plunging her free hand into her pocket out of the chill autumn air, she found the crushed envelope Beattie had deposited. She could feel the contents through the thin paper envelope. Money. A substantial amount if the weight was anything to go by. Putting the envelope inside the child's wrappings, she continued her flight while the twilight turned to dusk. Her first instinct was to flee as far from here as she could get, but where? The father's solicitor, Fairbourne, had the resources to find her almost anywhere in the world if he desired. And what of the girl child? She could not flee with both children for many reasons, forcing her to choose between them. The mother did not say why exactly, but she had the strongest feeling that the boy was in the most danger. Beattie would make provision for the girl, she had no doubt, but with whom? She was the only member of staff he had confided in. His loyalty to the family was beyond question or honour, but even he was concerned for the newborn twins. "The master had become unpredictable," he said. "Unpredictable and spiteful." The deeper his grief, the more malevolent he became.

He had seemed to grieve long before she died, but for what or whom she could not say. Only that this last crushing loss seemed to push him over some kind of threshold, from which she saw no way of returning.

Before she died, the mother had held the two babies close, whispering to them even as her life's blood drained from her, before handing them to Beattie and extracting his promise that they would be made safe. Only then did she succumb to her weakness. Her eyes drifted to somewhere far away as she whispered something in her native Welsh tongue before they closed forever.

She had seen and heard enough during her employment to know that something was shared between the children's parents. Some secret that only they were part of. It had brought them together like magnets and then pushed them apart. But the result of this union was two perfectly beautiful twins. Born out of tragedy, they were perhaps the only good thing that came from her time in the big house. Beattie had asked her to write him when she was settled so that he could provide her with a monthly stipend for them both, but she would not risk being discovered. The boy would have a happy, secure life; she would see to that, but he would never learn of his parents. Not from her. Not while she lived. The lights from the village loomed out of the darkness now. She had decided on her destination. She would have to wait a while for the last bus, but that was a risk she must take, and so she kept to the shadows. As long as she did not draw undue attention, she could slip away to safety, using her mother's maiden name from now on. She would decide on the boy's name during the journey home. Instead of Blodwen Huws, she would be Blodwyn Trevelyan.

∞∞∞∞∞

Charles Lester Seymour watched from the window as the housekeeper stole away with the child. It was no more than he had expected. Perhaps they had done the right thing. Gods rarely made good fathers. They lacked the moral aptitude for such endeavours. Having turned from the window, he poured himself a drink and sat at his desk in the library. He took the journals out of the drawer and added the last entry. He then locked the journals in his desk drawer and entered the nook. Seymour placed the keys in the smaller desk drawer and closed the door behind him as he left.

It would be decades before he was ready to put his plan into action. He would set the board during those long years of waiting and prepare the pieces. He must arrange an appointment with Fairbourne regarding the boy's future. After all, he would be the only male descendent of the long line of Seymour's. It was imperative that the boy inherit. His entire strategy depended on it. That was the first thing. The journals. They would be the key. If the boy grew to be anything like Seymour himself, or indeed his mother, he would not be able to resist the pull. The seduction would be irresistible to one such as him. The girl child was inconsequential. He had no use for her. She would be put up for anonymous adoption, having no part to play in his charade.

Next, he would need to ascend and prepare the other place. Only two people knew of its existence. And Morgan was dead. It was his alone now. But he had time. And patience. And cunning. It was the last that shocked him the most. His cunning. His desire to control this new Eden was as desolate as it was exhilarating. He refilled his glass, returned to his desk chair, and watched the sky darken as he considered his manipulations carefully.

Chapter Two

There are moments in time that can completely change the course of our lives and of which we are entirely unaware. Sitting in the waiting room, Gafyn Trevelyan, unaware of his pending moment, closed his eyes and listened to the rhythmic tap, tap, tap of the receptionist's false fingernails on her keyboard. He had already waited half an hour for this mysterious appointment, and only curiosity kept him in the seat, overwhelming the impatience that urged him to leave and make his way home. In the years to come, He often wondered where his life may have led to, if his impatience had won the day and led him home.

The receptionist said in a tired, expressionless voice, "Mr Fairbourne will see you now," She pointed to the door to her left.

Trevelyan rose and strode into the solicitor's office, almost colliding with Mr. Fairbourne as he made his way to greet him. Fairbourne clasped his free hand over Trevelyan's while still shaking like an overly pleasant stranger or an old friend, leaving him feeling uncomfortable. Fairbourne dressed immaculately in a suit and waistcoat with an air of confidence and seniority that completed the almost cliché appearance of a successful solicitor in his early sixties. Only his Masonic dress tie betrayed the illusion that he was about anything other than the business at hand.

"Please take a seat," he said as he motioned Trevelyan towards his desk. Fairbourne positioned himself on the other side and sat down. "I apologise for your overdue appointment, Mr. Trevelyan, but I had to make sure I had all the facts at hand regarding my instructions, paperwork, and such. All appears to be in order, so I suppose you must be wondering what this is all about." His eyebrows rose as he spoke.

"I must admit," said Trevelyan as he smiled, "I have been more than a little intrigued since your correspondence". Fairbourne smiled back, trying to hide his indifference, but then he caught himself short and continued.

"Then let's get straight to it, shall we?" He shuffled the papers before him, his eyes darting through the contents. "I have been instructed to impart some rather sad news to you, Mr. Trevelyan." He raised his eyes to meet Trevelyan's, awaiting a response. But Trevelyan was lost in thought. He had assumed the appointment was going to be bad news, not sad. Fairbourne returned to his documents and resumed. "It is my solemn responsibility to inform you of the passing of your father, Mr. Charles Lester Seymour, the third, on the Twenty first day of September this year... I understand that this may come as some surprise to you, and if you need a moment to gather yourself, please do." He paused and rose from his chair. "I find a drink useful at times like these. May I offer you a scotch or brandy?"

Trevelyan's mind was racing. He was not expecting this. "Err... whisky, large, please," he blurted, trying to comprehend.

Fairbourne could sense his confusion. He placed a large tumbler of scotch and ice before Trevelyan and said, "Can I speak frankly, Mr. Trevelyan?" before continuing without waiting for an answer. "Mr. Seymour has been a major client of ours for many years and a close and personal friend of mine. I was deeply saddened by his passing. His health had deteriorated in the last few years, and his death was not unexpected. He received the best medical home care available and passed painlessly in his own bed." His eyes met Trevelyan's. "But in all the time I knew him, I must confess I never knew he had a son. I cannot ever remember him ever mentioning that he had any children. He remained unmarried and, might I add, uninterested in anything outside of his passions. He had remained a recluse for the last ten years of his life and took no partners, romantic or otherwise, in the years preceding his hermitage."

Steadied a little by the whisky, Trevelyan tried to comprehend what Mr. Fairbourne was saying. He was led to believe by his mother that his father died before Trevelyan was born. The victim of a fatal car crash during their engagement that his mother never got over. He did not like to ask too many questions in his childhood, as he could see the pain in her eyes while she tried to answer without getting upset. He had so many questions that he did not know where to start. "How on earth did you track me down?" he asked, feeling this was as good a place to start as any. "I believed my father to be dead, or at least that is what my mother told me".

"Ah," said Fairbourne, "that proved to be rather difficult at first, but it was through your good mother that we were able to find you. She never married, which is fortunate in these affairs, and with the help of certain agencies we employ in such matters, we could trace her to..." He paused while he searched the paperwork before him and continued, "the Oakwood nursing home, close to here, actually." He reclined in his chair, no longer perusing his documents, and said with a measure of sympathy, "We were informed that your mother has advanced dementia and Alzheimer's disease and that she is beyond any of our inquiries but supplied your details as next of kin, and here we are." He sat forward to engage Trevelyan earnestly, saying, "I understand now that you are wholly unaware of these circumstances, so what I have to say next will come as a bombshell," he said, rising and taking Trevelyan's glass to refill. He did not continue until his guest had another large scotch before him and he, himself, had resumed his seat. "Mr. Trevelyan, you have inherited a vast fortune in the region of eight hundred million pounds sterling after taxes on revenues and such." More paper shuffling, "along with a substantial country seat in the Snowdonia range in northern Wales and all and any assets associated with it."

He paused to affect Trevelyan's attention once again and said, "I understand that this must come as a profound shock to you, and if I were in your position, I too would be speechless, to which end I have prepared a dossier detailing all the relative information and so forth for you to consider at your leisure."

After an hour of document signing and listening to the summary of the will concerning himself, Trevelyan noted there was no direct correspondence to him personally from his recently acquired father. He asked, "Did my father leave any personal letters that might explain his leaving all this to me? You must understand, Mr. Fairbourne, that until I walked in here an hour ago, I was a semi-successful artist with no real money, no prospects, and a future that did not include wealth and assets. Now I have more money than I could ever have imagined and a stately home! And yet I know nothing about him besides what you have told me today. Where was he when I was being raised by my mother alone? Did he know about my life? Did he know where I was and what I was doing? Why didn't he contact me in all this time?" Questions kept revolving through his head now that he had gotten over the initial shock, and the effects of the alcohol were beginning to show. Fairbourne looked sympathetic when he said, "All I can tell you with any certainty, dear boy, is that the will was written by my father some thirty years ago when he was captain of this ship." He raised his hands and opened his arms, gesturing to his surroundings. "And has remained unedited and sealed until opened the day after Mr. Seymour passed away, per his prior instructions. Which would suggest that he made arrangements for your inheritance shortly after your birth. In answer to your questions, I wouldn't like to speculate, and unfortunately, other than your mother, I can think of no one living that could shed any light."

He paused for a moment, then put his arm around Trevelyan's shoulder and guided him towards the door of his office as an act of finality. "On the bright side," he said, "you are now a wealthy man with the world as your playground. Should you find you require my services, please don't hesitate to contact me. I have put a business card in with your documentation, which I suggest you familiarise yourself with at your convenience. Any questions you may have..." He stopped, took Trevelyan's hand in his clasped grasp, and added, "regarding your estate or finances, they can be directed to the contacts listed within." With that, Trevelyan was back in the waiting room, still reeling from the news and the scotch.

Of all the thoughts whirling around his head in a tempest of confusion, one resounded above all the others. The only one he could fully comprehend. "I AM RICH. I AM STONE-COLD, STINKING RICH! I have an obscene amount of unearned and undeserved money bequeathed to me by either my anonymous lifelong absentee billionaire father, or some crazy old fart, and a case of mistaken identity thirty years ago that was never revealed." He wondered if someone out there with the same name and date of birth was expecting a fortune that would never arrive, although it seemed very unlikely.

∞∞∞∞

As Trevelyan stepped into the street from Fairbourne's building, the rush of traffic and people only added to his disorientation. He stumbled as he turned left and headed to the Oakwood nursing home to escape the noise and grime of the city. The fresh air had lightened his senses more than he expected, probably because he had skipped breakfast that morning in an effort not to be late for his appointment. Also, he was still in shock and more than a little bewildered. He was not hungry, only impatient to get home and take all the information in.

His next thought was Rose: 'Ah, sweet Rose.' A complicated flower, to be sure, but beautiful none the less, with a rare bloom for those she deemed worthy. He was not interested in her worthiness, though, only in her lovemaking. He was fond of her on a personal level, but she had too many problems in her life, both real and imagined, for his taste. Her mental instabilities were no secret, but not serious enough for his consideration. She had a tough childhood with messed up parents and, from an early age, preferred self harm as a way of dealing with life. He considered them to be 'friends with benefits,' as the phrase goes. Nothing more. Although he was acutely aware that she had much higher aspirations for him and that she was, he was sure, in love with him. She knew better than to make emotional or romantic gestures toward him, but the signs were there, all the same. The way she stroked his hair as they lay together. The passion that still lingered in her kisses long after their lovemaking was over. All these things and more he resolved to ignore because the situation, as it stood, suited him better than having a two-way relationship with all its encumbering responsibilities and levies on his time and person. He needed no one except himself. He knew she accepted his terms and conditions, hoping the time would come when he would succumb to her affections. Even through two abortions, she went along dutifully. Things were going to change now. And Rose did not figure in that future.

The noise receded as he chose quieter back streets to meander his way to Oakwood and his mother. He needed to speak to her about Charles Seymour. But first, he left Rose a message on her voicemail. He did not want to speak to her right now. He needed to get his thoughts straight before that. He would later wish he could remember the words he left her. So much that happened later that day could have been avoided if he had been a little more sensitive to her sensibilities and self-esteem. But he would recall using the words "last goodbyes". He all but floated the last thousand yards to Oakwood, wondering if mother dear would be awake and lucid enough for him to get some answers. Or scared and confused, as she seemed to be more often than not. The answer was neither. She was asleep. Or at least half asleep. Her eyes were closed as she muttered in her dreams. She appeared helpless, small, and defenceless lying there on that bed, in that room, in that place. Not at all the robust survivor of her generation that he called mother. A strong Welsh woman. Dignified and proud. But she was always kind and rewarding to those she loved, and she did love him; he had never doubted that. He could recall times in his youth when they lived in her childhood home. A small slate mining village beneath the Moelwyn mountains and the hanging valley of Cwmorthin. They would walk the old slate miner's paths that traversed the mountains and valleys in the area. She described to him the part her father had in the quarries and mines that roofed the world.

That was a world away from this semi-conscious and confused old lady lying in a bed she will never get out of. He found it difficult to know how to feel, sitting next to her bed, holding her hand, with a world of contradictions and questions demanding to be sated. She seemed so small and frail, almost transparent with age. Did she ever intend to tell him? Explain about Seymour and why Trevelyan had grown up without a father? He could understand the whole "died in a car accident" charade because it was better than whatever truth be told, especially when he was growing up. But she had the opportunity to unburden herself long after he turned eighteen and before she began her descent into ill health and dementia. She must have known at some point that he would discover the truth. One thing he had learned in life was that lies never lay buried. Not that it was a lie exactly, but a withholding of the truth. A truth he could have asked about growing up, but was reluctant to on many levels. His concern for his mother's feelings and the pain in her eyes when she thought about the past outweighed his curiosity about the small details that ultimately matter to a small boy with no father. If his father was some rich hermit, how come they had to struggle for everything that she could get for them both? They never went without food or a roof over their heads, but they never had it easy. His mother worked hard all of his life. She cleaned and cooked all day for other people. Then she went home and did it all again for him.

He just needed a reckoning... a confession seeking absolution, or at least an explanation. Perhaps on some level she could hear him, because, from time to time, she uttered rhetoric in Welsh that he could not fully understand. She had endeavoured to teach him Welsh when they lived in her home valley among the mountains, lakes, and rivers of Wales. But he was never the best pupil. He could make out the words 'mother' and 'sister' in Welsh as she muttered apologies to him in her dreams. "Sorry that he will be left alone after she is gone," but the rest was unintelligible.

Whose mother, whose sister? Nothing about his father. The drink had gnawed at his patience. It had been a long day, and he had a whirlwind rolling around inside his head.

This is pointless. He knew there would be no answers, and he was not disappointed. He did, however, think that he would feel a little better, less burdened by the secrets if they were out in the open. But he did not. Trevelyan sighed in forgiveness as he bent to kiss her forehead. And she found some peace in that because she smiled as a single tear rolled from her face to her pillow.

Chapter Three

Last goodbye? He sounded drunk, but Rose knew him better than that. Trey never got drunk before ten in the evening. He could get a little out there during the day sometimes, but never drunk. He liked to loosen up a bit before he would paint, a little wine, maybe a joint—but never so much as to dull his mind. It had been seventeen days and nights since they were last together. She had tried to get in touch, but he never returned her calls if she were to reach out to him. He only called when he wanted her, and she always wanted to say no, 'I'm busy' or 'I'm seeing someone else.' But she could never resist. Could never turn down the opportunity to be with him because during that time she would feel like she had finally found her home. In his arms. Safe and secure, if only for a brief time. When they were apart, she felt like an open wound. Vulnerable and exposed all the time. The way she had always felt since she was a child. But when she was with Trey, all that disappeared. Until she was apart again and those exposed nerves jangled. It was what she supposed love felt like. To yearn for someone with every part of your body and soul. If life had taught her anything, it was to grab a hold of the things you love and do not let go. Not without a fight. And she loved him. So much so that it often scared her when she was alone in her bed at night. Her thoughts betrayed her at every turn, throwing images of him with other women or, god forbid, a life without him at all.

It was in those dark moods that she would reach for the blade beside her bed and relieve her despair with blood.

She knew he did not reciprocate her feelings. But she believed that the times they were together belied his indifference to her. The love they made was proof of that. No one could make love that way and not be attached, body and soul. They were meant to be. She was sure of it. Even after the abortions she endured alone, she reasoned in his favour. They were her sacrifices for his happiness and the promise of a lasting togetherness. There was no mention of "last goodbyes" in that promise; there was no room for separation. She needed to take control for once in her life, instead of being led in the direction the world expected of her. Yes, she thought. It is time.

She gathered together the clouds of darkness that had begun to descend on her. She had work to do. While she worked, her hands steady, she contemplated what she would say when they embraced. They would embrace, she would see to that. She had to feel his arms wrapped around her if she had any chance of having the courage to see it through. With their eyes locked in an embrace of their own, he would not be anticipating her bravery. He would expect her to be her usual shy and compliant self, but this was too important to her to let it slip away. This would be her last chance to show him how much she loved him. And that she could not bear for him to leave her because she could not live without him. If she was brave, he would see that she was not the sum of her fears and weaknesses. That she could take action when it was required. When they were locked into that embrace and their eyes met, he would understand. That is when she would need courage most of all. She must cling to him so very, very tightly. To say exactly what it was she intended.

And it would not be 'Last Goodbye'.

∞∞∞∞

Still reeling under the intoxication and silent rebuttal from his mother. And the bombshell that landed in the middle of his day. Trevelyan slunk off home, leaving his mother asleep and at peace for the time being. After a short walk away from the throngs and traffic, he entered his front door and headed straight to his studio. It felt good to be in a familiar place, surrounded by his work. Feeling exhausted now, he slumped in his easy chair and closed his eyes for a moment. A tempest ravaged his thoughts. He poured himself a drink and looked at the dossier Fairbourne had amalgamated for him. True to his word, pretty much everything Trevelyan needed to know was there in black and white. He was unconcerned with the majority of the information. Mostly legal papers and deeds. Details of bank accounts and financial adviser contacts filled a single folder to bursting.

Finally, he found what he was searching for. He opened the manila folder marked 'Bryngaer', only to be greeted with an image of a spectacular mansion, all gables and windows, at the apex of a long gravel drive surrounded by a copse of trees. Gardens sprawled from the rear and drifted into wildflower meadows that bordered a slow moving, and wide stretch of river. Excitement welled up inside of him, and blessing his good fortune, he poured another scotch. Perusing the other pictures in the folder, he came across some photographs of the acres of land surrounding Bryngaer, showing the mountainous landscape in the background. The sky, dark and foreboding as it crossed the horizon. They struck him as familiar, as he had seen them somewhere before in a magazine or TV programme. He could not put his finger on it, but he was sure he had seen that landscape before, and more than once. He sat back in the chair, nursing the remains of his drink. As his eyes roamed the studio, his thoughts concluded he would soon have to move all this stuff to his new residence. There it was. The landscape in the pictures surrounding Bryngaer.

The sketch was not identical, but it was the same, sure enough. A figure concealed some details at the forefront of the scene. A young woman viewed from behind and to the right, showing her profile beneath a hooded cloak, staring off into the vista. Even the sky looked the same. Her long hair spilled from beneath the hood. Stretching out behind her, borne on unseen winds. In his reverie, he almost expected her hood to blow backward in response. Then the spell was broken, and the sounds of the day drifted in through the window and reasserted themselves and normality. Shifting his attention to the rest of the material within the dossier, he shuffled through the papers, not taking them in as his thoughts drifted off to Bryngaer and those majestic meadows by the river. He could see himself there. In the pictures. Walking through the cacophony of colour toward the riverbank. A life of luxury and leisure awaited him, starting tomorrow.

He wished he had not invited Rose over. He was more than a little giddy, and his mind was exhausted and racing simultaneously. Rose would not be happy about his change of fortune, and he instinctively knew she had already guessed that he planned to leave without her. 'Damn my flippancy,' he thought. He should have kept her in the dark and disappeared into a new life with no drama. But what was done was done. He decided he should enjoy the "Last goodbye" in the spirit he intended. Trevelyan would miss her, but only in the way you would miss a friendly stray cat. He was lost in thoughts of freedom he had never felt before. No longer are dreams to be imagined; but things to be attained and within his grasp. The abrupt ring of the lower doorbell brought him back to reality. He made his way to the buzzer, and without greeting or ceremony, he hit the button, allowing entry to the lower corridor that led to his place, and turned to pour them both a drink before she came through the door. In what seemed like longer than it should have, he finished his drink and poured another as he heard the door open behind him and Rose drift in.

He turned, only to be greeted by a soaked and bedraggled creature. Wild with distress and purpose, flinging herself toward him with outstretched arms. In his confusion, he could only spread his arms in anticipation and await her desperate embrace. But over her shoulder and through the window, he could perceive no deluge or cause for her appearance.

As she collided with him, he staggered back a little, bearing the force as she clamped her arms around him. Her face buried in his chest. She lifted her eyes to him and said, "We'll always be together now." The smell hit him. Burning his eyes and making him falter backward yet again.

PETROL. She was doused in PETROL!

Before his thoughts could turn into action, he heard the sound of stone on flint. And the world exploded into a blast of wrath. Like a shriek of fury, while their screams were engulfed in fire and flame.

Chapter Four

His first recollection after Rose's immolation is light. Everywhere, brightest argent. The thought arose that he was dead, and this was the here and ever after. "So be it," he mused, falling back into the wailing darkness.

The light again, dimmer now with murmured sounds, voices? Angels? Light again, only it is moving now. Rolling above him.

A realisation of motion, and then darkness and dreams of conflagration. For the longest time, he could only perceive the painful calling of the light and the hot, sweet embrace of darkness. Timeless oblivion carried him cradled in the arms of death. But the call of the light was too strong. He struggled to reach the surface of a dark and stormy ocean of unawareness. Repeatedly, he would break the surface with a scream, only to be swallowed back into the depths. Finally, he drifted, shipwrecked on a shore of pain. Awareness was agony. Relieved only by waves of foggy peace, he later learned was morphine. Eventually, the awareness grew, and the dreams receded, but the pain remained constant.

He saw shades of people passing through his field of non-vision, but the pain deterred any attempt at speech, if indeed he could speak at all. Attempting to move was a punishment he had learned to fear, and he lay as he was. But, between the morphine and his anguish, he found a purgatory between two hells.

He was soaring slowly, like a hawk. Spiralling, gliding through the clouds and down toward the island below. Green grasslands and greener hills, and in the middle of all this beauty, a walled town. No. Not a town. Four villages with walls of wood running between them created a walled defence around all at once. He saw buildings and a solitary windmill. Then he is between two rivers. Above a tower. He is drifting over a waterfall while cliffs stretched on either side of his vision. Far-reaching, snow-capped mountains lay ahead. He swoops above the forest and weaves across the river and past the lake to the castle between the white mountains. Then the ships and the blossom. He swooped lower still to watch the petals shuffle away on the breeze like little pink dancers across the pale white of the domed building below. And then... Darkness again. Not the crushing darkness, as before. A cavernous darkness. Cold and damp from ages past. Deep underground, the sound of falling water, and a soft glow in the air, the colour of amber. A small river of lava ran across the vast floor of the cavern, moving as it has done for aeons. He did not know how he knew this, but it was a fact as undeniable as the cavern in which he now floated like a disembodied thought. A gentle vibration he had not noticed before was slowly gaining ground on his senses. Concentrating on the west wall of the chamber at ground level, a burgeoning light was growing in the same spot as the vibration. A humming grew louder as it echoed off the chamber walls. As the pitch raised, the light became brighter still. Moving across the floor, creating a circle of amber flame. As the circle closed, the humming increased in frequency. Resounding across the chamber, drawing into the circle all the shadows cast by the rock light. Slowly they slithered, gathering like a black pool within the glowing amber circle. When there were no shadows left in the chamber, when all the darkness congregated together in the circle, it began to swirl and boil, taking shape. Elongating and forming into the rough outline of a tall man, but with none of the features. A man-shaped darkness, thrumming with a dark power. As the shape manifested itself, the humming reached a frantic pitch, until the very air strained. Culminating with a blast of fury, that sent a concussion through the bedrock walls of the cavern, threatening to bring the roof crashing down on the now fully formed figure of darkness below. All the darkness within that cavern now resided in the figure of a man. A figure made entirely of obsidian and distant stars. The figure raised its head. Its eyeless gaze fell upon the disembodied witness above. Snatching him from the atmosphere with a silent scream, Trevelyan was drawn into the cosmic darkness of the figure below, and the starry void that lay within. And then...

Pain. Awareness was pain. Still bandaged, bright light through the wrappings. Voices, a man and a woman. Receding now, the light grows dimmer. Darkness, for the longest time.

A voice calls him from the depths.

Softly at first, like the rustling of the leaves, growing slowly louder, bringing his senses to focus upon it. His name, someone was calling him from the other side of the darkness. Reluctant to move, he was forced to swallow; his mouth was so dry. Water dripped into his mouth, trickling gently down his throat. Bliss. Cool and comforting his thirst, but more pain as he swallowed again.

"Mr. Trevelyan, my name is Dr. Harper," came a man's voice, loamy and warm. "Please, do not attempt to talk. You have extensive injuries to your upper body and face, including smoke inhalation damage to your lungs and first-degree burns to your oesophagus and tongue. We have you in a private care facility, and you are our sole patient. We are a dedicated staff of twelve doctors and nurses, including myself, providing care around the clock. I am sure you have many questions and are compelled to try to speak. Again, I must advise you to remain silent for as long as possible. If you can understand me, please raise any finger on your left hand only." His brain stumbled. He understood well enough, but the pain was growing again, and his mind was desperate to escape back to the island and peace. He mustered his resolve and focused his thoughts on his left hand. It was then that he realised it was too easy... He did not choose his left hand as it was the only choice his brain delivered. His index finger twitched twice and then slowly raised itself from its resting place.

"Good," said Dr. Harper. "I will tell you as much as I know. Which unfortunately is not a great deal and does not include much good news, I'm afraid to say. We have put you in a coma-like state since your arrival here, a private rural burns retreat. This was the only way to ensure as much relief and comfort to you and rest for your body, to recover from the initial shock and damage from the accident."

Accident! They think I was in an accident! He instinctively tried to respond that some murderous bitch tried to kill him, and right now he almost wished she had! But even the thought of trying to articulate sent flares of pain across his mind.

Dr. Harper continued, "You have received fourth-degree burns to your right hand and arm. They are severely damaged and unsalvageable, I am sorry to say. Your upper body sustained third-degree burns from your navel, and your face is extensively disfigured with nerve and muscle tissue loss. Your physical condition is now stable, although we thought we might lose you some time ago. You have been here with us for six weeks. I'm afraid nothing could be done for your friend. She had died from her injuries before help could arrive. We were contacted by your solicitor, Mr. Fairbourne, once he realized you were in a hospital, and you were promptly transferred here. You have options where you can go from here, Mr. Trevelyan, regarding reconstructive facial surgery and grafts on the most severely damaged areas, but those will be for another time. All of your physical needs are being met by machines, but it remains for you to be as still as possible while your body heals. You are being suspended on a special tack that will move your position without your effort. This will allow us to heal the worst of your injuries without fear of further damage caused by friction. You will remain bandaged around the face to protect the remaining tissue, and we will continue to keep you under to minimise your pain and discomfort. We estimate another month or two before we can expect to remove your coverings and attempt at speech. Be assured you are in the best hands, and with time and rehabilitation, you should recover to the best of your ability. There is not much else I can tell you now except that the next time we speak, hopefully it will be under better circumstances. Farewell Mr. Trevelyan."

Time and the voice fell away, and he was once again plunged into the darkness. Broken only by dreams of drifting and soaring and mountains and valleys. He saw the hooded woman from his painting still gazing at the vista before her. All else was green, blue, and beautiful.

Harper's voice again. "Mr. Trevelyan, can you hear me?" Trevelyan swam upward toward the sound on a wave about to break. "Before we remove your facial covering, I must warn you that you have no eyelids with which to open or close your eyes. Again, I must urge you to refrain from speaking, for now at least. If you understand, please use your left hand again."

After much effort, he managed a wave of his left hand.

"We have dimmed the light, but it may still come as a shock, so I will remove it in stages. If you are ready, please let me know."

Once again, Trevelyan's thoughts soared leftward, with no hint of choice to the contrary, and he moved his hand again. As if dawn were breaking in slow motion, the rich, warm light revealed itself to Trevelyan's lidless eyes in a gentle stream. Blurry at first, but then clearing and focusing on the figure before him. The figure's eyes swam into focus first, deep and brown, the eyes of an older man who has seen many experiences, good and bad. "Shall I continue?" said Harper. Trevelyan flexed his hand again, and there was more light, soft, and rounded in his vision. It was a strange sensation, not being able to shut it out when he wanted to. Harper was aware as he strove to ease the process. By increments, he removed the covering.

He was in a richly decorated room that, apart from the medical equipment around the bed, looked like something from a small library, with a writing desk and antique bookshelves filled from top to bottom. Two large windows completed the ensemble, from which hung thick green velvet curtains. Dr Harper was to his left and behind him as he came into view, holding the blindfold he had been wearing. An African man in a white doctor's coat smiled down at him and said, "At last, we meet Mr. Trevelyan." He motioned with his hand to a straw he offered for him to drink from. "Slow at first, please. Take your time. I have suspended your tranquilliser for the time being. We have done as much for your physical recovery as we can. There will still be pain. For which you will receive medication, but it no longer serves any purpose to keep you sedated. Now you must begin the hard work to complete your recovery. You will still drift in and out of awareness, but this will, after a day or so, result in longer periods of awareness, which will need managing."

While Harper was speaking, Trevelyan continued to sip the water with the straw gripped between his teeth. He lifted his eyes to Harper's and managed to rasp, "Fuck you." Without lips, it sounded more like, "Foo," but Harper saw Trevelyan's eyes and understood. Several days passed as he swung in and out of awareness, but, as Harper promised, he was awake more than he was unconscious. The pain was almost unbearable at times. Hours dragged between his morphine doses. Although it dulled the ringing of his damaged nerves, he found it less effective as the days dragged on. The days blurred into weeks. Time lost any sense of meaning to Trevelyan. The pain that wracked his nerve endings receded a little. Enough to allow him to focus on the reality of his situation. Which was a different temper of the same pain that no medication could ease. With nothing to do except dwell on his circumstances, he contemplated the road that led him here. And sometimes he wished Rose had done a better job. She should have finished them both off. There and then in that studio. He once had a perfect future. He was king for a day! Until she took all that away from him. Because thinking of this future, the one in which she left him maimed and disfigured, seemed unbearable.

His physical body responded well to the treatment provided by Harper, who left Trevelyan to his own devices until the time came when he could be interviewed by the police. His room was dimmed for his comfort, but he had taken to wearing a blindfold and facial healing mask to hide his face from prying eyes and the horror and pity he saw there.

"If you think you can talk to the police now, Mr. Trevelyan, other than the rest of your treatment, I believe you can put the subject of your accident behind you. It has been nearly six months since you arrived here, and your progress has improved as much as we can hope for. I see no reason why we cannot wrap this interview up today once and for all and concentrate on your recovery and convalescence. So, if you are ready? I will show Detective Inspector Samuels in and leave you to finalise this unpleasant affair." With that, he left the room. Following an inaudible conversation beyond the door, Trevelyan heard someone enter and approach his bed.

"Good evening, Mr. Trevelyan." A voice said. "My name is Samuels. Detective Inspector Samuels. Might I take a few moments to talk to you regarding events preceding your accident and your relationship with a…" he took out a small pad in his breast pocket and concluded "Miss Rose Mullaney? May I?" He indicated the chair by the bookcase. Trevelyan nodded and Samuels moved the chair to nearer the bed.

"Doth my appearath offend you, Detective Thamuels?" Trevelyan rasped.

"On the contrary," he replied," I'm very glad to see you."

Trevelyan could not see him through the blindfold, but he got the distinct impression he was looking directly at him. "Having seen the crime scene, I am amazed you survived, Mr. Trevelyan!" There was a hint of respect in his voice instead of the pity Trevelyan had become used to from the brief encounters with the other medical staff. Samuels proceeded. "In the time during your recovery, we have been able to piece together most of the facts leading up to the," he paused, searching for an appropriate word—"accident". There it was again, thought Trevelyan. That word. Accident. Like no one was to blame. "If you could fill in a few blanks we are missing, I won't inconvenience you longer than necessary." He referred to his notepad again. "Miss Mullaney and yourself were in a relationship; was that correct?"

Trevelyan nodded. It seemed easier to admit that than how he viewed their entanglement.

"Was this both sexual and mutually exclusive at the time?" He nodded again for want of another gesture. It was too painful to shrug his shoulders. "With your consent," Samuels continued, "may I state the facts as we see them? If any are incorrect, Dr. Harper says you can communicate by raising your left hand if you prefer." Trevelyan once again nodded his acquiescence. "On the day in question, we know you attended an appointment with a solicitor, Mr. Fairbourne. He refrained from disclosing the nature of the appointment on legal privacy grounds, but added that the meeting lasted approximately an hour and a half. From there, you visited your late mother in her nursing home and arrived home around five o'clock p.m."

Trevelyan was stunned. He had not given a thought to his mother in the last six months, too preoccupied with his misfortune. He must have gasped audibly, because Samuels stopped talking and groaned. "You weren't informed about your mother's passing, were you?" he said. "My deepest apologies and my sympathies, Mr. Trevelyan; that was rather insensitive of me." Trevelyan did not know how to feel! Of course, he knew it was coming one day, but to find she had passed and he was unaware. That was unforgivable. Both of him, for not being with her and letting her die alone, and Harper for not telling him. He bit down on his anger and urged Samuels to continue by gesturing with his left hand. "Shortly after you arrived home, Miss Mullaney was admitted to the hallway leading to your apartment by yourself. She then made her way to your front door. The CCTV showed her carrying petrol containers. We found them discarded outside your home. The coroner concluded that the clothes she wore had an accelerant sewn into the linings. She fully intended to kill you both. What we need to know is the order of events after she entered your apartment. We know she was very distraught and probably unstable. We also know of her medical history and involuntary sectioning in the past and her habit of self-harm, but her aggression has always been directed at herself and not others." Samuels looked a little embarrassed when he asked, "Did something occur between you both that might have caused her to instigate this attack?" There. That is what he needed to hear. That she attacked him. Tried to kill him, in fact. How could he be to blame? He was the victim. But deep down inside, he knew he shared the blame. And that she was a victim as much as he was. He would never admit that to Samuels. He barely admitted it to himself.

So instead, he ground out the words, "Bith was craythy." And left it at that.

Chapter Five

Nestor awoke. Trembling and aghast at the apocalyptic nightmare that still clung to him. He closed his mind to the images of the man who desecrated the world even as they were dissipating, as dreams do in the pale light of dawn. He could not remember falling asleep. Or how long had passed since. He did not remember sitting beneath the tree that now rustled in the early morning breeze above him. But none of that mattered now. All that mattered was the dream and its consequences. How could this happen? How could this cataclysm come to be, and more urgently, how could it be stopped? Haunted by the scenes he had witnessed in his dream, he staggered to his feet and surveyed his surroundings for the first time. He stood within a small clearing amongst a bevy of tall, glorious green leafed trees. A bubbling river of silver and blue crystal water ran through the clearing. He wasted no time reviving himself by bathing his aching, feverish brow and drinking mouthfuls of cold water from his hands. Behind him and towering above the trees in the distance, craggy mountains dressed in green velvet reached the clear blue skies. Steadied now by the sobering effects of the cold mountain water, he gathered his thoughts about him like a cloak. He racked his memory to recall how he arrived here in this place. But every time he tried to concentrate, his mind would throw more images of death and destruction, until he could stand no more, let out a wail, and plunged his head once more into that cold, silvery blue absolution. His thoughts were fragmented. But the more he strove to bring all the pieces together, the more they drifted into a holocaust yet to come. How could he live with this knowledge? Because of that, at least he could be sure of. These were not ordinary dreams, or nightmares. These were prophecies. A glimpse of what would befall this land at the hands of a strange man from a strange place. He would arise in the east this wayfarer. A stranger travelling anonymously. Harbouring a power he cannot comprehend. His every step toward his goal is another step towards the unmaking of creation. He must be stopped. It would not come to pass during Nestor's lifetime. The dreams had promised him that much in sooth, but what of the generations to come? He must head east, yes, of course. East and to the Isle, but how to get there? If these dreams were prophecy, why then would they manifest in a wretch such as him? Someone of no consequence? Was he to warn the ones to come? Was he to spread his word and maybe the intended people were listening? Someone who could carry his mantle?

There was time yet, though. Plenty of time. The dreams must somehow provide for him in his endeavours. Else wise he would die sooner rather than later, a madman and happy for it. He accepted this task with vigour. Perhaps now that the dreams had shown him his path, they would become less traumatic. But somehow, he doubted this. Burdened with prophecy and purpose, he left the clearing as he must have arrived, barefoot and in rags.

He followed the river through the forests and then the grassy plains and abundant hills that spread before him. Rolling down toward the sea and the harbour town of Mor Gwyn. In the days it took to reach the coast, he had intermittent periods of lucidity and madness. Separated only by sleepless nights and dreams of destruction. In his madness, he would shout and curse the sky in a rage against the Wayfarer and the evil he wrought in his dreams. "All will be torn asunder; all will be brought to ruin," he cried, wringing his hands in anguish. In his more lucid moments, he still burned with the passion of salvation. But with a cunning, sharp intelligence, bent on his pilgrimage east. Once he reached the coast, he could work aboard a ship to gain passage across the western sea to the lands in the east. From there, his dreams would be his guide once he made landfall.

As Nestor approached the bridge that spans the river near the western docks, he could hear the hustle and bustle from the nearby town. A small gathering of people milling about at the bridge, unaware of his presence, continued haggling with the toll keep for passage across the swollen river.

"Only tradesmen may cross," yelled the toll keep above the cacophony of voices. A mountain of a man well chosen for his particular purpose. "Else wise, it's the river for you." With that, he picked up his thick wooden staff and brandished it at the crowd before him, saying, "Approach or be gone." Understanding the threat, the crowd thinned. A rowdy bunch of vagabonds and thieves seeking entrance to the harbour and its promise of enterprise. Nestor watched as everyone went about their business, and the toll keep went back to his ledgers. Some to making fires near the riverbank and scouting for food, while others contemplated the watery torrents and their chances of survival. He must cross the bridge. He must secure passage to the east. Nestor took his rest here and waited until dark. He settled back among the bracken, unseen by the remaining stragglers on the riverbank, and fell into a slumber that turned into nightmares. There he stood. The Wayfarer. His arms stretched toward the roof of an almighty cavern deep below the ground. Power etched the darkness in the swirling crucible that surrounded him. Not ordinary fire, but elemental fire. Driven by a torrent of unseen wind and flame as tumultuous as a stormy sea. Crashing against the rocks of the cave wall that surrounded him. His face was a scream of fury and madness, his eyes wild with command. The very stone beneath his feet began to soften and undulate with the rising heat. And the air thrummed with the promise of a world-ending detonation of power. Enough to bring about the unmaking of creation. And still, he drew more power to himself from the very earth. His potency screamed for release while the whirlwind of fire grew stronger. Until the air in the cave threatened to explode.

Nestor woke, his mouth stretched in a scream, but no sound came out. He looked around, alarmed he might have alerted others to his whereabouts. All was dark and silent. He peered above the bracken strewn around him and looked toward the bridge. The embers of dying campfires along the riverbank decried no movement. The figure of the toll keep stood at the apex of the bridge with his staff perched ready on his back, a burning torch in his hand. The sound of the rushing river drifted across the distance to Nestor as a reminder of his only course of action. He must cross the bridge. He must set sail for the east. More so now than ever after that haunting and crushing dream. He could still see that power crazed face. The silent, wretched scream. The desecration that was beginning beneath the ground. "It cannot be so. I will not let it be so. If, by my life or death, I can avert this unholy act, then I must begin now," he muttered to himself. His hunger made itself known by the growling noises coming from his middle. He could not remember the last time he ate. Only slaking his thirst and his hunger with river water got him here. He must secure some food if he is to survive and complete his purpose. The harbour. He must make the harbour. He raised himself to his feet and nearly fainted with weakness. His mind flashed with an image of the cursed stranger bathed in fire. His resolve gave him the strength he needed to make his way toward the bridge and the toll keep.

"Who goes?" challenged the toll keep as Nestor approached, dishevelled and ragged. "Who would risk the wrath of Talon toll keep?"

Nestor fell to his knees as Talon drew his staff from his back. "Mercy!" He panted, "I must reach the harbour".

"What business has a maggot such as you with the harbour?" He growled. "Be gone, vagabond. Or Talon will take your hands as a prize." With that, he put away his staff and removed a large knife from his belt.

"Mercy," Nestor pleaded, reaching out his hand to clutch Talon's tunic. Talon caught Nestor's arm and raised it, ready to strike with his knife. The moment he gripped Nestor's arm, a vision of fire and flame violently struck him. He saw a man with the power of apocalypse. Here to purge Hiraeth by fire. A madman's curse. In his mind, he saw his children and his wife, along with all those he loved, blown away to ashes. He released Nestor's arm and staggered backward, trying to find his feet. Failing and falling spread-eagled on the wooden floor of the bridge. Paralysed with horror, his eyes burned hot with tears from his damned vision. Nestor did not understand what had befallen the man who towered above him a moment ago. But he grasped enough to know that his nightmare had provided for him. He half walked, half staggered past the figure on the bridge. Then onwards toward the lights of the harbour beyond the hills.

∞∞∞∞∞

As he crested the last hills before Mor Gwyn harbour, an aerial view of the entire town greeted him, including the three docking ports. The largest lay nearest to him, with a single port further northward, and beyond that lay the last. The blue rooftops of the multitude of houses and buildings before him shimmered in the dawning light, revealing the houses on the periphery of the town had been built seamlessly together, creating a walled defence on both sides of the city gate. And as the shadows dimmed, a small copse of apple trees became visible between him and the walled town. He lurched forward, fell and rolled down the hillside, driven by hunger, until he lay within a few feet of the wind fallen fruit. Scrambling on his knees as fast as he could, he grasped the battered fruit with both hands. Without ceremony, he greedily swallowed chunks of wet fruit, barely stopping to breathe. After a few moments, he began to choke and retch, and so he slowed his actions, allowing him to savour the taste of fruit as the juice ran down his jaw and onto his rags. After eating his fill and stuffing what he could in the pockets of his rags, he made his way toward the sea, a short distance westward. Once there, he removed his ragged clothing and jumped into the cold, foaming waves of the shallows. Salt and cold stung his eyes as he immersed himself before resurfacing. Feeling invigorated, he grabbed a handful of seaweed and scrubbed at the grime accumulated since his first awakening in the forest cove. He emerged from the water as red as a lobster and shivering. He donned his rags and made his way from the shore, following the stone barrier of the walled town eastward. He began rubbing at his arms and legs as he went to bring them back to life.

Unannounced, he was blighted with a flashing image of the Wayfarer. Ablaze and wild and omnipotent.

The image dissolved as quickly as it appeared, leaving him suddenly cold in the wall's shadow. It was difficult to see his footing, so he stepped a few paces to his right and continued in the warming daylight. Just as he felt the warmth return to his bones, he stumbled over a root and went down hard on his knees, sprawling to the ground. Muttering curses, he nursed his grazed knees and turned to spit at the damned root. Before he could summon his saliva, he saw it was no root at all but a rib bone protruding from the ground. He inspected the area and saw the remains of an arm and hand in a sleeve. He cleared the detritus around the skeleton he revealed on the ground beside him and extricated it from the earth. He discarded the bones, shook out of the garments, and stood to look at his reward. A wool lined leather tunic, and strong waterproof leather jerkins. Mouldy but otherwise intact. What is more, it fit him comfortably and would keep him dry and warmer than his rags, which he quickly discarded. He imagined he looked a different fellow now to the wretch that wandered out of the woods to throw himself on the mercy of Talon toll keep. If he was to gain passage eastward, then he had better look as though he at least belonged among the citizens and not the beggars. He allowed himself a wry smile as he made his way to the city gate. Once again, the dreams have proved themselves sooth worthy. As he approached the gate, he saw two sentries armed and armoured guarding it. Neither seemed particularly vigilant, as they were both leaning on their spears, chatting to two women that Nestor presumed to be 'daughters of desire.' Emboldened by the power of the dreams, he approached the gatemen, exclaiming, "Help! Help. You there, Gatemen Talon toll keep has sent me seeking aid."

The sentries eyed the barefoot man hobbling his way toward them with more than a little disdain. "What aid does Talon need from us? The man is built like a mountain," said the largest of the two, but still half the size of Talon.

"Wine merchants seeking to barter their way into the city besiege him. Even the thirst of such a mountain of a man must surely be quenched by an avalanche of wine," he quipped. "He urged me to fetch you that I may watch the gate while you help him relieve the merchants of their burden."

The second of the sentry men laughed as he said, "And who might you be that Talon toll keep trusts our gate and gold too while we depart our posts?"

"Twas I who offered the highest bribe, and therefore first to pass. After which, he was awash with dozens of merchants who had seen my ploy plying him with their wares. I tried to intervene on his behalf, but the crowd took me off my feet, and I lost my shoes in the rush. When I gained his side again, he urged me to leave my horse and cargo with him and hurry here to ask your aid while he holds the bridge. And that you will bring my horse and wagon on your return." Nestor looked ragged and exhausted enough for it to be believable. His clothes, though dirty from the road, were of good quality, even if worn.

"I will not leave the gate undefended," said the large one, "but Orid here can go. And when he returns, we will seek you out in the 'Buckled Barrel Inn' in the town centre. Tell 'Gormund' that you are a guest of 'Hagmar of the Gate,' and he will serve you a brew until I arrive with your belongings." With that, he removed a large metal key from his waistband and turned the lock in the black metal gate, and swung it open for Nestor to pass.

"Good grace to you then, till we meet again," said Nestor almost too confidently as he strolled into the harbour town of Mor Gwyn with new clothes, a full belly, and a purpose to fulfil. He lifted his face to the air and above the smell of spices and cooking food, he caught the salt of the ocean and made his way toward the harbours.

Chapter Six

Bryngaer sat nestled within a cwm. A valley closed by mountains to the east, west, and north, built over a bronze age settlement surrounded by natural defences. The river ran straight from the mountain, through the Bryngaer estate towards the coast. It had been over a month since he had said goodbye to Dr. Harper and the staff. His recovery was progressing as well as hoped, and it was decided that he would benefit from the mountain air and the change of scenery. Trevelyan's Burns team had created a treatment room in Bryngaer, utilising the empty bedroom next to the one he had chosen for himself. Framing the rugged mountains and overlooking the gardens and meadows that extended toward the riverbank. He would also have a live in nurse and therapist rolled into one in the delightful form of Miss Evelyn Munroe. A dark-haired, aquiline eyed beauty, dedicated to Trevelyan's recovery, both physical and psychological. He had been against Dr. Harper's recommendations for surgery on his face and upper body and the complete removal of his black and withered right arm and hand. He had agreed to the facial prosthetic under the guise of its healing properties. His true reasoning was that it would hide his deformities from himself when he caught his reflection in the glass of the windows or bookcases as he passed them. His decision was born from many weeks of self-searching and no small amount of guilt that he carried with him. Not survivor's guilt, that was for the blameless victims. His guilt was well deserved and a long time in the making.

He had a long time to think about the pre-windfall days. The freedoms of being an artist suited him. Never a social creature, he had kept his circle small by choice and was making a living between selling his art and teaching lessons to a few bright and talented youngsters. He was not untalented himself. But he was too entrenched in the mundane to reach the dizzying heights of passion and fervour required for a masterpiece. He was happy producing art that was easy on the intellect as it was on the eye. But Rose had burned that old life down. It lay shattered in tiny fragments, all the pieces lost to each other. He did not recognise that life any more than he recognised himself. In those first days of awareness, he found himself trapped between pain, fear, and anger. Of the three, it was anger that dominated. He could use it to override the pain and push away the fear when it arose. It became his shield when he was in the company of others. The staff ignored his wrath and smiled in his presence, but no one dared look him in the eyes. Unwilling to gaze upon his countenance in case their horror belied their professionalism. Dr. Harper suffered the brunt of his rage and did so with grace. Trevelyan told him as much as he was leaving for Bryngaer. He thanked him for his kindness, and patience, and his care. He also donated a cheque for several hundred thousand pounds with the help of Fairbourne. This was for a brand new recreation room. Complete with cinema and music studio for the use of staff and patients. Dr. Harper appeared humbled at his generosity and recommended Evelyn Munroe to him as a personal carer.

∞∞∞∞∞

After the hospital, Bryngaer was literally a breath of fresh air that soothed his scorched lungs. He recalled marvelling at the house and its position as he was driven through the wrought-iron gates and onto the crisp gravel drive that led up to the house. He had chosen the rooms he required for himself from the extensive property portfolio sent to him by Fairbourne. A bedroom, study, studio, treatment room, and a reading room and were all accessed from one room to another so Trevelyan could move through his quarters without fear of bumping into any of the dozen staff. He had prepared a statement to the staff after his arrival. Stating that his privacy is to be respected above all else. In the meantime, to please go about their duties referring any queries or requests to Beattie, the old steward. The only staff member to serve both father and son at Bryngaer. No one knew the house better. Or its day-to-day requirements. Beattie had requested permission to remain living in his rooms on the ground floor of the west wing due to his age and seniority. Trevelyan was happy to agree to this and felt better that he had only one point of contact for the time being, other than Evelyn, whose rooms were below his in the east wing. He would arrange a meeting with Beattie soon to set out his requirements.

In the meantime, he retired straight to his new quarters and roamed from room to room, exploring his new domain. His art was lost in the fire, with only a few scorched canvases surviving. Evelyn was not expected to arrive for another two days, and so Trevelyan had some time to settle into his new lifestyle. That of a hermit, like his father and grandfather. Keeping to himself, he took his meals at the door and left the rest of the world to take care of itself. He still had to take certain medication daily for the pain and discomfort of his existence. Other than that, he had time to reflect on all that had transpired without interruption. For the first time in many months, Trevelyan was alone. In his own space, away from people and the distractions they inevitably incur. The pain medication was keeping the beast at bay for the most part. Although its minions ran along the frayed and damaged nerves of his neck and face unchecked. Causing uncontrollable twitches and jerks that sent flashes of pain that disappeared as soon as they arose. Exhausted by the journey and the medication, Trevelyan had arranged for Beattie to attend to him in his rooms at nine o'clock that evening for a brief introduction and an opportunity to answer questions either of them might have for the other. That allowed four hours in which Trevelyan could rest and prepare himself for Beattie. He closed the large heavy curtains with his good arm and made his way to the enormous fourposter bed that awaited him. He lay himself down, still clothed except for his shoes. He took the blindfold from his shirt pocket and covered his lidless eyes. His thoughts travelled to and fro between the past and the present. He could not help but smile when he realised the irony of his position. Richer than he had dared dream and all the poorer for it. He could have had it all if he had not left that message for Rose. If he had done this. If he had not done that. None of it mattered now.

So why? Why did she do it? What was it that pushed her over the edge of sanity to do such a thing? But even as he formulated the question, he knew the answer. Someone, although he could not recall whom, once said, "You can blame the world and everyone in it. But if you look at things long enough, you realise you brought it all on yourself!" As much as he hated to admit it, he knew that at least a part of that was true. His flippancy and dismissive attitude. His unwillingness to deal with situations he knew would grow out of his control. His inability to engage with people sincerely and objectively. Instead, he treated the world as his playground and the people in it as toys to be picked up and then discarded at whim. He accepted his part in Rose's immolation, but he could not yet forgive her. The overshadowing of his mother's death caused him much grief. And then there came the inevitable guilt. These thoughts held him prisoner until they thinned, blurred and melted away, only to be replaced by the balm of sleep.

∞∞∞∞

A quick series of raps on his bedroom door awakened him. Dammit, how long had he been asleep? Pain flared in his neck and face as he rose to respond. "Is that you, Beattie?" He asked the closed door.

"Indeed, Mr. Trevelyan. It is nine o'clock, as arranged. Would you prefer I came back a little later?" the voice beyond the door replied, with no hint of reproach.

"No, not at all. Give me two minutes, please," replied Trevelyan. He removed the blindfold and gathered a dressing gown that hung on the door to wrap around his now crumpled clothes. Dimming the lights in the room, he found his facemask, put it on and pulled the hood of his gown over his head. He retired to the seat in the darkest corner of the room and said in a raised voice, "Please. Come in."

The door opened, and a well-dressed, but short and balding old man with a dignified air entered the room. He peered through the gloominess in search of his employer.

"I apologise for the lighting, Beattie. My eyes are damaged, and the light hurts," said Trevelyan. Following the sound of the voice, Beattie turned to face the shadowy figure seated in the corner.

" Not at all, Mr. Trevelyan." He smiled. "Although the rest of me may be slowing down, it seems my eyesight persists. My knees, however, are happy to comply." He paused. "May I sit?"

"Please do," Trevelyan replied, and added, "Do I call you Mr. Beattie, or is there another name you would prefer?"

The old man took a seat at the table across from where Trevelyan sat and replied, "Beattie will do just fine, Mr. Trevelyan. My first name is James, but here at Bryngaer, I'm 'Old Man Beattie.'" His voice was warm and friendly, with no recognisable accent that Trevelyan could discern. But his eloquence betrayed his attempt at sounding of a lower station than he was bred into.

"Then please call me Gafyn. Mr. Trevelyan is my father's name." As soon as the words left Trevelyan's lipless mouth, he realised it sounded uncouth. "My apologies, Beattie. My humour can be inappropriate sometimes. I believe you worked for my father for many years." He paused. It was the first time he had referred to Seymour as his father to anyone else. "I didn't intend any disrespect," he finished.

"I have been here at Bryngaer in one fashion or another for nearly sixty years now," he said, choosing to ignore Trevelyan's flippancy. His eyes seemed fixed on the space before him. "My father was head gardener when I was a boy. I would often stay here during the summers to help him. Then, when I came of age, my father retired and I replaced him. That was in your grandfather's time. When your father returned from his travels, he took residency here after his father passed and raised me to his steward. A position I held for many years now. With this position comes a certain formality, which I would find impossible to refuse." Then he raised his eyes, looked at Trevelyan, and smiled. "So, if you could excuse an old man his habits, I would be more comfortable with Mr. Trevelyan."

"Of course," said Trevelyan, meeting his smile behind his mask.

"A most suitable room has been arranged for Miss Munroe beneath this very room. Should you need any assistance a phone has been installed between the two rooms. All you need to do is lift the receiver and await a response. I have taken the liberty of providing Miss Munroe with rooms sharing the same view as yourself. A mere formality when receiving guests, but it can provide a change of conversation should the need arise." With all the formalities over, both Trevelyan and Beattie discussed the day to day running of the household. Trevelyan found he liked the old man's easy and solid manner. His response to Trevelyan's questions showed his seniority in his role. Trevelyan had every confidence that his and Beattie's relationship would work out splendidly. Trevelyan explained he would prefer to hold regular meetings between them daily before Beattie retired for the night. Any items for discussion could be raised and appraised in a timely fashion. Trevelyan did not mention that he liked the old man's company and would look forward to their daily catch up. Time seemed to pass by quickly. When they had finished with the business at hand, it was ten forty-five. Trevelyan began feeling the pain creep back into his traumatised nerves. He thanked Beattie and arranged for him to attend again the next night at the same time. Trevelyan suggested perhaps Beattie could rustle up a nightcap or two while they discuss matters. This being agreed, Beattie bid Trevelyan goodnight and left Trevelyan tired but content. He liked Beattie and was glad he accepted his offer of a nightcap of an evening before retiring for the night. Perhaps it was his lack of a father figure growing up. Or perhaps, because he had no contact with anyone outside of his care team and DI. Samuels.

∞∞∞∞

The following day brought rain. Lashing against his window as he woke, urging him to peer outside. The far mountains disappeared and reappeared through the cloud, and the rain swept sideways, driven by the chilly winter wind. He took his breakfast at the large bay window overlooking the gardens, still dressed in his gown and rumpled clothes. He would like to wander the grounds when the weather allowed. He had never left London before, preferring the anonymity of the crowds of strangers, all going about their business in their thongs. Bryngaer was a world and more away from London, and he was eager to experience the fresh mountain air. But that would have to wait for another day. Today was a day for settling into his new situation, and he opted to rearrange his studio so that he could paint by the large balcony window. He was still learning how to manage with no right arm or hand, and so he wrapped them beneath his clothing to avoid injury. The damage to his arm was severe. The nerves were scorched beyond the ability of the human body to regenerate. But thankfully, there was no pain because the nerves were dead. Dr. Harper was aghast at his decision not to undergo facial reconstruction and a prosthetic arm. But Trevelyan still felt that he had the right of it. They could not understand his guilt, and he was unwilling to explain it. It went far beyond guilt, but he had no other words for how he felt. Aside from his physical injuries and his difficult recovery from his psychological injuries and emotional trauma, it was the guilt that weighed on his spirit. The guilt he felt toward Rose for his arrogance, the guilt he felt concerning his mother and her passing. He had compartmentalised everything except the guilt. That he owned. That he could understand and process. And it was for that reason he decided against surgery. It would take a miracle of science and talent to right the ruin of his face and arm. He could buy the best that the medical profession could offer. But he could never right the wrong that he did to Rose or the wrong that she had returned on him. He would never be the same. He had a new life now. And that required a new Gafyn Trevelyan. His previous ambitions of success and wealth were granted through circumstance and not hard work or talent, and so he remained untested and unchallenged. The only challenges available to him now were adapting and compensating for his injuries. The guilt helped him through that by punishing him. And that punishment required acceptance for it to work. So, he accepted his withered and blasted limb and his ruined face as a part of that punishment. He would have to start his treatment in earnest within the coming days, and he wondered how that might fit into his self-sacrifice.

Evelyn Munroe would arrive tomorrow. From the information provided by Dr. Harper, she was both dedicated and gifted in her rehabilitation methods. Trevelyan was not sure that he needed rehabilitation. In fact, overall, with all things considered, he felt he had dealt with the whole traumatic business very well. He had hoped to continue his own self recovery, but Harper pointed out that he would require medication that only a professional could prescribe. And regular visits to medical facilities. A live in medical and psychological healer seemed the lesser of two evils if only for a short time. He understood he suffered from PTSD, along with the other trauma related stresses, which left him without control of his emotions most of the time. He kept himself distracted from his thoughts and moods by reading whatever literature on the bookshelves in his room he could relate to. He read from Byron and Shelley until after lunch. Feeling inspired by such creative literary minds, he tried to create for himself in his studio. But he could not effectively use his left arm or hand for art, and the effort increased his frustration to a borderline rage within minutes. He caught himself and elected to spend the rest of the day at the bay window, watching the mountains melt away and return through the clouds. His mood simmered below the surface of his contemplations.

Chapter Seven

He was glad of Beattie's knock on his door to enquire if there was anything he may require before their evening meeting. Maybe it was his anger that he had nowhere else to direct but on himself. Or maybe it was because he felt it was time for him to embrace his deformities that led him to bid Beattie to enter without first concealing his disfigurements with his mask and hood. Then, suddenly self-conscious, his anger was supplanted by his vanity. He turned before Beattie could enter and donned his cowl, drawing it over his ruined face and kept to the shadows once more. Beattie entered and dipped his head to the figure in the darkness. "I have taken the liberty of arranging a welcome dinner in honour of Miss Munroe's arrival tomorrow. In keeping with the traditions of Bryngaer, guests are greeted and celebrated in the dining hall on the first day of their arrival. As we are a little short staffed, I have elected a three course instead of the usual five. I have a copy of the menu. If you would like to make any changes, it would be prudent to do so now. If not, I shall inform the kitchen to make their preparations this evening ready for tomorrow."

"I'm sure you have everything in hand, Beattie." Trevelyan sighed from his darkened position. He was tired and dismayed with himself. His emotions were haywire today. He could slip from a quiet rage into indifference and exhaustion in a single moment. Dr. Harper had warned him this may happen. A symptom of the PTSD wild mood swings and intolerances to certain situations and people. "I hoped we may play a little chess with our meeting this evening, Beattie." He continued. "It has been so long since I played and would welcome the distraction if you could find the time?"

"Of course, Mr Trevelyan. Your father has an excellent set in the library. Would you like me to have it brought to your rooms after you have taken your evening meal?" Beattie enquired.

"If you could show me the way, I would be happy to fetch it myself. I have read all the poetry I can stand for now," Trevelyan replied.

"Of course, Mr Trevelyan." Beattie lowered his head again and turned to lead the way. Bryngaer was a rabbit warren of hallways and stairs. Without Beattie's guidance, Trevelyan would have soon become lost. "With your permission, I will instruct the staff to use the service stairs to the house.

There are many, and all the house can be reached without using the main thoroughfare which I have left for your sole use, so you will not be…" Beattie seemed to search for the right word… "Disturbed," he finished.

"Thank you, Beattie. I would be lost without you, both figuratively and literally." Silence met Trevelyan's attempt at a little light humour. He decided he would have to pull the stick out of Beattie's arse a little at a time if he ever hoped to get past the formalities of the man. After a few minutes, Beattie stood before two beautifully crafted wooden doors carved with two large dragons engaged in battle beneath a mountain. He turned the key in the large brass lock and pushed on the heavy doors, which slowly swung open with no effort on Beattie's part. He turned and met Trevelyan with a smile that was hard to read as he held out the door key to him.

"Mr Seymour would spend many hours here in his studies," he offered. "I'm sure you will find something more interesting than the romantics within these bookcases." His eyes smiled as he spoke. Without hesitation, he added, "If that will be all for now, I have a few things to see too before our meeting this evening."

"Of course, Beattie, thank you," Trevelyan replied. Beattie disappeared between the wooden doors and back into the hallway. Trevelyan made his way into his father's study. A desk loomed in the right-hand corner of a large room lined with oak bookcases against every wall. Only the large windows were unencumbered. A fireplace made ready stood to the left beneath a large picture of Bryngaer taken from above, showing its true grandeur amid the trees and landscape surrounding it. Trevelyan browsed through the bookcases, running his good hand across the spines of the books that had gathered no dust. Two small tables with a carved wooden chair at each sat on either side of a beautiful Persian rug that stretched the length of the room and ended before the fireplace. His father's desk was uncluttered and unused for some time. Trevelyan slumped down into his father's chair with a sigh. It suddenly struck him he did not know what his father looked like. He had seen no photographs nor portraits he always supposed rich old men had in their studies or elsewhere on display. In fact, he had seen nothing at all that alluded to his father's countenance. I will ask Beattie about that this evening, Trevelyan thought. Surely there must be something with his father's face, even from his youth. He sat back in the chair and perused his father's desk. Letter headed paper depicting Bryngaer and three lion symbols graced the desk and elaborate pens and pencils sat within their holders. Beneath the desktop were two drawers on either side of his legs. He tried them both, but they were locked. He searched the desk for any sign of a key, but found nothing. Trevelyan rose and circumnavigated the library. He perused the books on the shelves, looking for something to lose himself between now and Beattie's visit later that evening. There seemed to be no real classification to the randomness of the books. Classics mixed in with history books, literature, and encyclopaedias. He rearranged the books while he was here and cleared the shelves of the bookcase he was nearest to. He placed the books on the small reading table nearby. Not a speck of dust or fluff could be seen, considering the library had gone unused since before his father's death. He continued in this manor until all the bookcases were emptied. Books rested upon the reading tables and the floor when none could fit elsewhere. Trevelyan had no real interest in arranging the bookcases but found that the lack of organisation disturbed him. He had nothing better to do. Besides, he found he felt normal here. Surrounded by bookcases and desks in this room. He felt like a story, surrounded by the stories of others. There was a strange comfort in that. He returned books to the shelves collating them not alphabetically but by subject and size over several hours. As the time for his meal arrived, he left the task unfinished and picked a copy of 'The Tales of King Arthur' before he made his way back through the dragon doors. They closed with a gentle sigh as he turned the key to lock them and replaced it in his pocket. He felt a little more comfortable wandering the halls, knowing he would not bump into any staff. He silently thanked Beattie again for his foresight and thoughtfulness. As he wandered the halls and stairways, he accidentally found his way back to his room and lay back on his bed to read for a short while.

∞∞∞∞

He awoke before nine o'clock and readied himself. It was then he realised he had forgotten to get the chessboard from the library. He had no desire to play chess this evening. He hoped Beattie could tell him a little about his father while they shared a whisky or two instead. He prepared his chair near to the shade in the room's corner and positioned the table and guest chair a little way off to his left. As he shielded his twisted right arm from view, he heard Beattie's footsteps approaching down the hallway. He waited a moment before shouting, "Come straight in Beattie, the door's unlocked." As promised, Beattie entered the bedroom with two tumblers, a decanter of what appeared to be whisky, and a small ice bucket. All balanced perfectly on a silver tray. He placed them on the table before turning to close the door. "I forgot to fetch the chessboard when I left the library, I'm afraid, Beattie. I wondered instead if you would tell me a little about my father over a drink or two?"

"I fear I could only tell what you already know, Mr. Trevelyan." He sighed while he seated himself and crossed one leg over the other.

"I really know nothing, Beattie. Other than he arranged for me to inherit while I was still a newborn and that he died in his bed in relative peace. I live here in his house and spend his fortune, and yet I know little to nothing about the man himself!" he replied, trying not to sound glib.

"I can tell you what little I know, Mr. Trevelyan. But I'm afraid it probably won't help you come to know the 'man himself,' as you say. But I can tell you about the Seymour Family since the days of my father," Beattie said. He poured two measures into the glasses and added a little ice. "Your father and Mr. Seymour senior didn't get along, I'm afraid to say. Your father was a little rebellious after the death of your grandmother. By the time he became a teenager, that rebelliousness had led to a complete disregard of his father's principles and future plans. When he came of age, your grandfather had despaired of your father and allowed him to live his life as he pleased. As long as he did not return to Bryngaer. Your father travelled far and wide for thirty years before returning to Bryngaer after your grandfather passed. During that time, I believe your grandfather would have forgiven your father his transgressions, had your father returned while he still lived, but that was not to be. Your father had spent a long time in the east before he returned to the west. And longer still before he returned here. By the time Bryngaer had a new master, your grandfather had passed a year hence. Your father attended several meetings with Mr Fairbourne, the younger. He had, by then, taken over the legal practice from his father. It was decided that Mr. Charles Seymour Jr. would not take over the reins of industry and business as his father had intended. Instead, he elected several boards to manage the interests of the Seymour dynasty, while he retired here to Bryngaer and immersed himself in personal interests that would consume him."

"Personal interests?" asked Trevelyan, as he sipped on his drink. The ice cooled his throat while the whisky soothed his nerves.

Beattie paused as he took a sip of his own drink and gazed at the wall ahead of him, lost in memory. "Your father was a student of eastern philosophies before he returned westward. He continued his studies in Europe and eventually here at Bryngaer. He collected many volumes of work from around the western hemisphere. Particularly works of Welsh history and mythology." His focus returned as he turned to Trevelyan. "I don't know if you are aware, Mr. Trevelyan. Here in the Snowdonia range, there are many historical, or at least legendary, locations pertaining to local folk stories and such. I remember my mother telling me stories about the mountains surrounding Bryngaer, and the heros and beasts that dwelt there." Trevelyan pictured an infant Beattie on his mother's knee listening to fairy tales. He reached for the decanter and ice to refill their glasses. Beattie continued. "His collections are still there in the library should you wish to learn more, and his private study contained many such tomes and papers relating to his absorptions. All of which were removed before your arrival and stored in the nook within the library."

"Nook?" asked Trevelyan, his interest aroused.

"Ah yes," replied Beattie. "Forgive me, Mr. Trevelyan. With so much to organise and staff shortages, it completely slipped my mind. The middle bookcase on the western wall can be opened with a sharp pull on the top shelf. It swings open to reveal your father's reading room and personal documents. He left no instructions on what was to be done with them after his passing, and so I thought it best that they are kept safe."

"Talking of personal effects, Beattie, there no portraits or photographs of my father anywhere in the house, only my grandfather. In fact, I have no idea what my father looked like. Do you know where I might find any?" Trevelyan said hesitantly.

"I confess I can't say." Beattie admitted. "As he was away from Bryngaer for most of his years, and because of his father's wrath, his likeness was removed from the house and disposed of shortly after his departure. After his return, I don't believe he had any desire for such trivialities. Whatever personal papers he left were boxed and deposited in the nook. Perhaps you may try there?"

"Did you know my mother, Beattie?" Trevelyan asked, as he seemed to exhaust the subject of his father.

"Alas, not well." He replied. Trevelyan thought his eyes suggested otherwise. "I believe she left your father's service around the time of your birth."

Trevelyan caught himself mid sip. "You mean my mother WORKED for him?" he said, louder than he intended.

"Indeed. She was the housekeeper here for many years. She worked for your grandfather before he passed. She stayed on for a couple more years before leaving." Beattie looked embarrassed to be discussing such matters and shifted awkwardly in his seat.

"So, my father got her pregnant before dismissing her, you mean?" Trevelyan's anger rose sharply, but he subdued it. Redirecting his anger at his dead father rather than Beattie, who looked suitably shamed. "I'm sorry, Beattie. Since the incident, I have had trouble controlling my anger. That was not directed at you. I am angry at my father for doing such a thing," he finished apologetically.

Beattie seemed to defend his previous employer when he said. "I truly do not know the situation between Mr. Seymour Jr. and your mother. I have never known him to act in a manner unbecoming to his station or mistreat any of his staff in any way. The only affiliation I knew your father enjoy with a member of the fairer sex was Miss Llewelyn, his research assistant. And as far as I am aware, that was purely academic." The mention of his father's assistant seemed to sadden Beattie. He seemed far away for a moment before he continued. "You must understand, Mr. Trevelyan. My relationship with your family has always been a working one. By that I mean, my family has been employed by yours for several generations. My interactions with your forebears were solely within the terms of my employment. And as such, remained only professional until the end." The old man seemed upset.

"Of course, Beattie. Again, I apologise if my questions have seemed inappropriate. I have so little information on my father's life it frustrates me a little," Trevelyan said earnestly.

"Not at all Mr. Trevelyan. I am sorry I couldn't be more help," returned Beattie. "If you would excuse me, I am feeling the burden of my years tonight. We have a busy day tomorrow with Miss Munroe's arrival and I fear our nightcap has succeeded in its purpose." He smiled weakly. His eyes seemed far away still and drooped sadly as he gathered the remains of the refreshments on the tray and bid Trevelyan good evening. After he was gone, Trevelyan undressed. He took his copy of the Arthurian tales and climbed into his bed, unable to sleep. As he read, his mind wandered. He decided tomorrow, as soon as he woke, he would investigate the reading room in the library and his father's collection.

∞∞∞∞

Trevelyan awoke to the sound of torrential rain and wind outside his bedroom window that rattled during the largest gusts. Today was the day of Evelyn's arrival. He was nervous about having somebody staying here at Bryngaer. Especially someone he would have to interact with every day for some time to come. He had very much enjoyed his isolation from all except Beattie, and wondered how he was to adapt to this new element in his life. He would be expected to reveal his deformities and to troll out all his psychological babble that someone outside of his mind might understand. It seemed an impossible task, and he could feel the stress creeping into his furrowed brow already. Perhaps he could convince her that all was well and cut short her stay. But he would have to be on his best behaviour and resist his outbursts of anger that have slipped out of late. He was always alone, except for the time he spent with Beattie. There was no one else to witness these spontaneous eruptions over some trivial matter. He must keep a lid on them for as long as they were together. Dressed and about as ready for the day as he could be, he opened his bedroom door and made his way down to the library. Armed with Beattie's description, he used the time he had to distract himself until she arrived. He drew the large key from his pocket, unlocked the dragon doors of the library, and beheld the mess he had created the day before. He located the bookcase identified by Beattie. He cleared a path between it and the table full of books and took hold of the top shelf with his only good hand. Using his weight, he tugged and swung the door on its concealed hinges. A masterpiece of design, the bookcase opened, revealing a well-adorned study. Complete with reading desk and chair, drinks cabinet and standing glass lamp. On the desk and scattered around the floor were boxes of papers and folders in no particular order. With his right arm strapped to his chest, he sat himself cross-legged and began flicking through the mounds of papers in the nearest box. To his dismay, the first box consisted only of receipts to various booksellers and archivists, which he discarded behind him. He moved on to the next box. A brief survey produced nothing of interest. There were a few correspondences between his father and an organisation called 'The Theta Society'. They discussed something called 'the tree' and its planetary correspondences. Whatever that meant. So he put these to one side and continued to the next box. Here he found letters from a Morgan Llewelyn. around thirty of them. They contained much the same type of content as the letters to The Theta Society. These he put together with the others, deciding that anything of interest he will take to his rooms and read at his convenience. As he pressed through the boxes, his 'Interest' pile was growing. After collecting the items that caught his eye, he gathered them together and put them on the desk beside him. He sat at the desk, noting that it was almost the same as the desk in the library. The checked the drawers either side of his legs. They were unlocked. He reached across with his left hand to open the right-hand drawer. Within were a small bunch of keys and a faded picture. On closer inspection of the picture, Trevelyan could make out of a thin elfin faced woman. He guessed she was in her early thirties. She had a wide smile with a shock of bright red hair and emerald eyes. An image of Rose clouded his mind's eye, and he struggled to push it away. Concentrating instead on the face of the woman in the picture. Her hair was brushed back behind her ears, revealing her high cheek bones and thin red lips. She was attractive and attired in a loose-fitting red summer dress contrasting starkly with her pale white features.

    He put the picture down on the desk and turned his attention to the left-hand drawer. Inside was a small notebook and pen and nothing else. Flicking through the notebook, Trevelyan found symbols and scrawlings along with references to other resources, siting passages and paragraphs. These he put on top of the picture on the desk and examined the small bunch of keys he now held in his hand. He closed the right-hand drawer and, trying the different keys, he found one that locked it perfectly. Using the same key, locked the left-hand drawer too. He stood, collected the items on the desk, and left the reading room. Closing the empty bookcase door behind him, he made his way to the desk in the library. Seating himself, he tried one key after another until he heard the tumble of the lock in the left drawer. He slid it open. Here, he found, wrapped in a soft, sweet-smelling cloth, two leather journals. He rose from his chair and emptied one of the boxes of receipts and began putting his new treasures inside. Once finished, he desperately wanted to return to his rooms and read through them. But there would be time enough for that. So instead, he continued replacing the books on the shelves until the library looked, once more, organised and tidy. A quick glance at the sun midway through the sky told him it was time to have lunch. Miss Munroe arrived within the hour.

Chapter Eight

Trevelyan finished his lunch and checked the clock. It read one in the afternoon. She should be here anytime now, he mused. He took his lunch in his studio, sitting by the window overlooking the gardens and the distant mountains. Wind and rain swept across the landscape in waves, hiding the sun from view. At about a thousand feet above sea level, Bryngaer had its own weather because of the rugged mountains that surrounded it on three sides. A few miles in any direction would leave the mountains behind and drop steeply to the coast. The winds would lessen and the rain would thin, till blue skies would creep between the clouds and let the sun peek through. He dressed and was about as ready as he could be for Evelyn's arrival. In the meantime, he extracted the first of the leather bound journals and examined the lock. All the keys he had found were far too big for the miniature lock. As he tried to force it open, he noticed a loose leaf of paper within the journal. With a few minutes' delicate effort, he freed it from the journal and opened it on the desk.

The Journals of Charles L Seymour

Have finally arrived back at Bryngaer after almost thirty years of travel from east to west. I was nineteen when last I was here. As I sit at my desk to write this, I am now forty-eight years old. My father has passed, and I am now heir to my family home. Charles Winston Seymour passed peacefully in his bed almost a year ago, aged eighty-eight. Our differences prevented any form of reconciliation in the years since I left. Other than a generous yearly allowance that allowed me to indulge my passions and curiosities around the world, I have all but dispensed with my past. My father had high expectations for my career and social standing. After my schooling, he had such noble plans for my inclusion in the various industries and businesses he had accumulated over his many years of success. To his great dismay, I did not share his ideas for my future, and I did not hold back in telling him so. My father was not used to being disagreed with. Especially by an 'Ingrate' like myself. After several years and disappointments, he finally gave up on his aspirations of me and allowed me to live my life as I wished. I endured no loss of finances or heritage due to the fact I was his only child. My mother died of consumption when I was still very young. My father was too consumed with grief to consider women from then on. He lived the rest of his days here at Bryngaer, accumulating his wealth and building his empire. An empire which now belongs to me. A board was elected to manage this empire, as I declined to take the reins myself.

I have a greater work in mind.

During my travels, I discovered an unknown desire within myself for knowledge. My travels in Tibet and Asia revealed to me a spiritual culture I had underestimated. One that was not embraced here in the west. I was born into a life of materialism and sought something other than material ambitions and prosperity. I studied with many eastern mystery schools. While these were stimulating and productive, I felt a detachment from them on a cultural level as a westerner. This prompted my curiosity into what, if anything, would be the western mysteries? Evolved from the cultural histories and beliefs of my ancestral past? Many years would pass as my understanding grew. I studied the Greek and Egyptian mysteries in depth, but from an academic point of view. Never connecting with them on an instinctual level. Then I discovered The Matter of Britain. Specifically, the Arthurian mysteries and, through them, the Mabinogion. Here was a culture that I felt a connection to. I was born and raised at Bryngaer. A vast mansion with acres of forest estate amid the Snowdonia range in north Wales. I had lost touch with my Welsh heritage and was delighted to learn of the hidden and secret knowledge of this tradition. I halted all my other studies and outside interests. I immersed myself into tales and myths with links to locations throughout Britain but mostly concentrated on Wales and Snowdonia, in particular. I longed to return here and conduct my research in my homeland, but while my father remained alive, that could not be. Until now.

I have within me the concept of creation.

Not a physical creation in the material world. A mystical creation on another plane of consciousness. My studies have opened my awareness of the vibrational aspect of manifest creation. There is too much detailed and precise information relating to my studies, research, and unique purpose to deal with on these pages. But a brief inspection of quantum theory, string theory, and many other scientific and spiritual texts will illuminate my concept. I will endeavour to explain these steps and methods I employed as they are encountered and overcome. I will record my failures along with my successes, if any. My proposal is this. Employing my own magical system of ceremonial magic, developed over the last thirty years using different resources that I will detail later, I will create a world not unlike our own. In a purely elemental and vibrational plane of *existence on the outer levels of consciousness. I will imbibe this world with Celtic principles, using nature as a catalyst in the manner of the three rays of ancient Celtic magic and the ancient Jewish Qabbalistic tradition of the tree of life.*

C.L. Seymour

Trevelyan re read the letter again. It was not at all what he expected, although he was not exactly sure what he expected. Certainly not references to "otherworlds" or whatever the 'concept of creation' might be. Also, the mention of the 'tree' again, as did his father's letters from The Theta Society. Trevelyan's interest was piqued now, and he felt a tremor run through his stomach. A little adrenaline caused his excitement to rise. A feeling he had not experienced in many months. As he read the letter a third time, he heard the gravel crunching outside his window. Looking out, he saw the big black Mercedes grind to a halt outside the main doors of Bryngaer. He put the letter to one side, along with the bound journals, and sighed wearily as he rose from his seat. He checked his appearance in the mirror before placing his white plastic prosthetic mask over his scorched features and pulled the cowl over his head as far as it would go. He left his studio and made his way toward the grand staircase that led to the foyer.

Beattie stood facing the main doors with his arms behind his back and his hands clasped together. Two very young porters raced outside in the howling rain to extract Miss Munroe's belongings from the car. Beattie took an umbrella placed conveniently by the doors and, opening it, met Evelyn as she hurried out of the rain. Trevelyan could hear Beattie welcome Miss Monroe as he ushered her into the foyer under the umbrella. Beattie then returned outside to gather the smaller items himself. Trevelyan remained out of sight on the west landing at the top of the stairs, suddenly coy about descending. As he watched Evelyn remove her wet coat, he was struck by the image of a desolate and soaking Rose. It was not the first time she had appeared to him while he was awake. A phantom of his trauma. She was standing on the east landing, staring at him. He looked back at Evelyn and back to the east landing, but Rose was gone. Of course she was gone, he thought. She was never there! Not the most auspicious start to his act of mental equilibrium. He would have to keep a lid on his wild imagination if he was to forestall Miss Munroe, and have her return to wherever it was she had come from as soon as possible. He watched her from his hiding place atop the stairs for a moment while she shook her coat dry. He suddenly realised that this would be his first interaction with a woman since Rose. A shiver ran down his spine. Beattie had returned to the foyer and greeted Miss Munroe as only Beattie could. Trevelyan was in awe of his composure and professionalism and assumed that Miss Munroe was too. As if Beattie could hear his thoughts, he raised his eyes and met his gaze. Trevelyan felt like a naughty schoolboy caught eavesdropping and spurred his legs into motion, descending the staircase to Beattie and the waiting Evelyn.

Evelyn was taller and younger than he expected. Having read Harper's recommendation and her corresponding qualifications, he guessed she would be at least ten years older. She had a soft, round, and very attractive face with long, loose, flowing brunette hair falling to her shoulders. Trevelyan felt uncomfortable with her attractiveness. His coyness struck again as he extended his left hand in welcome. She took his hand in hers and shook it, her gaze moving across his mask beneath the cowl.

"Thank you, Mr. Trevelyan," she exclaimed as she looked about the vast foyer in amazement. "I had no idea I would be staying in such beautiful surroundings," she said, as her smile widened. "It was a spectacular journey for a city girl," she quipped.

"You should see it on a good day," he said, cringing behind his mask.

Beattie rescued him by announcing that Miss Munroe's rooms were ready and if she would follow him, he would show her around Bryngaer before leaving her at her quarters. Trevelyan took his opportunity to slink back to his studio after bleating that he would see her at dinner and to feel at home here. He was unfamiliar with entertaining strangers when he was whole and good-looking. Now he felt like a freakish child trying to act like a man.

Dinner was at seven o'clock, leaving him three hours to himself. He threw himself on his bed and before he could castigate himself for his wretched existence; he fell into a shallow and fitless sleep. He dreamed of that far stretching landscape from his coma dreams, draped in the early morning mist. A red glow coloured the mist before him, growing brighter the nearer he approached. Like the rising of the sun, it glowed until, finally, an incandescent figure loomed out of the fog. Rose. It was Rose… and she was burning! Her lips clenched in a silent scream as the conflagration engulfed her. "We will always be together," the flames announced, and her booming voice echoed, "NOW WAKE UP!"

Trevelyan awoke with a start. Sweating profusely. He swung his legs off the bed, sitting motionless for a few moments while he gathered his wits. Checking the time, he saw he still had an hour before dinner with Evelyn. So, he seated himself before the window once again and gazed at the storm lashing the trees outside. Dazed still from his sudden awakening, he took the leather-bound journal the note had slipped from and placed it on the floor at his feet. Removing the large library key from his pocket, he placed his foot on the bottom of the journal, securing it to the floor. With his left hand, he jammed the key beneath the strap that stretched across the covers. With a sharp jerk, he broke the small hasp attaching the two together. He released his foot on the journal and replaced it on the table where it fell open, revealing the pages within. Trevelyan noted the receding daylight and closed his curtains against the weather outside. He needed something to distract him from the image of Rose ablaze in his dream. He picked up the journal and flicked the pages until he reached the beginning. The loose page he had pulled out earlier was the first page in the journal. He flattened it out and read it yet again. Returning it to its rightful place, he continued on the next page.

May 19th 1965

I have established a comprehensive library of books that I require. With only a few exceptions due to the rarity of such texts, I have begun to build correspondences between the three rays and the tree of life. I will include all methods and techniques in detail within the appendix at the back of the diaries. Briefly put, the tree will provide the structure of unity dividing into duality. These are then balanced by the middle pillar. The deities and elemental forms of Celtic tradition will then clothe the branches of the tree. Thus, can I bring, bind and focus the forces through controlled visualisation and ceremonial magic. Creating balance for channelling the power I intend for conception. Once I have my system in place with its hierarchies and correspondent archetypes, I can then experiment with the ceremonial magic techniques until I can marry the two together. But there my Great Work, as I have begun to refer to my dedications, must come to a halt until I can find the physical counterpart required to complete my system. A female priestess, instinctual and mysterious as the moon. I cannot seek her out or acquire her myself or through my influence. She must arrive of her own volition and unknowing of my Great Work. If, after laying out my ideas and ambitions, she agrees to the role of priestess, my purpose may succeed. It is fundamental in securing the permission of the great gods if you are to attempt such a work. This is approved or denied by their will alone. There was still much work to be done before the time will arise for my priestess to light my way. With this in mind, I reached out to several occult fraternities for clarification on certain principles and methods. I insisted on written correspondence only to separate the wheat from the chaff. I am at present receiving inspired advice and learned opinions from a correspondent called Morgan. He has been invaluable in his translations and interpretations of my requests for clarification and has of late become curious about my intentions. I must tread with care.

Trevelyan was intrigued by what he read, but he was unsure of what it was his father was actually trying to accomplish. Whatever it was, he had gone to great lengths and expense to pursue this goal. As he understood it, Charles L. Seymour was trying to create a kind of 'Narnia' on some astral plane or something. It did not seem to make much sense, but somehow Trevelyan became more engrossed in the idea as he thought about it. It seemed surreal. But in as far as experiences go, he had lived the 'surreal' and so suspended whatever beliefs he held and read on.

23rd September 1965

I have of late taken to morning walks along the river toward the mountains and the forest. Today is the Autumn Equinox, and the nights shall draw in as the season changes and the weather becomes cooler, but the changing colours of the landscape are spectacular to behold. I love it here and, if it is within my power, I shall endeavour to recreate it within my new Eden. After, I return and take my breakfast. I then retire to my library and study and return to the Great Work. My system is almost complete. I have researched different aspects of ritualisation drawn from those great minds and spiritual pioneers of The Order of the Golden Dawn. An organisation derived from the Rosicrucians around the turn of the twentieth century. Founded when three Freemasons signed a pledge of fidelity on 12 February 1888. The Golden Dawn existed as one coherent association from 1888 to 1901 with many distinguished members and great minds of their time. Other occult society members had an enormous influence on my work. Especially Dion Fortune, who shares some of my instinct for nature-based magic, and who established her own society. By forging an alloy of these systems and methods, I will have a working formula to control and direct the forces I intend to summon. Once again, my pen pal and fellow spiritual Infidel Morgan has set me in the right direction. I have become quite fond of receiving his letters and the observations he expresses with a passion equal only to my own. I have considered breaking my no visitors rule for him alone. I feel I could accomplish much more if he could share at least some of my research without giving my goal away and not having to rely on the postal service for prompt responses. I find the telephone a vulgar distraction and would enjoy the company and conversation of a fellow spiritual thinker for a couple of days if he would agree to a weekend here at Bryngaer as my most welcome guest. I may invite him on my next correspondence. In the meantime, I have much to compile and prepare.

Here was something Trevelyan could use as an entry point to his father's way of thinking. It surprised him at how the idea of some 'otherworld' for want of a better terminology seemed to tug on his imagination, and he found it a welcome distraction. His father would have reading material in his library that would shed some light on the references contained in the journal.

Chapter Nine

Time was pressing on now and he must prepare for his meal and formal introduction to Evelyn without the safety valve of Beattie to rescue him again. He would have to entertain Evelyn by himself, which filled him with dread. He imagined what it would be like for her, sitting opposite 'The Phantom of the Opera' at dinner. Trevelyan thought this is going to be a disaster! Dinner was a little awkward. Only because Trevelyan's nerves seemed to get the better of him. He was never a social creature even before Rose dropped a firebomb in the middle of his life. Now he only seemed comfortable in his own company. Or that of Beattie. He was growing to appreciate Beattie's easy manner. There was no pity in his voice or his eyes when they shared their nightcaps. Evelyn, on the other hand, was an expert in professional empathy. Not quite condescending enough to be rude, while still maintaining an air of sympathy. He supposed it was one of those things in life that if you had not experienced personally, you were always going to be on the other side of the glass, so to speak.

She outlined her treatment plan and agreed on morning and evening sessions. The mornings were to be for physical treatments. His pain management and physiotherapy. Evenings for psychological evaluation and psychiatric therapy. It surprised him at how nervous he was because she was a woman. An attractive woman that offended his vanity, or what was left of it. As she spoke of how she would like their rehabilitation programme to progress, he considered to himself how, if he was not the deformed, guilt ravaged creature he had now become, he would have tried to flirt or at least impress her. But he was no longer a slave to his ego. In that way, at least Rose had brought him some kind of freedom. Another thing he noticed was in Evelyn's company, Rose never seemed far away. Almost like she was hiding in the room somewhere listening to their conversation and plotting her revenge. The thought sent a shiver down his spine, and he realised that Evelyn had stopped talking and seemed to await some kind of response from him. He was seated far away enough from her that she could not see beneath the cowl he now wore all the time. It was a part of his defence protocols.

"I asked how your pain medication is working out for you," she said, as if he was hard of hearing. The dark mood was creeping up on him as she spoke, creating reasons to lose his temper. She was being perfectly reasonable, and he was looking for a reason to dislike her because she was an attractive woman. He would be expected to share intimate thoughts and feelings with her over their time together. Just like Rose.

"It leaves me a little foggy sometimes," he replied, trying to sound as cordial as possible. "But it allows me to get through my day," he concluded.

"Well, we can look at your current medication and see if there are alternatives," she replied with a smile. She sighed, and he could feel her gaze on him, making him shuffle in his seat. "May I ask you a question, Mr. Trevelyan?" she asked.

He almost barked, 'Mr. Trevelyan is my father,' but remembered his promise of best behaviour and elected instead for, "Please...call me Gafyn."

"Gafyn, may I be blunt with you?" she asked. He was a little surprised by her change of approach. From cliché sympathy to straight forward tactics. He nodded his acquiescence.

"I have read your medical reports on the extent of your injuries. You were removed from General and quickly treated under Dr. Harper. This undoubtedly saved your life. General is a good hospital but understaffed and unskilled in the kind of emergency treatment you required. I would be tempted to say you're lucky to be alive, but I'm sure you have mixed feelings about that." She left that last remark hanging in the air.

He was tempted to look at her, but he felt that if he did, he would fall into some kind of trap and so remained silent. He could feel her eyes on him, searching for a breach in his defences.

"I know you wish I was a million miles away from here, spewing pity on some other roasted wretch, but I'm not. I'm here. I have read the psych report. You have refused any corrective surgery to your chest and face. I also know you have chosen to keep that twisted and charred branch of an arm out of some kind of self-inflicted punishment. Whatever it is you feel guilty for, you resent me for being not only an unwelcome intrusion on your seclusion, but for having the audacity to be of the same gender that put you in this situation." All this was spoken quite matter of fact without a trace of animosity or bitterness. Trevelyan was taken aback. Struggling with how to respond, he blurted, "You forgot to mention your bedside manner," and for the first time in months, he smiled. She let out a small laugh, and the tension between them fell away. The rest of the evening went much better. Trevelyan unclenched a little in her company because of her candour and ability at being able to read her patient. He appreciated her cutting through the false sympathy bullshit, but felt a little violated that she could see into him and through the walls he built against her. They spoke of Bryngaer and her wish to wander the grounds if the weather improved. She told him a little about her background and journey into medicine until it was time for Trevelyan and Beattie's meeting in his rooms. After bidding each other a good night and arranging to start physical treatment the following morning, they went their separate ways at the bottom of the stairs, Trevelyan to his rooms and Evelyn to hers on the ground floor beneath his.

During their night cap discussion, Trevelyan asked Beattie if Charles Seymour had any particular religious inclinations, to which he replied, "If Mr. Seymour followed any particular faith, he gave no indication of so doing. But having travelled extensively, he enjoyed the study of various forms of worship." That seemed to be the extent of his knowledge. Beattie spoke of closing the parts of the house that were unused during the winter, as was practise and had Trevelyan sign a few invoices for the felling of several of the trees on the grounds that had become weakened over the years and posed a danger in high winds. After finishing their drinks, Beattie prepared to retire for the night and took the tray as he made his way to the door.

"Miss Munroe seems very nice, wouldn't you say, Mr. Trevelyan?" he said before he left the room.

Trevelyan replied, "A Rose by any other name, Beattie Old Boy," he said cryptically, enjoying the private joke. Beattie, indulgent as ever, replied, "Of course, Mr. Trevelyan," and disappeared through the door.

'Alone at last,' Trevelyan declared to himself, eager to return to his father's journal. He slumped into the chair by the curtained bay window and took it up once more.

11th November 1965

Having invited Morgan to weekend here in my last letter, I received response today that he would look forward to a weekend before Christmas arrives and I have arranged a car to collect him and bring him here this coming Friday. I feel relieved that he accepted and look forward to an evening or two discussing magic and psychology over whiskies and cigars. He also included some 'Path working' suggestions. Directed Visualisations used in meditation for me to try before his arrival on the fifteenth. I think I shall enjoy the break from my Great Work, which can be mentally exhausting after months of solitary study.

19th November 1965

My fellow 'Infidel' Morgan has returned to London this morning after a very auspicious few days. **Miss** *Morgan Llewelyn arrived on Friday as arranged, and my shock and delight must have been palpable to her as I met her car on the driveway.*

Miss Llewelyn! Didn't Beattie mention her? He continued reading.

In my arrogance, I believed Morgan to be a man due to His ambitious thinking and rare intellect. The question of gender never entered our correspondences, and I did not relate his instincts in the realm of magic to be female when, in retrospect, they most clearly were. I have been blinded by my work and my ignorance. I cannot easily describe the days and nights that followed her arrival and was reluctant to part company until she promised to return for a longer stay. I am bewitched by her beauty and spirit. A warm and kind face with emerald eyes and the most wonderful shock of bright red hair worn in length down her back. We are of a similar age and share a Welsh background, although hers was an agricultural background of generations working on the land, whereas mine was a line of Moguls and aristocrats. She began teaching me Welsh over breakfast each morning. Once again, my ignorance shames me. We spent our days walking the hills and valleys of Snowdonia and evenings drinking single malt whisky and long discussions on occult and spiritual practices until late into the night. We hardly got through any of the tasks I had planned for us as I was having such a good time in her company and felt a breath of fresh air run through myself and Bryngaer. I was immensely attracted to her although I tried to disguise my affection so as not to infringe on this kinship of magic but could not help feeling the old gods had smiled on me and my Great Work and that perhaps this was my priestess come to me in my hour of need. In fact, I feel sure of it.

The cosmos has blessed my endeavours and sent her to me to complete my creation. I can hardly hide my excitement and have thrown myself into her suggestions in the hope I will be able to present my idea to her sometime in the near future. I have no reason to think I will not see her again, as she seemed to fall in love with Bryngaer and the landscape surrounding us and despairs of the city and its legions of lost souls. I hope that after a short time she might accept an invitation to stay here for a season as my assistant research partner, which will meet her financial requirements and my ambitions.

Trevelyan stopped reading and returned the journal back to the table. It was getting late and, seeing as Beattie had extended his apologies and cancelled tonight's nightcap and chat due to poor health, Trevelyan undressed and got into his bed and contemplated the day's events. Evelyn was a surprise to him, to be sure. She was not at all what he expected. Her forth right attitude seemed to get the best results from him, and he presumed to expect more of the same. They would meet in the treatment room shortly after breakfast and would continue until lunchtime. Thereafter, Trevelyan's time was his own until five o'clock, when they would once again meet in the treatment room for an hour or so of therapy and discussion. He was reluctant to extend an invitation to walk the grounds together outside of the prescribed hours and so would suggest using the time they spent in therapy on walks beside the river or across the meadow instead of the treatment room, which he was already growing to dislike. Or perhaps his studio surrounded by his art, where he felt safe.

His thoughts then wandered to his father and Morgan Llewelyn. He tried to comprehend what it was his father was hoping to create. If he understood correctly, the information gleaned between the journal and the notes and diary entries his father intended to use a power born of the sexual chemistry and natural laws of attraction between them both and amplify it many times over by certain occult principles and what he termed 'constructive visualisation' to build an alternative world somewhere outside the realm of matter, independent of our own world here in reality. This world would be much like the world we inhabit, but a nature-based world subject to a Celtic-like ideology. Was it even possible? Seymour and Morgan seemed to think so. He lay back on his pillow, using his left hand to position his dead right arm across his chest and imagined what such a world might look like, during which he fell into a shallow, protracted sleep.

Chapter Ten

He dreamed of Rose. Arms outstretched and ablaze, drifting toward him through a sea of mist. Like a burning image of Christ on the cross. As she got nearer, he could see her scorched features turning black with the heat of the flames. Her naked body blistering. Her hair a bright conflagration. She was screaming something soundlessly as she passed him, floating on the mist. He reached out to her in his anguish, trying to hear what she cried out. Their eyes locked. Their fingertips brushed each other's as she drifted past him. In that instant, he, too, burst into flames. Before he could let out a scream, he was transported across the sea and through the mist, toward dark mountains and volcanoes, across a blackened plateau cracked and fractured by lava. Still ablaze, his vision swept past the volcanoes and plunged down beneath the black mountains. Back into that subterranean cavern where he witnessed the birth of a being of darkness and stars. The cavern, lit only by the lava and rock light, now embodied what appeared to be a round, vertical, spinning portal of green fire. Contained between two horn like shapes of rock protruding from the ground. He could feel power thrumming in the musty air emanating from this portal. Knelt before it, in abeyance, was the dark figure receiving some kind of instruction that Trevelyan could not understand. The air inside the cavern seemed to throb and vibrate to the sound of the voice beyond the portal. Suddenly, he felt a crushing pressure surrounding him as the dark figure raised his hand, pointing to where Trevelyan watched. In that moment, it was as though he winked out of existence. Became a disembodied thought, travelling across an ocean of space and time and slowly dissolving into the aether.

He awoke bathed in sweat and took a moment to compose himself. A quick glance at the clock beside his bed showed it was three in the morning. The dreams were becoming more frequent and intense, and Trevelyan could not help but feel they were somehow connected. He could feel Rose's presence so acutely sometimes. It was almost as though she were watching him from behind his own eyes. Lurking like some kind of unholy monster waiting to be summoned from whatever hell it came from. His nerves were becoming more frayed as time went by. He put his unsettled manner, and the incumbent nature of these dreams, down to the fact that he would soon have to discuss with Evelyn his inner feelings and trauma. Reliving the moment, she burned his life to the ground and gave him back a life that was broken. He wrapped a dressing gown around himself, made his way to the window, and pulled the curtain back. There was no light pollution at Bryngaer, isolated as it was. He could see a night full of stars blinking in and out by the passing of unseen clouds. Although still tired, he slumped into the window seat, turned on the lamp beside him, and picked up the journal once more. He was maybe half way through and had been perusing the diaries that gave straightforward instructions for the strange magical practices employed by Seymour and Morgan. He poured himself a generous measure of scotch into a glass and continued to read.

January 30th 1966

Morgan and I have continued our correspondence along much the same lines as previously noted. She persists in impressing me with not only her knowledge, but also her perception of its value to me. Our letters have become more personal and gone is the formality since her stay here. In my last missive, I offered her a full-time position here as my research assistant with a generous salary and the promise of working on a unique metaphysical project. If she would attend me here at Bryngaer for another weekend, as before, I will allay her curiosity, which has been growing ever more indomitable, and explain to her in detail, how her help has quickened my purpose and what it is I intend to do. There is little else I can do now except refine my theory and await her reply.

February 14th 1966

Morgan accepted my invitation to weekend here once more. Understandably, she requires more information on the project before she can decide on whether to accept my offer. Arrangements were made, and she will arrive tomorrow evening, giving me four days in which to explain my premise and show her the magical system I have built and the commensurate ceremonial ritual with which to implement it. My only misgiving is how to approach the subject of creating the forces that will be required and the manner of summoning and use of those forces. As a high priestess, she will embody the attributes of the feminine principal. I, as the high priest, will likewise embody the male principal. It will be the cyclic exchange of energy built between us that will power the machine, in a manner of speaking. We must raise these forces using a form of magic, namely sex magic.

This is not as deplorable as it may sound to the uninitiated. The forces generated by a priest and priestess are, at a very basic level, the same forces of attraction that are displayed in nature. Except that initiates amplify these forces of attraction. Direct them for a given purpose. The greater the attraction, the greater the force, meaning the greater the result. Normal sexual congress dallies with these forces imperceptibly. Climax by either partner will cause the forces to dissipate, but, to the initiated, these forces, when raised, are sustained using Tantric methods prolonging the act itself. Thus, allowing them to increase subliminally without dissipation. They can then be channelled by acts of ritual and visualisation, to attain the magician's purpose. I have included all my notes and material in the diaries that accompany these journals. It may be that she rejects both my premise and my job offer, in which case I shall, of course, accept with humility, but in terms of my Great Work, I will be bereft.

Trevelyan returned the journal to the table, his eyes sore and tired. The scotch soothed his nerves enough for him to relax a little. He had never considered sex to be anything more than a basic urge. In the manner that Seymour described, it became something more sacred and instinctual. Had Rose interpreted their lovemaking in a similar fashion? If so, then he understood her a little better. Even though he still considered her crazy. How could he have been so blind to what was going on around him back then? Rose, clearly unbalanced and fragile, required compassion from him instead of the complacency she received. It was as though he were deaf and blind to all that surrounded him unless it affected him personally. His selfishness staggered him. It was in these moments he saw himself as he was. Or at least had been. His ego was lessened now. His vanity only revealed itself in his urge to hide his ugliness from those who would see him. Did it take a desperate and tragic act like Rose's to make him see himself through her eyes? He felt his shame and guilt descend as the early morning sun rose. He dressed despondently to await the day.

He refused his breakfast. His appetite had gone with the morning mist. He went, instead, to the library to search through some of his father's books. He made a small pile on the reading table to occupy himself with after morning physiotherapy. He selected several titles by Dion Fortune, and others mentioned in his father's journals and diaries. As he passed the time in the library, he found his excitement rising at the thought of Seymour creating an 'otherworld.' He marvelled at the sheer audacity of playing god. This excitement lightened his mood a little, and he arrived at the treatment room a little before Evelyn. He was eager now to get started so he could resume his investigation of Seymour's books. He took a notepad and pen from Evelyn's desk and held onto them for note taking when he returned to the library. He wondered if he should mention the journals to Evelyn, but decided against it. It was good to have a secret to himself, and it felt like the only connection he had with a father that he deemed was always beyond reach. He did not have to wait long for Evelyn's arrival, and she appeared surprised, and a little elated, that Trevelyan, indicating his commitment to their first session, had arrived before her. They dallied for a minute or two with greetings, and Evelyn seated herself at her desk while Trevelyan seated himself opposite her. She began by reading through Dr. Harper's notes aloud so that Trevelyan could intercede on any point at any time.

"When you were admitted to General by the emergency services, you were in terrible shape," she said earnestly, her eyes never leaving the report. "They didn't expect you to survive the initial examination, let alone make a recovery," she added. "They were certain any attempt at separation would be fatal for you and gave your chances at less than seven percent."

"Separation?" Trevelyan asked, not understanding.

Evelyn raised her eyes from the page and considered Trevelyan for a moment before leaning back in her chair. "Normally I wouldn't recommend discussing post trauma treatment with a patient. But then, most patients don't refuse corrective surgery or amputation when it is necessary. Seeing as the information is readily available if you should stumble across it at some future point in time, I may as well be straightforward with you from the beginning." She sighed without waiting for Trevelyan to respond and continued. "Both you and the other victim, Miss Mullaney, were fused together at the torso from the intense heat of the accelerant she had secreted about her clothing during the fire. It was Harper's surgery that separated the tissue, saving your life on the operating table several times."

"You mean we were melted together?" Trevelyan asked, horrified.

"I'm afraid so," Evelyn replied, breaking eye contact with him.

He was speechless. Appalled! Nothing could have prepared him for this. When Evelyn spoke, she left out any hint of pity from her words. "I only tell you now because we are to embark on very intense trauma therapy. And I need you to be aware of all the facets of your situation if we are to progress. If you were denied this information and were to discover it after we complete treatment, it would undo all the work I hope we can achieve."

Trevelyan barely heard Evelyn as Rose loomed into vision in his mind. Her eyes on his. Locked in her embrace. "We'll always be together now," she said. Trevelyan continued his session with Evelyn, but hardly a word was spoken between them. Evelyn completed her physical examination in silence. She realised the impact her words had upon his mood. Trevelyan answered the questions she had for him, but, ultimately, she cut their session short so that he could process the information. They agreed to not discuss it during their counselling sessions in the evening. It could wait for a while. There were other problems to address first before she had him dive into his personal quagmire of left over feelings of Rose and immolation. Before they parted for the afternoon, Evelyn explained to Trevelyan that she would be in her rooms until later that evening, working on a recovery plan. If he felt he needed to talk, or just some company, then he should not hesitate to knock on her door. Both of them knew that was unlikely to happen. He supposed she felt a little guilty for her bombshell, but he understood it gained neither of them anything to withhold relative information from each other.

He returned to the library rather than his rooms. He spent an hour or two browsing through the pile of books he had deposited on the library table. They created a welcome distraction to the world wind of emotions that cyclone through his mind. Was she still a part of him? Her flesh merged with his? The thought distressed and comforted him at the same time. His life had become so much of a compromise between opposing emotions since the tragedy that he had concluded he could not resolve these extremities that lay within him, and he should not even try. There was no 'middle ground' between his old life and his new. Somewhere he could call 'no-man's-land.' Somewhere a delicate peace could be forged. They were two conflicting halves of the same whole. So, he decided to walk the thin line of oblivion that bordered between them. Too much on either side, and he threatened the thin veil of sanity that he could shroud himself in.

Restlessly, he watched the wind blow the rain past the window and the trees sway in unison to the sound of the storm as they danced. A mood as black as the clouds that shrouded the grey mountains in the distance fell upon him. He gathered the books he could carry in his good arm and, after locking the library doors, he shuffled back to his rooms and Seymour's journal.

Chapter Eleven

Afon Eigion arose into view as the Dauntless rounded the peninsular nearest the first of the fingers of land that protruded from the mainland. They were headed for the first 'finger' of five. An inlet surrounded on both sides by sheer cliffs. Ships would pass beneath the suspended wooden walkways, stretching the span between the two cliffs. The floating wooden harbours that the ships would dock at sat below cutaways hewn into the rock above, creating cargo holds and small warehouses where goods could be loaded and unloaded from above. The suspended walkways allowed access to the other ships in the harbours where the cliffs met the sea. Stairs led from each dock to meet the walkways, allowing passengers to board and depart without hampering the business of cargo and trade. Nestor disembarked the Dauntless shoeless and content. He climbed the stairs to the nearest walkway. He stood motionless for a moment and tried to decide which direction felt 'right.' He elected to travel east all that time ago and saw no reason why he should not continue to do so. He placed his feet, one in front of the other on the long zig zagging climb up the cliffs on to the boardwalk. After the steep steps, he reached the cliff top between two mighty rivers that cascaded over the edge and down, past the harbour below. There were many people gathered at the cliff edge. Some making their way down to the harbour with bundles of fruit and vegetables or tools of some trade or other. He made his way between the crowds. Several minutes later, he was alone and headed along a well-trodden path towards the woods. It felt good to be on dry land again. He had eaten his fill that morning before leaving the ship as he did not know when his next meal may be. He felt a little sad to be leaving the Dauntless and the reprieve from having to endure his dreams and visions, which he felt brooding under the surface of his growing fever. Just before he reached the trees, he noticed a horse and cart ahead. The horse was busy grazing the scraps of grass that bordered the path. Sat upright, against the wheel of the wagon, was a plump well-dressed figure drawing in the dust between his legs. He seemed to be waiting for someone or something.

Nestor paused. He was about to bypass the fat man and leave the path when the figure lifted an arm and waved at Nestor. As though he had been awaiting his arrival. Nestor looked behind to see if perchance this stranger was hailing someone there, but saw no one. "Ahoy there!" shouted the figure, gathering his feet beneath him and using the cartwheel to pull his corpulent frame up from his seated position. Nestor remained motionless, not sure what to do next. The fat man dusted off his clothes and hailed Nestor once again. "You there," he shouted, beckoning Nestor forward. Cautiously, Nestor continued along the path, drawing nearer to the stranger. A short and extremely fat man dressed in black and silver with a black cloak billowing out behind him in the wind greeted him as he approached. His short, thin silver hair, groomed backwards across his sweating brow, revealed a pair of beady, gleaming eyes above a wide, fox-like grin and a thousand chins that wobbled as he spoke. "Good day, my fine fellow," he said with a voice deep and resonant. He licked his lips like some kind of reptile, and his eyes never once remained still. He stepped away from the wagon blocking Nestor's path and opened his arms as he bent as far as his corpulent body would allow in a bow, designed to humble Nestor into conversation. "My name is Gideon Slay," he exclaimed, his eyes bright with humour at the sound of his own name. "I have waited long for your arrival, my prophet. I have been sent to assist in your travels to the east."

Nestor could not hide his shock or concern as he said, "Sent!... by whom?." The stranger scared him.

Gideon Slay replied, "A mutual friend who shares your concern for the preservation of this world."

Nestor eyed Gideon with intense suspicion, and he backed slowly away from the man before him. "I have no friends," he said earnestly.

"Who then would have me await your arrival with clothes and provisions for your journey east if not a friend, hmmmm?" Gideon licked his lips again. "Come now," he implored. "I see your feet are unshod and you lack the clothing for a long journey. Here," he beckoned Nestor to the wagon. "I have all you may need and the pleasure of my company to boot," he said, still smiling.

"How did you know where to find me?" Nestor asked warily.

"There is one who knows, my prophet. One who sees. Like you do. One who would stay the hand of destruction if he could," smirked Gideon. "One who names you friend," he finished with a low bow as before.

Unconvinced of the stranger's intentions and unprepared to be named 'friend,' Nestor challenged Gideon. "Name this friend then or be gone," he insisted.

"Then I will name him in All Sooth," declared Gideon. "Diras! lord of the Westerlands." As he spoke, his voice seemed to reverberate across the space between them. "And, Wayfarers bane." As Gideon named Nestor's foe, 'Wayfarer,' it was all Nestor could do not to fall at Gideon's feet in gratitude. "Then it is true!" he gasped. Relief flooded through him like a balm. "I feared I had lost all reason."

Gideon's grin spread as he took Nestor, almost weeping, into his arms and guided him to the waiting wagon. "On the contrary," Gideon soothed, his words sweet with pity. "You are most beloved of my lord and master. T'was he himself sent me to you. Many were the days and long the journey that has led me here."

As he spoke, Gideon removed the new clothes from the wagon and furnished Nestor with the finest leather boots and attire he had ever seen before. Much alike in quality to that of Gideon's himself. Removing the mouldy clothes, he found on the corpse during his attempt at gaining entry to Mor Gwyn, Nestor donned the fine silk and rough spun tunic and leggings. He then pulled on his fine knee-length boots while Gideon attached his cloak and fitted a golden torque about his neck.

"There," said Gideon in a satisfied voice. "Much more befitting a man of your status."

He was clearly patronising Nestor, who was much more interested in admiring himself in his new attire, than paying attention to the malevolent tone creeping into Gideon's voice. "There is food and wine aplenty on board and the road is waiting," he announced. He ushered Nestor aboard the wagon. Gideon Slay mounted and took the reins, urging the horse into motion toward the road that meandered out of sight as it entered the forest ahead. Gideon Slay whistled to himself as the cart hobbled down the road that lay between the trees. A haunting tune that made Nestor feel sad. Gideon hailed the passersby in an over friendly manner, which received no reply except suspicious glares. Nestor had not expected help from any quarter and was most concerned that someone knew of his purpose and his destination. That Gideon was acting on behalf of his 'Friend' and master,

Diras, Nestor had no doubt, but who exactly was Diras?. Nestor was sure he had never become acquainted with anyone of that name even before he awoke to his new purpose. A purpose shared, it seemed. Nestor had no inclination of travelling with Gideon until he had mentioned 'the Wayfarer.'

It was not inconceivable that he was one of many. Others who shared the warning of 'the Wayfarer,' but somehow Nestor knew that was not true... Gideon stopped his whistling and briefly looked at Nestor as though he could hear his fears. A grin that seemed never ending spread across his fat face. "Suspicion lines your face, my prophet. How may I allay your fears? I have spoken of my master, Lord Diras, have I not? Perhaps I should tell you of him, that you may be safe in the knowledge that he only means to aid you in your quest, hmmmmm? He licked his lips again and continued, "My lord and master, Diras, has laid claim to the western mountains. Building his fortress deep below the fiery mountains, he names Dinas Diras. It was there that first he saw the stranger you name Wayfarer, he that walks between the worlds. As a spectre, he witnessed my lord and master's birth. Again, he appeared, as my master Lord Diras spoke with his god. He was cast away for his impertinence." Gideon laughed at the thought and licked his lips. "My lord and master has seen you too, my fine fellow." He glanced at Nestor, his grin unchanged. "And the omens you were witness to." Gideon shook his head in mock dismay, all the while still wearing his sick grin. "'Gideon' he lamented when he learned of your struggles. You must go to him in haste. For here goes a pious fellow with an inglorious burden. He will require much aid if he is to succeed in saving Hiraeth from this wretched apparition. The 'god' has decreed it. So it must be done! So you see, my prophet... you are serving the god's will. It is with a joyful refrain that I offer up my service to you, beloved of my lord and master."

Nestor listened patiently to Gideon as they rolled along the road toward the green mountains ahead. He contemplated speaking of his dreams to this fat lizard of a man who had bound their fates in the name of a common cause. He had spoken to no man of what he had witnessed in his dreams of the future.

"How is it that you know where I am travelling? I do not know myself. My dreams and augurs drive me eastward to an island, but I have as yet no destination," he said, still a little wary of Gideon.

"Ahh... Of course. Apologies, my prophet. My lord and master, Diras, dreams deep and long beneath the fiery mountains. He has seen much of the Wayfarer." A sneer crept into his voice, although his grin was unchanged. "He has seen the apocalypse he brings; he has devised a defence of several measures that shall aid Hiraeth's faithful defenders when the time for his arrival is upon us."

Gideon allowed a moment for Nestor to ask him to elaborate, but instead Nestor sat unmoving and listened intently. "He entrusts these defences to no one but you, my prophet. For only you have endured the dreams. Only you know of what he speaks."

Gideon allowed a hint of admiration to creep into his voice, but Nestor could not tell if it was genuine or feigned.

"I would speak of them with you if you would allow, my prophet. The road is long, and there are many miles to go."

Nestor nodded his approval for him to continue, and Gideon licked his lips as he told of his lord and master's ambitions for Nestor. And his dreams.

Chapter Twelve

March 28th 1966

I am elevated to say that Morgan has agreed to become my research assistant. More importantly, my high priestess.

We spent our days walking in the chilly spring air among the woodlands and valleys surrounding Bryngaer when the weather was agreeable. Or taking long lunches in the library, pouring over some of my source materials. The evenings were once again spent in front of the fire in my study, drinking whisky and falling deep into conversation.

On the first night, I grabbed the bull by the horns, so to speak, after my second scotch and related my work over the last year and a half and the reasons for doing so. I asked Morgan to remain silent until I had exhausted my woefully inadequate explanation of how I meant to achieve my goal.

When I explained my theory of using sex magik to build enough power to achieve 'abstractive conception' (my termination), she remained absolutely silent, raising only an eyebrow in mock surprise. After I had given her all the facts and theories as best I could, she remained unsmiling, and my heart sank. Until I looked into her eyes and saw the smile there, her lips concealed. In that moment, I felt the greatest love I have ever felt for another living soul, accompanied by a humility I have never experienced before. She let the moment linger before stating that she had decided to accept my offer long before she agreed to hear me out and had terminated her employment and accommodation a month since. Then she laughed at the look on my face, relishing my surprise. And so it was that Morgan Llewelyn came to live at Bryngaer. And together, we embarked on a journey of profound discovery.

✕

APRIL 3RD 1966

I have left Morgan to her own devices for the last couple of days. Both to familiarise herself with Bryngaer, and to read through my notes and research armed with the knowledge of my intent. We would dine together in the evenings and retire to the study for the rest of the night, but her days were spent in contemplation and study. I have not been idle during our days apart. I have begun designing a temple room in which to perform the necessary rituals detailed in the diaries. In essence, a space needs to be created in which to perform the Great Work. Away from the mundane world. A place used only for ritual and spiritual practice. This space must be specially prepared by purification and other means before it can be used for the Great Work. When Morgan feels ready to take the next step with me, I shall bring her into the 'sanctum' as it shall be referred to in these journals, so that we can design our temple to complement the nature based Celtic system we have designed. I could not have conceived it alone without Morgan's help, even if that help was innocently given.

During my childhood at Bryngaer, I was often left to my own devices, especially during mother's illness. Perhaps that is where my solitary wanderings derive from in later life. I had learned to use the servant's stairs that lurked hidden behind alcoves and hallways, leading from the different wings to the ground floor kitchens. Bryngaer has seen several generations of families before the Seymours descended on her. There were several alterations to these hidden passageways. Armed with my childhood memories and a good torch, I slipped behind the walls of Bryngaer and explored her secrets. Eventually, I discovered the very place I sought. Perfect in almost every way and far removed from the mundane world. I have now located and secured the foundation of my will to create. From here, I can finally put my years of learning into practice. It will not be long now, and my excitement grows every day.

Seymour had his sanctum hidden away here at Bryngaer! Of course! It made sense. Bryngaer was immense. Trevelyan had explored only a third of the house itself, and less of the grounds surrounding it. Somewhere in this house is Seymour's sanctum. Untouched since the last time Seymour himself had occupied it. This was what he needed. A distraction within a distraction. Something to throw himself into as a reward for the intrusion of Evelyn.

June 3rd 1966

The sanctum is now ready to begin the Great Work. All preparation is detailed in the diaries along with the correspondent symbols and names of power. The temple itself will change in its symbology and colouring, as will the robes I have procured in relation to the forces that will be summoned on each occasion. Morgan feels she is ready to move on to the next step of practical work. She has been invaluable once more in the design and creation of the sanctum, utilising her feminine instincts to marvellous effect. Tonight will be our first attempt at drawing in the elemental forces I plan to weave together.

My calculations indicate the time to begin would be between the hours of three and four am to align the planetary aspect. All the staff would be absent until around six a.m., and so, we are likely not to disturb anyone with any chants or vibrational god names. I have endeavoured to soundproof our little hideaway. The space I have selected has been ritually purified and is now a sanctified area. Cleared of any unwelcome influence and separated among the many planes of existence from the mundane world we call home. The deities of the four elements of Earth, Air, Fire, and Water will be invoked to attend us. Using my system of Celtic and Jewish magik combined, we will bind these forces to the power we create as priest and priestess. This will yield a plane of existence among the many other planes on which to build our world, hidden from view and unbeknownst by any but Morgan and myself. There we shall plant the seed of creation and bring it to life by an act of Love and Will.

September 23rd 1966

Over the past several months, we have put all the elemental forces in place, created all the corresponding forces in a cyclic pattern and visualised the necessary thought forms. All that now remains is to charge the seed with a spark of life. Gods willing, it will grow within the pattern of creation that we have intended. Until we breathe life into our cosmic child, it remains unknown whether we have been successful. All is ready for the great rite to commence. Our foundations are solid, and our resolve is steady. Both Morgan and I are confident in our ambition, and we are ready to bring a light where there is only darkness. May that light remain. Tonight is the Autumn Equinox, a time of equilibrium amongst the heavens. A perfect occasion to make our attempt.

It was almost time for his evening session with Evelyn, so Trevelyan returned the journal to the table. While he changed clothing, he considered what he had read in Seymour's journals so far. He was eager to continue reading, but that would have to wait. Perhaps Beattie could shed a little light on the matter of the secret room? Trevelyan resolved to ask him at their usual meeting this evening if he was feeling better. In the meantime, he had Evelyn and his psychotherapy session shortly. His nerves jangled, thinking about trying to relate all that was going on beneath his personality, his dark moods and guilt. The apparition of Rose in his waking life, as well as his dreams. When she appeared during the day, he knew it was his fevered mind conjuring her up to accuse and berate him. More often than not, he would ignore her to the best of his ability. Rose's appearances did not scare or traumatise him. On the contrary, he accepted her as a symptom of his old life colliding with his new life as a burn victim. Like his scars and disfigurement, it was the price he paid for surviving. It seemed a little like a betrayal to mention her to Evelyn. Rose would not appreciate him talking about her to another woman. An attractive one at that. He decided he would keep Rose's presence to himself. Evelyn would never understand. She would rationalise and call her visits an unresolved facet of his trauma, and she would probably be right.

However, he found her visits more of a comfort than a problem that needs to be solved. Having her around him allowed him to feel that a little of his previous life had not abandoned him. She also held his guilt and shame up before him so he might not forget his culpability and become the blameless victim everyone expects him to be. Having dressed and readied himself with mask and cowl, he opened the bedroom door and said to no one in particular, "After you," before walking through and making his way to his studio for his appointment. As he arrived, he saw Evelyn was already there. She had her paperwork spread before her on his desk and was looking at the few pieces of art that had survived the fire. His latest left-handed attempts he kept hidden inside a closet. She was looking at the painting of the woman gazing toward the mountains. "Make me an offer," he said, forcing a smile as she turned toward him.

"Like you need the money," she said with a little laugh, and then a little sheepishly, "I wasn't sure if you would keep today's appointment after this morning," she said, not making eye contact with him.

"How could I resist?" he said, matching her humour.

She smiled back. Gratitude shone in her eyes. "Are you flirting with me, Mr. Trevelyan?" she said coyly.

"When you've got a face like a dropped pizza, it pays to have charisma," he said, slumping into his easy chair after turning it to face Evelyn as she sat at her desk.

She smiled again, but awkwardly this time. She motioned toward the painting of the gazing woman with the long red hair. "Was that painted since you've been here at Bryngaer?" she asked. "I recognise the mountains in the background."

He wiggled his stump of a right arm at her and was about to reply with something inappropriately witty but declined and replied instead, "Impossible, I'm afraid. My career as an artist has ended," but added in explanation, "I painted that several years ago before I ever set eyes on Bryngaer, one of those spooky coincidences, I suppose. It was the only piece of my work to survive the fire."

"That's a pity," she said earnestly. "You had talent."

A silence fell between them that Trevelyan felt he should fill somehow. "I thought I should be honest with you from the beginning," he said. "I don't think I'm ready to tell you about a lot of what's going on in my head. There are some things that I can discuss but there are some things I will not talk about."

"That's ok," she replied. "I don't expect you to let me in there on day one."

"No. That's not what I mean," he said. "Some of the stuff rattling about up here," he pointed at his head, "I will never find the words that you could understand. Stuff about Rose and what she did to me." He paused for a second before continuing. "About what I did to her." He left it hanging in the air between them, waiting for her to ask him to elaborate. When she did not, he continued, a little more confident. "I didn't harm her or anything like that," he confessed, "But I could have been more supportive and less selfish," he admitted.

"We are not doing this so that I understand everything that occurred between the two of you before the..." she paused, trying to find a word that did not cast blame or trivialise what happened.

"Marriage?" Trevelyan suggested sardonically. "That's what she thought it was," he said, staring at the floor.

Evelyn let him indulge his self-pity for a moment or two before continuing. "Tragedy, I was going to say, but it's interesting that you think that," she said, making a note in her folder. "I'm more concerned with the consequences, not the actions," she explained softly. "The trauma that you carry every day, 'rattling around' as you put it." I believe it all ties into your refusal for surgery and amputation. You wear it like a dark medallion for all to see. Yet you still hide your disfigurements behind masks and hoods."

"I told you," he said, trying to conceal his anger, "I don't want to talk about that stuff."

It was not that he did not want to talk about it if he was being honest with himself. It was not knowing where to start. Not knowing what to say. He understood little of it himself, but he accepted the guilt without question. Because at some level, at some time, he could have averted all that happened if he had only shown a little compassion toward Rose. He could not change what happened, but he could take responsibility for it. He could use it to punish himself for his transgressions, and he would let no one take that away from him. He had to own those feelings and make his own peace with them. Or else he would just be a 'baked potato' living as a rich recluse. A walking, talking cliché.

Evelyn saw his mood darken as he sat in front of her, lost in his thoughts. She elected to change the subject in an effort to lift him out of the mire of despair he made for himself. "How about we take a walk outside?" she suggested. "I promise not to pry if you promise to be good company." She raised a weak smile as she spoke, disarming him, and he felt sorry for her. She had an impossible task ahead of her. He could never divulge his visions of Rose. She would see them simply as a symptom of his trauma. But they were more than that. Rose was more important to him now than she ever was before the 'tragedy.'. If he was honest with himself, she was his only friend. Other than perhaps, Beattie. But that friendship was born of necessity. Rose was a companion not of choice exactly, but of a sense of shared experience. She understood him in a way no one else ever had. Even now, and she had called him on his bullshit.

They wandered the grounds for an hour. Crossing the meadow to the river and along the bank to the trees. Evelyn was as good as her word and only talked of his medication and if he felt it was helping. To which he offered his approval, even if he did not really mean it. The sky was becoming quite dark as they made their way back to the house, and a chill was creeping into the air as the sun set behind the mountains. They said their goodnights at the staircase and went their separate ways. They both took dinner in their respective rooms, leaving Trevelyan free to continue reading Seymour's journals.

Chapter Thirteen

Trevelyan finished dinner alone in his room. With an hour before Beattie arrived for their nightcap, he continued reading Seymour's journal.

September 24th 1966

I shall endeavour to describe the events of last night to the best of my ability. We built the circle around us using a blue flame and invoked the quarters by inscription of the pentagrams in the usual manner. We summoned the elemental deities, each at its relative cardinal point. Using intense visualisation techniques, we built our temple and resonated the required frequency to contact the etheric plane we had chosen. There we visualised ourselves as beings of pure light. We faced each other, our hands raised toward each other at shoulder height, as close as possible without touching. We then built our force of attraction between our palms to begin with. Attuned to each other and the force we created. As that force built, it took the shape of a spiral of power between our naked bodies. A vortex, cycling round and round, gathering momentum and power to itself until it took on a life of its own and became difficult to contain. Within this vortex of power, Morgan and I made exquisite love. Our ethereal energies whipped together between our palms and spread to encompass our entire bodies, yet stayed within the circle of blue flame. Our ecstasies reached a feverous pitch, and we both dissolved into a peak beyond orgasm. Still focused on our intent, we released that power through the seed of creation and into the ether. As the power broke and our bodies slumped to the floor, some of the power that we created still vibrated between us. Before it dissipated, we made love, a deep and resonating golden copulation. It engulfed our bodies in the blue flame of the circle and ended with a soul shattering climax that felt like it shook the foundations of the earth. Startled and breathless, we stared at each other for a long time. Morgan broke into a delicious laugh that melted any remnants of power, and left us exhausted, with a peace that seemed to last for days afterward. I still can feel it now as I write these words. My body feels like it is oscillating at a frequency invisible to the human eye. Like I am present through all the levels of manifestation. More real than I have ever felt before. Morgan and I have become inseparable since our night on the temple floor. We share a togetherness that neither of us has experienced previously. All that remains now is to wait. If the ritual was successful, we should feel it on an instinctual level first. Having never attempted something of this nature before, the results are unknowable. We shall need to be vigilant to our dreams and reveries.

I have attempted to experience our creation since its conception. But I can only seem to view it from the outside. In my imagination, the wellspring from where the birth of this new world has sprung, all I see is the elemental powers still converging on one another, creating a cauldron of theory. A good sign. As we are both still recovering from our expenditure of energy, we have not left my room and do not intend to for several days. We spend hours resting in each other's arms and making slow and lazy love to one another, but without climax. There is still much work to be done.

Trevelyan stopped reading for a moment to let what he read sink in. It would seem that Seymour and Morgan had some success. That they had, between them, created a new world. Even if it was not a material one. He reflected for a moment on what it could mean to be a creator of worlds. To be like a god. He continued to read.

October 31st 1966

Our reoperation is now complete and we are ready to ascend to our creation. We have both felt its touch over the past month and we are both pulled toward it in our dreams. Tonight we shall draw the circle and attempt to experience what we have built.

November 1st 1966

It is with a bitter disappointment that I write these words. It seems our creation is a resounding success. We have conceived between us a world of majestic natural beauty.

Alas, as its creators, we cannot inhabit our creation! The infinite cannot exist within a finite universe.

By the very nature of our art, we are excluded from its bounty. If we were to try, the very forces we used to create would be its undoing. It seems god cannot visit his creation without destroying it in the attempt. An unforeseen legacy of creation. But perhaps, like god, we can send an avatar on our behalf? Morgan does not seem as disappointed as me and is content knowing that we have succeeded. I, however, am bitterly resentful that all the work over the past several years has been taken from me. What use is a world that cannot be experienced first-hand? A creation that cannot be put to any practical use. I have hidden my discord from Morgan, but my guess is that she knows, at least on some level.

She urges me to be content to watch it grow and evolve as an entity of its own. To nurture it with love and care. But I cannot help feeling a little cheated. Almost like an unspoken promise was made and broken. Morgan has named our creation 'Hiraeth,' a Welsh word meaning to long for a place that never was. Nostalgia for a place we cannot return. It is an echo of something lost and our grief for them. A most fitting name. And so Hiraeth is what we called our lost world.

If god himself is not welcome in his creation, he can create someone who is. After much thought and discussion, Morgan believes we can create avatars that can exist in Hiraeth on our behalf. We could create them using the same methods as Hiraeth itself. To create an entity that can subsist within the confines of Hiraeth and perform certain tasks dependent upon the intention used in their creation. These entities we have called 'Incarnates'. Some are male, some are female, and some have attributes of both or neither, depending on their purpose. These incarnates are independent beings of free will. Following an inherent driving force imbibed in them from their creation. For instance, Morgan created a female Incarnate she named 'Anwedd,' to live amongst the forests. Anwedd has the power of growth and protection. To care for the forests and wild places of Hiraeth. An earth elemental, she appears dressed in the green foliage of the deep woods. Her hair loamy brown and stiff like bracken. Morgan also incarnated the tree. Having no sun or moon, Hiraeth required a source of light and warmth. Morgan Incarnated a very special tree. This tree contained enormous power that was perfectly balanced. She placed this tree where it cannot be found. It contains the cycles of the day and night and also the seasons. The tree brings forth light at daybreak with spring on its branches. That turns to summer by midday, then autumn as evening begins and finally winter for the dead of night. Starting over again and again. This replaces the sun. The weather systems are brought forth with the subtle alignments of the branches. It is a creation of pure intuition and balance and one of which I could never succeed. Morgan surpasses me at every turn. Hiraeth truly is more her child than mine now. She has nurtured and loved our child, paying detail to all the little nuances of life that we take for granted. She hither too, created forests and mountains. Rivers and oceans with such alacrity and authenticity that they are a wonder to behold, even when viewed through the eyes of an incarnate. Of which there are many now. All created to govern, nurture, and protect the energies of the element they inhabit.

There are incarnates for every facet of nature. Although there is, as yet, no way of populating this world with denizens of wildlife, we are working on a formula that predicts a solution. Or should I say Morgan is? I have become despondent and uninterested in Hiraeth. Offering only suggestions and insights that seem uninspired and doing no practical work of my own. Morgan, however, has taken the reins in completing our work. She is organising and refining the power created by our passion to imitate and, at times, completely surpass the natural beauty of our real world. I would sometimes wander Hiraeth using an incarnate that approximated me. Created just for me to inhabit and explore. But this only seemed to deepen my feelings of separation and loss for the world I wanted to experience. I disposed of this incarnate cruelly to spite myself. The only incarnate I have created that I have not suffered to die is the 'Testament,' created shortly after Hiraeth's genesis as a living record of all that passes within this creation of ours. Having no material presence in Hiraeth, he retains an appearance should he deign to show himself and is omnipresent but not omnipotent. He exists solely as an observer, with the will to communicate in the form of answers to direct questions. His creation was necessary because of the time dilation between Hiraeth and home. Several days in Hiraeth may amount to mere hours in our real world. So, when we were away from Hiraeth, we needed a record of what had transpired in our absence. He is autonomous in his existence and can be summoned at the monoliths near any of the various portals that Morgan and I use to deploy incarnates. We can question him regarding occurrences during our absence.

I have learned much about the nature of the creator and his creation. I no longer wonder why god allows the world he created to lose its way. It is because he just does not care. As my discontent grows, so does the gulf between Morgan and myself. She, being so engrossed in her work, has not as yet noticed my indifference. She spends hours relating her success to me, only deepening my resentment. I have not the heart to disclose my feelings to her and so I smile, and feign my enthusiasm, and make excuses for my absence.

Trevelyan was dumbstruck. They have created another world on another level of existence! This seemed almost unbelievable to him. As he read about Seymour's plans and ambitions, he found it hard to believe that they could have succeeded as they did. It was incredible. Seymour's disappointment was palpable to Trevelyan. His need for ultimate control of his realised dream betrayed his good intentions to create. Seymour must have seen himself as some kind of benevolent god until he realised he could not control that which he had made. Which, in turn, has soured his willingness to complete his goal. Trevelyan wondered if our god felt the same towards us as he cast us from the garden of Eden. Glancing at the time, he saw that Beattie would soon be here with a whisky or two before he retired for the evening. He returned the journals to the table by the window and donned his mask and cowl. As he waited, he wondered how Beattie was feeling now. He had been out of action for two days because of ill health. Trevelyan considered he should suggest to Beattie that he take some time to himself and forego his responsibilities at Bryngaer in favour of a comfortable retirement. He elected to raise the subject with Beattie over their nightcap.

∞∞∞∞

As the clock struck nine, he heard Beattie making his way down the hall toward his rooms, the clinking of ice in glass and the slow shuffling steps. Without waiting for Beattie to knock, Trevelyan opened the door and relieved Beattie of the tray and invited him to sit in his usual chair by the table. Beattie spoke of the day to day of Bryngaer, and the staff requirements. Trevelyan signed the invoices for the regular expenses, and the cost of the upkeep of the acres of land surrounding, such as tree felling and fence maintenance. There was some livestock at Bryngaer. Sheep with a few horses and cattle all supervised by the farm manager. After they had completed business, they spoke of Evelyn and how she was settling in and if there was any sign of how long of a stay she intended. Trevelyan admitted that as far as Evelyn Munroe was concerned, he knew little. Dr. Harper's recommendations and patient details guided her, and she seemed very diligent and professional in her treatments and manner. They both agreed that it was nice to have a woman's friendly disposition about the house. As they paused their conversation to refill their glasses, Trevelyan took the opportunity to ask Beattie about his recent ill health and if he felt he needed a break from his duties. Beattie's response was to reassure Trevelyan that his ailments were because of his age and nothing serious to be concerned about. Bryngaer was in his family's blood for generations, and he would probably die in the performance of his duties and would have it no other way. Trevelyan accepted his candour and struck while the iron was hot. He asked Beattie if he had any knowledge of the service staircases and where they led. He hoped he may have some direct information that Trevelyan could act upon, but Beattie only knew of the main through fares throughout the house that led to the landings and hallways between the rooms they served. "Only, there was one occasion," said Beattie in his recall. "Mr. Seymour Jr. was in his bedroom dressing before the tall mirror and, as I recall, having a little difficulty with his tie. I passed his room while on the way to the housekeeper's closet next door, which took less than a moment or two, and when I passed the room again, Mr. Seymour was nowhere to be seen. I briefly checked his room, but it was unoccupied. I presumed we must have missed each other in the hall, and he used the service stairs that led to the kitchens, but the chef had not seen him all morning. He appeared sometime later, and the incident went unremarked upon." All the time Beattie spoke, he seemed lost in memory, and, as he finished, he caught himself and gathered the used glasses and filled the tray. "If that will be all, Mr. Trevelyan, I will retire for the night. I'm afraid a nightcap or two makes me rather sleepy these days."

Trevelyan uttered his approval and held the door for Beattie to retire to his quarters. All the while considering their conversation. He had the same bedroom as Seymour, and the very same mirror stood by the bedroom door to his left. After Beattie departed, he stood before the mirror, trying to avoid looking at himself. He examined the frame and the wall on which it hung. It would make complete sense for Seymour's sanctum to be accessible from his room. Away from prying eyes. He ran his left hand around the frame, hoping to find some kind of button or switch to press releasing a secret door, but there was nothing. He stepped a little closer to the mirror, searching for some clue and finding nothing. He admitted to himself it was a long shot and sighed heavily as he put his forehead against the glass and sagged.

Click.

There it was... he stepped back, and the mirror swung open like a door, revealing a narrow wooden staircase leading into darkness. He swung the mirror back to its original position against the wall and he heard the click again as the mirror/door secured itself closed. He pushed on the mirror again firmly, and once again he heard the click and the mirror swung open. A simple mechanism on the back of the mirror secured and released with a simple push. It was devilishly cunning. Trevelyan searched for a light source he could investigate with. A cold draught exited the stairway, rushing into the room replacing the warmer air. Trevelyan found the matches and candles in the cupboard stored for those fierce winters that can cause power outages. He wrapped his gown around him as he lit the candle and climbed the small narrow staircase into the darkness.

Chapter Fourteen

The candle flickered in the darkness, threatening to blow itself out. Trevelyan reached behind him and pulled the mirror/door closed, stopping the draught and steadying the flame. As he climbed the narrow wooden staircase, he could see only a few steps ahead as the staircase climbed steeply. Within a moment or two, he reached the top of the staircase and swung the candle around to throw some light on his surroundings. He observed a small alcove furnished with two chairs and two coat hangers. On which were draped two robes of what looked like expensive fine silk. This was a small dressing room, he guessed. He turned clockwise. Behind him, to his right, he saw a small hallway next to the narrow stairs leading to a small room. If he calculated correctly, the small room sat directly above his bedroom. He made his way down the hall, and the candle shed light on the small room in front of him. He had to duck to get through the low arch of the doorway and stepped into a small windowless hexagonal room. The walls were covered in strange sigils, each different from the others. On the floor was inscribed a circle within a circle. Strange glyphs bordered the outer circle like the rim of a wheel. Several neat piles of books stood between the outer circle and the sigiled walls. Half-used candles situated around the room were waiting to be lit once more. Trevelyan lit each of the various candles from his own and waited for the darkness to recede. The room had been unused for a long time. Dust covered all the surfaces and the floor. A musty smell of incense permeated the air. It was cold here, and Trevelyan returned to his room after gathering some books from the top of the piles and descended the narrow stairs. He pushed on the mirror/door and was back in his warm bedroom in a few moments. He seated himself at the table by the window and examined the books he had collected. The first was a study on the astral body and how to travel. The next was a treatise on The Western Mystery Tradition, but it was the last two books he had picked up that interested him most. Two leather bound diaries with tiny keys already in the respective locks. These must be the diaries. Seymour put all his formulas and ceremonial instructions in.

The journals were his thoughts and feelings, his dreams and disappointments. These diaries were a 'how to' guide on ascending to this mysterious world called Hiraeth. Trevelyan turned the key in the lock of the topmost diary and flicked through the pages. They contained diagrams of sigils and symbols alongside notes scribbled hurriedly. The other diary was much the same. Between the two, it would be possible, with the correct amount of study from the other books scattered throughout the sanctum, to reproduce Seymour's ceremony. It would be possible to visit this world his father had conceived off and Morgan had fallen in love with. He had before him on the table a secret account of the means and methods to ascend to another world on another plane of consciousness. It was at that moment that Trevelyan had decided that was exactly what he intended to do.

Trevelyan undressed and, after the usual arm binding ritual, settled into bed. He correlated the journals to the diaries to see the timeline of events from the beginning. He worked his way through the two references until they were up to the point he had last read in the journals. Seeking a better understanding of the forces and powers needed to accomplish such a grand idea, he bookmarked the diaries and put them away in his bedside drawer. It was after three in the morning, but his mind was full of Seymour's fantastic passion, and so he continued to read the journals.

December 25th 1966

Morgan has announced that she is pregnant! She saved the news till today as a gift and broke the news with a baby's rattle wrapped as a present. It was all I could do not to vomit in disgust! A child!! I bleated some exclamations of joy, but inside I am furious! I have never, nor ever will hold any desire to be a parent. I am the last in my line. Still, I do not care to waste the rest of my life suffering a child to grow as spoilt and ultimately lonely as I became in my younger days. I have not enough love in me to do otherwise. I am at a crossroads. Morgan is beside herself with joy and will become insufferable in the coming months, of that I have no doubt. Although I love her, I am unsure on how to proceed. Our lovemaking since the creation of Hiraeth has been without climax as we used the energies generated to further our aim. The only time conception could have occurred was after we released the vortex, creating Hiraeth, and fell victim to the powers we created and made love with such passionate intensity. I have wondered if that is the cause of our inability to personally experience Hiraeth, like some kind of energy displacement. I must think on this further.

Pregnant! Morgan was pregnant! Trevelyan had not considered this. Nor did he suppose had Seymour. There had been no mention of contraception elsewhere in the journals, and they had had sex, at least for a short time. It was at least unsurprising. Trevelyan was not sure if this meant he had a sibling somewhere?

January 6th 1967

Morgan has excelled herself in the works that she has done in Hiraeth. Even my lack of enthusiasm cannot diminish her accomplishments. She has created a world that resembles ours four or five thousand years ago. She has mastered the creation of the seas and the land. The seasons and the climate. She has even approximated a kind of evolution of sorts that has brought forth small instances of original life. I use the word 'original' because they were born in Hiraeth, within its bounds, and not incarnates created from our focus of thought. They are a natural occurrence of the culmination and cyclic nature of the forces we have employed.

These small lifeforms are advancing into bigger, and more diverse species that should ultimately create a population here in Hiraeth. Not unlike our own.

Although I marvel at what she has created from the duality of our persons, I do not feel any love for it. My resentment has deepened as the marvel of what Hiraeth has become flourishes. My estrangement is the fault of no one but myself, yet I cannot overcome it. Morgan is content to let Hiraeth thrive under its own governance, apart from the Incarnates, used as guardians of the natural elements. She has no desire to impose her will upon it and instead has nurtured it with love.

The dream I held of creating a world of my own was to be able to walk amongst my creation and build it as I saw fit. My resentment has not diminished because of Morgan's successes. She has noticed my aversion to Hiraeth, if not my reasons why. Perhaps the reason for her brilliance with Hiraeth is the fact that she is pregnant. Growing life inside must have a positive effect on the outcome of her attempts at creating the same on the planes.

Trevelyan could not help wondering where Morgan is now and what became of her child. Perhaps, due to Seymour's deepening resentment toward Hiraeth, they parted company.

March 29th 1967

Morgan is glowing in her expectancy. As much as it pains me to say she suits pregnancy, and motherhood will become her, I know. The care and love she has lavished on Hiraeth is proof of that. It is a living wonder to behold. Even through the eyes of the ghosts that I inhabit as they walk the lands and forests and mountains and seas. It fills me with awe and revulsion. Amazement and despair. I cannot reconcile my broken heart and continue to distance myself from both Hiraeth and Morgan.

While she sleeps, I inhabit a ghost of myself and spend days and nights there, marvelling at what lies beyond my grasp. I have seen birds both small and large, alike in every way as the birds we have here in the real world but with different plumage and colourings. Stags and wild beasts of the forests and plains. Fish of various sizes and colours in both the freshwater rivers and the salt foam seas. Fruit grows on certain trees and wild crops of wheat and barley come and go with the seasons. What Morgan has accomplished is nothing short of a miracle. I continue to aid her by providing the male polarity she requires to bring about the changes that are occurring more frequently now. But I do not participate in the employment of those forces. Or the designs used to propagate the fertile landscape.

Instead, I secretly seek a way to take part in Hiraeth without the use of incarnate ghosts. I can observe from any location, like some omnipresent eye, but only as a disembodied entity of no material significance. I have also secreted a portal that I may use unnoticed by Morgan for my solitary travels in this torment of paradise. It allows me a little personal control over a particular environment that, through the use of various incarnates, I can accumulate elemental power to myself. Unknown to Morgan. I have, as yet, found no proper use for this power. Should I find a flaw in the contradiction of the infinite/finite problem, I have a storehouse of theurgy at my disposal?

Morgan has been feeling the strain of gestation on both planes of existence. She has, of late, been confined to her bed at the behest of the local doctor. Her pregnancy advances well and although she is larger than expected at this stage of pregnancy, she is well, and healthy, even if tired. She is aware of my withdrawal from her and Hiraeth. She accepts this as my coming to terms with both her unexpected conception, and all that implies in both our futures, and my obvious disillusionment with Hiraeth. When I try to talk to her about all my misgivings, she brushes them off as my reluctance to become a parent because of my personal experience with my father. And my disappointment at not being worshipped as a god. She says both with a sideways smile, trusting to the fact that I will come around once the child is here, but I do not share her sentiments. I am not ready to become a father. I am still a child myself, even at my age. I cannot see the blessing of a child, only the burden.

Trevelyan stopped reading for a moment. Seymour had a real problem with Hiraeth and the pregnant Morgan. He could understand his fear of parenthood. Trevelyan had his ghosts from the past that shared common ground with Seymour's misgivings.

June 20th 1967

Morgan has been bedridden for the last three months of her pregnancy. She is due anytime now. During this time, Morgan has ascended to Hiraeth and create the Incarnates she has required to complete the dream that once we shared, from her sickbed. She has built a temple akin to, and potent as, the sanctum above my rooms without ever having to leave her bed. She has built a temple of her own on the outer planes. This temple has no material existence in our world but is still as effective in its purpose. Morgan has hit upon the notion that a temple need not be here in the physical realm at all. The sole purpose of the temple, and the symbols, sigils, and colour correspondences is to focus the mind on the Great Work and provide a sanctified space from which to work. Morgan has become adept at continuing the Great Work to its completion. She has no need of ceremonial trappings or aids to focus her intentions. She can ascend to her temple on the planes built over the last several months in her mind alone.

She has described to me the steps to take that I may build a temple of pure thought of my own. A place I can visit whenever I need by closing my eyes and remaining undisturbed. There are no limits in the scope of this temple, other than the limits of one's imagination. I have included these steps in the diaries that accompany these journals. Morgan has revolutionised my Great Work, for which I am truly grateful. But my resentment has surpassed my ability to deny it now, and my broken purpose has deposed my reason. I have no intention of becoming a parent and will press upon Morgan the need for her to depart Bryngaer and my life forever. I do not believe that she will oppose me on this as we have grown further apart day by day until we have hardly any contact with one another anymore. Beattie keeps me appraised of her condition when I ask, and she remains in her rooms, spending her time in Hiraeth, or being attended by the doctor on his daily visits now. Hiraeth will remain in Morgan's hands as much as it does in mine, although it is only a stranger to me now. The forces we used to create Hiraeth have become independent from us now and continue to serve Hiraeth in a cyclic pattern. Renewing with each cycle. If we were to refrain from attending Hiraeth, it would continue on its own without our input. In fact, there is little left to do according to my last conversation with Morgan. There are peoples now. Tribes that are autonomous to one another, and a renewing environment to support them. Ad infinitum.

I have not ascended to Hiraeth in quite some time, as I now realise that I will be forever exiled from the paradise it has become. No theurgy of mine can undo what has been done. Even if I wished to do so. It is a macrocosm of its own now. The future remains uncertain in as much as Morgan and I are concerned. I shall ensure that she has a luxuriant home for herself and the child. A generous annual income that she need never work again. I have no wish for shared custody or visitation rights. I have agreed to name the child as heir to the Seymour fortune when the time comes. I cannot express my disappointment in my work and myself. Nor my bitterness and frustration over the events of the last years. I have considered attempting another creation. But I fear this would be futile, as the results would undoubtedly be the same. When I consider the last few years and the dreams I had, I am filled with wrath at the outcome of all my hard work and expectations. I now regret my ambitions and the acquaintance they brought. It has become a madness in me that threatens to erupt should my resolve fail. Damn Hiraeth and Morgan, too.

My madness took me. My brooding heart would not relent, and my madness overwhelmed me in my weakness. Curious, I ascended to Hiraeth and observed the paradise it has become. I wandered disembodied above the landscape below and saw for myself the peoples that had populated Hiraeth. Scattered clans living in small communities, co-existing with the environment they share. These were my children. I was their father and yet I could not reach out to them. They could never know me. Nor the dreams of their conception I once held to be impossible! I was wroth to look upon them in their ignorance. That Morgan had accomplished all this with no help from me was both wondrous and infuriating.

It was then that my madness erupted. Lost in a fury of resentment, I threw power down upon them all. From the realm of Infinity, I poured my malice and hate into blasts of theurgy and hurled it down upon the heads of all Morgan's beloved and sacred creatures in a whirlwind of destruction. It must have been only moments before my reason returned, but as I gazed on the burned and blackened landscape that scourged the northern hemisphere of Hiraeth, I recoiled in shame and horror. What have I done?

Trevelyan held his breath as he read the last paragraph. He could tell that Seymour had a problem with Morgan and Hiraeth, but he never expected this. What could have possessed Seymour to do such a thing? He had held certain sympathies for Seymour on reading the journals, even to the extent of his resentment toward Morgan and his apathy to his impending parenthood. But this was unforgiveable, selfish, and arrogant. Traits shared by Trevelyan himself.

Chapter Fifteen

June 21st 1967

Morgan is dead! Died in childbirth! I awoke this morning in shame and guilt after my actions last night. I looked out the window to see an ambulance and the doctor's car outside the main entrance on the drive. I dressed and rushed to Morgan's quarters, where I was met by Beattie in the hallway. His face was as solemn as I have ever seen it before. He explained that the doctor was called in the early hours of this morning as Morgan haemorrhaged uncontrollably. The doctor immediately called for an ambulance, but it was too late. Morgan passed away before the ambulance crew could arrive. Doctor Evans managed to save the twins. Twins no less. One girl. One boy. I am in shock.

Could I be responsible for her death by my dark actions on the previous night? The doctor insists that it was a rare complication that no one could have foreseen, but I can't help but feel responsible. Perhaps my actions caused some kind of rebound effect on Morgan, causing this tragedy. The doctor asked if I would like to meet my son and daughter, but all I could do was to give him a horrified look and walk away. I have given instructions that the children are to be adopted. This may seem cruel and unforgiving, but I have no love for children. Even my own. I fear that should the darkness take me again, perhaps I might do them harm! And I was in shock after the events of the previous night. How could all we worked for end like this? I feel a certain amount of guilt over the fact that from my point of view. All my previous worries have resolved themselves. No Morgan. No children. All is as it was before I had even heard the name of Morgan Llewelyn.

In the eyes of the doctors and house staff, I am seen as the grief-stricken lord of the manor. Victim of unforeseen circumstances. But I know the real truth. Morgan's death lay at my feet. The consequences of my attempted destruction of Hiraeth, or whatever it was I thought I was doing. I retired to my rooms for the day and took no food or drink. I wept like I have never wept before. Not for Morgan or for those two small children. My tears were for myself. My grief and ultimate relief were abhorrent to me. It was then that I learned to hate myself.

June 23rd 1967

I have met with Fairbourne this afternoon, in order to provide care for the children away from Bryngaer and myself. I cannot be responsible for their safety. He is to draw up a will in the event of my death. All of my personal wealth and properties will go to the boy. The girl child has been put up for anonymous adoption. It seemed the best course of action to take. I have learned to live with my shame but cannot face life outside of Bryngaer. I have become a recluse, keeping to my quarters for the most part. I seldom ascend to Hiraeth now. The last time was a week ago without the use of an incarnate. I observed the damage I had wrought on the night Morgan died. In my disembodied state, I drifted across the landscape while the denizens of Hiraeth lived and died beneath me. The northern hemisphere was blasted beyond recognition. No tree or blade of grass has attempted to grow on these cursed lands. The mountains of the northwest were blackened and burned, becoming unstable volcanos that scorched the surrounding earth. To the northeast, the scorched ground has collapsed, leaving a bottomless chasm, its mouth a frozen, silent scream at the sky.

It has been a week since I ascended to Hiraeth and have sworn to never do so again. I shall leave it to its own devices and trust that our magik will, at some point, disperse itself after many years. Hiraeth will return the forces we borrowed from the universe, back to whence they came. My shame looms large today, and I have called an end to my journals. I have drawn a line beneath this entire enterprise and continue to hide away from the rest of the world here at Bryngaer. I have locked away the journals and diaries and no one living knows of the miracle myself and Morgan created out there on the far planes of existence. The only remnants of Hiraeth exist in my dreams and nightmares now. Which I share with no one. May the god that created this world have mercy on me when I could have no mercy on those that I have created. In both the otherworld and this.

C Seymour

Trevelyan was aghast! Morgan dead! Twins! What the hell is going on? Was he was adopted?! He had a dreadful foreboding of what was to come, but his mind could not catch up with his thoughts. He felt the same as he did in Fairbourne's office when he heard the news of his windfall. Before his life went up in flames. All subsequent pages were empty. Trevelyan was beside himself. Morgan was his birth mother! He had a twin sister! His mother was Seymour's housekeeper and his ADOPTIVE mother! Suddenly, he recalled sitting with his mother in her room in the nursing home before he left to meet Rose and his impending doom. She had been mumbling in Welsh, but he distinctly heard her say mother and sister in her ramblings. He put it down to her mental awareness and his drunken state. She was trying to tell him he had a twin sister, and she was not his biological mother! Realisation came crashing down upon his head, and the room spun. He reached out with his good arm and, grasping nothing but air, went crashing to the floor.

He awoke to Evelyn's concerned face looking down at him. He was sprawled on the floor of his room, and his head ached from the impact with the floor. Evelyn assured him there was no blood and helped him to his feet, and then to his bed. He was aware he had no mask or cowl on, but Evelyn's countenance did not display any revulsion or horror. Only concern. She explained she had heard him fall from her room below his. After knocking on his door that went unanswered, she abruptly made her way in and found him passed out. She offered him a glass of water to drink and sat with him on his bed. He was acutely aware his disfigurements were visible. When his vision had returned to normal, he covered his features, and still a little shaky, thanked Evelyn for her prompt response.

"What happened?" she asked. Her eyebrows narrowed as concern etched her face.

"Nothing. Just a dizzy spell," he replied, his voice still a little shaky.

"I would like to give you a full check over tomorrow morning if that's ok. Blood sugar, blood pressure, that type of thing," she said.

"I'm sure it's nothing," Trevelyan replied, feeling a little better now. Evelyn made him promise to see her in the morning at nine sharp for a full examination. He agreed, more out of a need to be alone than any concern for his health. They said their goodnights and parted company until their meeting in the morning. Trevelyan remained in his bed, still shaken by the fall, and the news that Morgan was his real mother. He was born from some kind of experiment rather than any kind of loving partnership. His mind swam with so many thoughts, he struggled to keep them in his head. Was there some kind of way to find his sister? How could this have been kept from him for so long? In fact, if he had not found the journals in the nook so long ago, he would never have discovered any of this. He needed a drink or three before he could ever hope to calm himself to sleep. He poured himself a large scotch from the tumbler in the studio and sat looking out of the bay window into the darkness for the next hour. After a second large drink, he sighed and shuffled his way back to his bed and fell into a deep and dreamless sleep.

∞∞∞∞

It had been two weeks now since his collapse on the bedroom floor. Evelyn was satisfied it was a one-off event and conceded that, considering the extent of his injuries, he was recovering well physically. His pain had receded, and he was a little more willing to let Evelyn inspect his disfigured face and arm for any signs of infection or inflammation. It was her calm patience that won him over in the end. After she had seen him unmasked in his bedroom, he felt a little easier in sharing his deformities. He was still unwilling initially, but with her winning attitude and gentle persuasion, he yielded to her. She was more concerned with his PTSD and his mental faculties than the physical. Through her gentle questioning and probing, he gave up a little of what was rolling round his head from the tragedy. But nothing about his recent findings on his true birth. Or that his dreams almost always contain burning Rose. Or that she appears to him sometimes during his waking hours, uninvited. Instead, he admitted to Evelyn that he suffered from anxiety and depression, which was, "Only to be expected," she said. His feelings of guilt and remorse about the part he played in his own downfall he kept to himself. When he was not in "session" with Evelyn, they would sometimes wander the estate together, discussing the landscape, the seasons, or whatever subject they fell upon that was not treatment related. He enjoyed the walks. She was good company and had a wicked sense of humour that was endearing. They spoke a little about their past and childhood. All the while Trevelyan keeping his true heritage a secret. She told him a little about herself and how she became this "angel of mercy." The times he was alone, he poured over Seymour's diaries and instructions and familiarised himself with the sanctum and its furnishings. He sifted through the library and collected any books he thought might prove instructive, or books that Seymour referenced in his writings. It was his sole occupation, other than his regular sessions with Evelyn and his nightcap with Beattie. He had decided against tasking Beattie about Morgan or his twin sister. He figured that Seymour would have kept these events to himself. Or if Beattie did have any knowledge, he would probably remain silent through some act of duty of loyalty. On the occasions he brought up the subject of Morgan,

Beattie would always repeat the same diatribe that she was 'Seymour's research partner' and that she and her baby died during childbirth from complications. He would never eschew that Seymour was the father, or that Trevelyan was the child that was adopted by the housekeeper. In his position as steward for all these many years, he refrained from any personal opinions of his employers or their private lives. But his eyes, when he spoke, would sometimes seem far away with the ghosts of the past. The more he read the material that Seymour referenced and the books he had selected, the more he understood the nature of the forces Morgan and Seymour raised and how they employed them. So much was beyond him still, but he was beginning to make a little sense out of this mystery, and it excited him. He wanted to see what they had created. Where he had come from and why. It was all he could think about sometimes, and he decided he would attempt to ascend when he felt he was ready.

∞∞∞∞

This was how he passed his days and nights over the following weeks. After breakfast, he would meet with Evelyn in her treatment room for physical examination and medicine review. Then he would retire to the library or his bedroom to read. After lunch, Evelyn and he would take a walk through the meadow to the river if the weather was good. Or play a little chess before Evelyn's psych session. Then dinner, after which they would talk for an hour or so before retiring for the evening. Trevelyan would read a little more on arriving at his rooms and wait for his nightcap with Beattie. Life seemed to settle into some kind of normality and routine. After Beattie retired for the night and Trevelyan knew he would not be disturbed, he would spend a couple of hours in the sanctum, familiarising himself with the ritual of ascension that Seymour had detailed in his diaries. Evelyn was due to return to London for the weekend shortly. She had a meeting with Dr. Harper to attend regarding Trevelyan's recovery and a few personal items to take care of. Trevelyan decided that this would be the perfect time to attempt his ascension to Hiraeth.

He would be uninterrupted for several days, which should be enough time to complete his attempt. His understanding of the ritual was almost complete. Even though he had never thought to try anything like this before, he felt he had done himself some justice in his capacity to juggle the various concepts required for such an undertaking. And so, counting the days to Evelyn's departure, he continued to involve himself with Evelyn's schedule and Beattie's attendance. In the meantime, he lost himself in a reverie of another world.

Chapter Sixteen

The day of Evelyn's departure had finally arrived. As melancholy as Trevelyan was to see her leave, he was as eager to begin preparations for the evening and for his first ascension. He saw her off at the main hall after lunch. The driver honked the horn, and she waved from the window. He made his way to his room and took notes from the various books from the library. These, accompanied with the diaries, should be enough for him to make his attempt. He gathered all the necessary items he thought he may need and slipped behind the mirror/door and up the narrow staircase. He had read that in order for the work to succeed, the petitioner must remove his mundane garb and don a consecrated robe, preferably in the colours of the forces he wished to obtain. Trevelyan stripped from his jeans and shirt and donned Seymour or Morgan's orange robe that hung in the small dressing area. As he pulled it over his head, he could smell the incense and oils that were used so long ago. Already, the smell of the robe and the deliberate shedding of the mundane world seemed to elevate his senses to a higher pitch. He gathered his notes around him and sat himself on the floor dead centre of the inscribed circle. He took a couple of minutes to read through his notes and, laying them at his feet, he stood and drew the circle of power around himself.

He had been practicing this part of the ritual over the last several weeks. Designed to encapsulate the power of the will and the imagination, he would conjure, in his imagination, a string of pale blue flame outlining the circle as he drew his hand around its circumference. After completing the circle, he would summon the four elements from their cardinal points to attend. This was done by visualising the archetype of that element, and by vibrating the names of power. He then, using the pointed finger of his left hand, drawn a pentagram at each of the cardinal points in the air before him. Visualising them ablaze with the same colour flame as the circle. Once completed, the circle was sealed in a conflagration of unearthly pale blue flame. The cardinal pentagrams hovering in the air between him and the outer circle. The air within the sanctum changed, becoming taut, like it was being strained to thin. Trevelyan glanced at Seymour's notes and built an image of a door within the inner circle. He recreated the dragon doors of the library until they stood before him, materialised from the air. With a tremendous effort of pure willpower, he detached himself from his physical body and stepped towards the awaiting dragon doors. Without as much as a glance behind himself, he pushed on the doors until they swung open into darkness and with a moment of trepidation, he stiffened his resolve and stepped through the doorway.

∞∞∞∞

Trevelyan had stepped into a world of vibrant colour. Much more intense than the real world, even in the twilight. He could feel the grass beneath his bare feet. The leaves on the many trees displayed autumn colours. He turned to look behind him, but the dragon doors were nowhere to be seen. Instead, a shimmering in the air, not unlike the thermals created on a hot day, stood where the dragon doors had opened. He found himself in a small copse surrounded by tall trees. A narrow path lay before him, leading further into the landscape. He could detect the smell of flowers that bordered the treeline on both sides, sweet and heady as the wind teased them. He looked above him to the sky, a dark blue but growing darker as he watched. He guessed it to be evening, but there was no sign of a setting sun, so it was difficult to tell. The resonant hues amazed him. They seemed so... alive. He instinctually reached out to touch the leaves on the tree with his right hand. He could not believe it. His hand, his arm. He was complete! He reached up to his face and where before his scars ran deep, there was nothing! This was completely unexpected. He was a being of thought and light now. His physical body was left behind and his imagination had given himself a new one. He marvelled at his newness. He took a deep breath of air that did not exist into his lungs that were not there. The contradiction of standing here astounded him, in this place that should not exist. But that was just it. It was real. It did exist. He reached again for the leaves on the tree. They were real sure enough. He curled his toes into the lush green grass beneath his feet. Real, once again. His surroundings were alive, and he could feel it as he touched them. As though they welcomed his touch. It was almost as though something passed between them during contact, and he instinctually knew them.

He started forward along the path that led further into the copse. The light was fading as he walked. He progressed a short distance down the path before he picked up on some new vibration. Something that lay ahead of him. He could sense it up ahead, a kind of very low-pitched reverberation.

It was almost dark now, but he could still see the path ahead. The tone of the pitch shifted as he seemed to draw nearer to it. Peering into the dimness, he could see a feint glow ahead. Cautiously, he approached the source of the glow. It was a monolith. The reverberation changed to a rhythmic thrumming barely audible, but still palpable. It seemed to reach out to him, with tendrils of eldritch power teasing at his mind, drawing him closer. The monolith stood like a solitary fang protruding from the ground and glowing rhythmically in time to the thrumming he felt in his head. The tendrils had brought him before the giant stone, and as the darkness grew around him, the glow from the monolith seemed to brighten in answer. He reached his good right hand out to touch the monolith, but before he made contact, the thrumming stopped. He paused. Thin threads of silver light spread from his fingers, illuminating symbols and sigils inscribed on the stone. Within half a heartbeat, a figure manifested itself from the middle of the monolith. He stepped back in shock and stumbled, falling on his rump, his arms outstretched. The figure took the shape of a tattered old man in a dirty and torn robe. His hair and beard were a tangle of grey and white. His face was ancient. Etched with deep wrinkles and the furrows of time. His scrawny hand clutching a twisted wooden staff. He stepped from the stone. "Greetings, Wayfarer," the old man announced, looking directly at Trevelyan.

"Ermm... Hello," Trevelyan answered, a little bemused. The pair stood facing each other in the dimming light. The old man waited patiently, but silently. "My name is Gafyn Trevelyan. Who are you?"

"I am Tyst," replied the old man, immediately returning to his silence.

"Tyst, where am I exactly?"

"You stand before me at the Monolith of Wayfarers Isle," replied Tyst. More silence.

Trevelyan was unsure of what to say next. It was getting dark.

"Are we alone? Is anyone else here?" asked Trevelyan.

Tyst seemed to incline his head a little in response. Much like a confused dog. "There are others on the Isle," he offered but without explanation.

"Others? Who are they? Where are they," Trevelyan asked perplexed.

"As to their names, I know not. Only their purpose and location. To the west is the settlement of Mid Ward and 'Nestor's Keep.' Further to the coast lies the 'Western Ward.' These are the nearest of the peoples of Wayfarers

Isle. The rest lie to the north and east." He lapsed into silence once more. Trevelyan was still a little confused, and the surrounding darkness did not help matters much. He could only make out the old man's figure several feet in front of him. But, even if he could not see him, Trevelyan could feel the old man's presence. Tyst seemed more solid than his surroundings and more palpable to Trevelyan's senses. Unsure of what to do next, Trevelyan sat and put his back against the monolith. He looked at Tyst. The old man looked exhausted with age, but he held a warm smile and patient eyes as though he was used to waiting long periods of time in contemplation. Trevelyan felt uncomfortable with the silence between them.

For want of something to say he asked. "Tell me about yourself Tyst". The old man seemed to come alive as his face grew animated and the warm smile grew into a wide grin.

"I am Tyst," he began. "Testament of Hiraeth." As he spoke, he opened his arms as if he embraced the surrounding copse. "I was born from the first twilight and will persist until the last light of the breaking world. My purpose is to stand witness to all that transpires within Hiraeth. I have within me all the histories and chronicles from the time of the first light. I was born ancient but have grown wise. Over countless centuries have I endured. Silent until your summons." He returned his arms to rest on his staff and his eyes settled on Trevelyan.

"How did I summon you Tyst?" Trevelyan asked.

"By your very presence," Tyst replied, still smiling.

Trevelyan stopped to think for a moment. He needed a different approach. "Then who am I?" he asked.

"You are 'the Wayfarer.' He whose arrival was prophesied by Nestor centuries ago. The walker between the worlds and bringer of doom," he announced, still smiling.

Trevelyan was speechless! Bringer of doom? Wayfarer? And who was Nestor? How had he been prophesied? He needed more information and time to think. He would glean what he could from Tyst and then make his way back to the portal and Bryngaer. "Tell me about Nestor and his prophecy, Tyst" he asked.

"Nothing is known of Nestor before his gift of prophecy," began Tyst. "Only that he came from the east around five centuries ago. Accompanied by a rich merchant and dreams of death and destruction for Hiraeth, at the hands of a stranger he called 'Wayfarer.' Nestor, along with the merchant, created the Sentinel Guard and the Citadel, purposed with capturing and enslaving the Wayfarer before he can unleash his wrath. He enlisted men to serve him. Fathers and then their sons. Together they built the wards and towers over the lowlands of Wayfarers Isle that this stranger may not progress further. Nestor died ravaged and insane after many years of prophecy. He recorded all his dreams and visions regarding the Wayfarer in tomes and passed them on to his sacred order, who remained in faith until a century ago. They disbanded to devote themselves to the land and raised families. But they taught their sons of the Wayfarer, a portent of doom, until they may be called to service once more. The tomes of Nestor's prophecy went to the Citadel for safekeeping and study by the Nestorian priests. For his dreams were mysterious and far-reaching in their warnings and amendments." Tyst lapsed once more into silence and smiled at Trevelyan. How could this be possible, Trevelyan wondered. How could he be prophesied as a danger to Hiraeth when he had never been here before? This was unexpected. He was not sure what to expect when he ascended, but he did not expect to be labelled as a bringer of death! How could he become a destructive force? He needed time to think.

"Tyst, will you accompany me back to where I entered Hiraeth? I need to return home and I have a few more questions for you."

"Most assuredly," he replied and straightened himself, using his staff, smiling amiably all the while. Trevelyan gathered himself to himself in his mind and prioritised the questions he had for Tyst. It was a short walk back to the portal and so began with his most pressing question.

"How could I be a danger to Hiraeth Tyst? I don't understand," he asked, almost to himself.

"You are a being of great power," said Tyst.

"Power? What do you mean?" Trevelyan asked confused.

"The power of manifest creation," Tyst replied, as he hobbled along beside Trevelyan.

"How can that be dangerous?" said Trevelyan, as the shimmering emerged from the darkness.

"The power of creation by its very nature speaks to the power of destruction. One cannot exist without the other. It is the natural order of life," said Tyst, and as he spoke, Trevelyan saw his predicament.

"I have no wish to destroy. So, why would I do so?" Trevelyan replied.

"Wishes and desire are for others to contend with," Tyst replied. "I am not burdened so. To that I cannot answer. But, in my many years of observation, I have seen good men commit acts of great evil from a desire to do good. Passion and despair make poor bedfellows to power." As Tyst finished speaking, he looked at Trevelyan with only kindness in his eyes and not the judgement Trevelyan expected to see. They had reached Trevelyan's destination.

"Will I see you again, Tyst?" Trevelyan asked.

"Most assuredly, Wayfarer," replied Tyst, bowing grandly.

With that, he melted away into the darkness before Trevelyan's eyes, leaving him alone. Trevelyan took a moment to gather his thoughts. All this is too incredible to comprehend, he thought to himself and, taking a last long look at the darkness, he stepped through the portal and back to Bryngaer. When next he opened his eyes, he was lying on his back in the circle within the sanctum. Back in his twisted and burned body.

Trevelyan descended the narrow staircase leading from the sanctum and back through the mirror door to his rooms in Bryngaer. He had much to contemplate. He still struggled to understand how his ascension to Hiraeth could have been expected. Tyst said that Nestor had arrived on the island five hundred years ago. How could he have known where Trevelyan would ascend? There was nothing suggesting any prophecy in Seymour's journals. He took a moment to let it all sink in. It was incredible. *I have just been to a world that no one knows exists except me! A world as real as the one I inhabit now. No... that's not quite true, is it,* he mused to himself. The colours, the sounds, the fragrance of wildflowers. If he closed his eyes, he could recall the heady aroma carried on the breeze. Hiraeth seemed to be more REAL than this world. The vibrancy and colours were astounding. *The night air is clean and sweet and cool.* The leaves on the trees and the grass beneath his feet all seemed more tangible than anything in this world, more alive!

He glanced at the time. It was less than a few minutes since he ascended from the sanctum above his rooms in Bryngaer. It seemed like he was there for at least an hour or two. His talk with Tyst and his brief sojourn in Hiraeth took almost no time at all here in our world. He wondered how long an hour here would be in Hiraeth, but his mind was too blown to calculate. While he dressed for bed, binding his black and ravaged stump to his charred and mangled chest, he donned his bed robe and reflected on all that had led him here, to this moment. I had all started in Fairbourne's office that day. The day of the windfall and the fire. How two events such as that could converge on the same person on the same day filled him with a terror he had not thought possible. Destiny? Or Fate? He had been foretold in Hiraeth, regardless of the implications. Surely fate must have a hand in this. Any small difference that day would have spared him so much mental anguish and physical pain. But if they had not happened, he would not have found himself able to walk between two worlds. Each was as real as the other. He reached across the table next to the bed and turned off the light, preferring the darkness and silence of the night. He was asleep within minutes.

    Hiraeth called to him in his dreams, but he resisted feverishly. Rose beckoned him too. He could hear her whispering his name in the darkness of a dream. Urging him to follow the sound of her voice to a room. Not any room but the sanctum above his bedroom. Within the circle inscribed upon the floor, a small orange glow lit the sanctum. Growing larger and brighter until it became a blazing flame, and still it grew. Defining itself into the burning figure of the Rose of his dreams. Resplendent in flame and purged of her madness, she screamed silently at him. Pleading with him, her eyes a dancing flame. She lifted her arms like a bird's wings, outstretched and palms down on either side. She held them there for a moment before turning her palms toward the ceiling. She raised them above her head in their perfect arc and slapped her hands together in a furious gout of fire, her eyes never leaving him. As the palms of her hands met, the world winked out in a thunderclap. And he was alone once more, floating in the darkness of the days of his recovery. Rose's piercing scream suddenly shattered the peace coming from everywhere around him. One word echoed in the darkness..."Beware!"

Chapter Seventeen

Trevelyan woke feeling a little uneasy about his dream. That was the second time Rose had visited him, warning him of some impending doom. As he dressed, he considered the previous day's events and his ascension, Tyst and Hiraeth. If he stopped to think about it, he would probably convince himself that he was going insane. But he could not refute the authenticity of Hiraeth. How real it felt when he was there. The sweet-smelling breeze, the cold stone monolith, and, of course, his conversation with Tyst. He closed his eyes and recalled the scene as Tyst bid him farewell, and he took his last look before he returned home to Bryngaer. The movement of the trees in the darkness and the feel of the soft fresh earth beneath his feet. And a night sky with no stars...! He had just realised. The sky, when he arrived was turning to dusk and by the time he returned to the portal, it was fully dark. But there were no stars in that inky firmament. With no hint of them to come.

While Seymour brooded in his disappointment, Morgan had solved the problem of the duality of day and night and the seasons with the creation of "the tree." The light and warmth of the day, and the changing seasons, along with the night and the colder months, were overseen by the tree. Hidden somewhere in Hiraeth, presumably to prevent interference from unwanted sources. It all worked beautifully, it seemed, but the sky appeared empty and bleak without a moon and stars. Otherwise, it seemed that they had, between them, created an almost perfect rendering of the world, without the trappings of a modern progressive society and its inherent technology. From what Tyst had told him, Wayfarer's Isle was populated well enough. Nestor had seen to that. He was unclear on so many facets of Hiraeth, that he decided he would ascend again today and question Tyst some more. Trevelyan thought he had solved at least some of the mystery of Tyst by recalling their conversation. Tyst remained poised but silent until asked a question. When the answer to that question was fulfilled, he lapsed back into his affable silence once more. Seymour had created Tyst apart from the other "incarnates" as a document of the history of Hiraeth. He would be a solitary witness to all the events that occur within Hiraeth and could be summoned and questioned regarding them when either Morgan or Seymour would ascend.

It would seem that time runs much slower in Hiraeth than it does in Trevelyan's world. Hours could pass in Hiraeth, and only moments could slip away in the real world. If, for some reason, they had not ascended in a day or two, Hiraeth could have moved on by decades… or more. It was only early now; if Trevelyan were to hang a 'do not disturb' on his door, he would have the entire day to himself. That could amount to a lot longer in Hiraeth, and he could get answers to some of his questions. He was eager to explore this secret world of his. It was a welcome distraction from the circumstances of his birth. Their birth, actually. Because somewhere out there, he had a twin sister who knew nothing about her true heritage or parents. He had no idea where to search for her. Money was no obstacle, but he had considered that perhaps she was happy in her world and her life. Was it justified that Trevelyan should come along and upend all that? Look at the effect such a bombshell had on his life! All these thoughts he pushed down until he felt ready to deal with them. In the meantime, he had a world that did not exactly welcome him. But it had made him whole. At least while he was over there. The shock of discovering himself whole and unburned was almost unbelievable. He had the use of two arms and hands, and his features were as they were before the immolation and ruin. He felt complete in a way he had not felt in the last year. With a little buzz of excitement gnawing in his stomach, Trevelyan gathered his notes and diaries once more, and ascended the narrow stairs to the sanctum. He silently discarded his clothes, slipped on the perfumed robe, and entered the sanctum and the circle. As before, he summoned the quarters and invoked the elementals. He inscribed the circle and the pentagrams, and when he was ready, he built the dragon doors before him. He pushed them in his mind and was gone. Once again, he stepped through the dragon doors and into a paradise of colour, sound, and aromas.

The day was resplendent. With a clear blue sky above, but no sun to give an indication of time. It was a warm and balmy summer day. Insects buzzed around the blooms beneath the trees that lined the copse. Thick, straight, ancient trees, like broad oaks but with much larger leaves, towered above him. He retraced his path to the monolith and Tyst, taking in the small details around him. The lush grass beneath his bare feet, the cool breeze enveloping his perfect body. The scented air that he drew deep into his lungs and released slowly filled him with a tranquillity he had rarely experienced. It really was a wonder that had been created, and as he strolled aimlessly along the path between the trees, he marvelled at its complexity. He understood now Seymour's grief at not being able to personally experience Hiraeth, as Trevelyan could. Resorting to his "Incarnates" to explore. Like a second-hand memory of someone else's dream. But that begged the question of how Trevelyan could ascend within Hiraeth, when Seymour could not. Perhaps Tyst would have the answers, although Trevelyan was not sure of Tyst's awareness of his creators. Or their origin? With this in mind, he quickened his step and made his way to the monolith. He could see the way before him clearer now in the daylight, and the monolith emerged into view near a junction in the path. As the path turned to the left and the monolith, it also forked right and round a bend in the line of trees it lay between. Ignoring the right-hand bend in the path for now, Trevelyan approached the monolith and, once again, felt the tingling sensation through his body. This time he could hear a barely perceptible singing...like the sound of gentle bells. In the space of a heartbeat, Tyst materialised from the monolith and stepped into the bright daylight. The old man bowed low, his arms outstretched to Trevelyan in silent greeting, and stood leaning on his gnarled staff, smiling. Trevelyan was taken aback a little by the grandeur of the bow, and awkwardly attempted to do the same in return, failing ungraciously.

"Hello, Tyst," he said and waited.

Tyst continued to smile, but his eyes shone a little brighter in response. Confirming Trevelyan's guess that he could not speak unless in answer to a direct question.

"I was hoping to explore Hiraeth a little today. Would you care to accompany me if you are not too...?" Trevelyan was not sure exactly which word he was looking for but settled on "busy?"

Tyst straightened his back, still leaning on his staff, and stood poised but remained silent. "Of course," thought Trevelyan. That was not a direct question. He unconsciously cleared his throat with an embarrassed cough and tried again. "Do you have time to answer some more of my questions, Tyst?" he said more directly.

"Time, I have Wayfarer. Answers, I fear, are contingent upon the query." He replied cryptically, although still smiling.

Trevelyan took that to mean that he should frame his questions thoughtfully if he wished to get an accurate answer. He jumped into the deep end first. "Tyst, can you tell me why I can exist in both my world and Hiraeth and travel between the two?"

"It is within my means to relate the answer to you if that is your intent," he replied as if to underline his previous statement.

Trevelyan sighed and rethought his question, and then continued, "How is it I can travel between my world and Hiraeth?" he said as about direct as he could.

The old man became animated and began, "Wayfarer, you have within you a spark that remains from the creation of Hiraeth many aeons ago. 'Your world,' as you call it, is our Infinity. But within you is a fragment of the finite world of Hiraeth. It is this that allows your presence here, and alas, the power of apocalypse that you bear."

"How do I have the power of apocalypse?" Trevelyan asked not understanding.

"You bring with you the power of the infinite world you inhabit into the finite world you presently occupy. This power, if unleashed, would be the doom of which Nestor prophesied," stated Tyst, without judgement.

Startled, Trevelyan finally grasped his predicament. His very presence here was a threat to its continuity, and his arrival had been foretold. Defences had been employed, and Nestorian monks ensured his capture if he were to be discovered. He took a moment to frame his next question as direct as he could, without leaving room for interpretation in terms of an answer. "If I was to be discovered, would I be put to death?" he asked tentatively.

"That in all sooth I cannot answer." Said Tyst with a hint of sadness in his eyes. "The Nestorian monks disbanded ages ago. Their descendants still live, but whether they are of the faith, I cannot say. The world has moved on since then, and apart from Nestor's writings in the far Citadel, naught remains of his visions." That seemed reasonable. He may be able to pass among the denizens of Hiraeth anonymously if he keeps his wits about him. When it came down to it, he had two choices. He could return to Bryngaer and deformity, thus ensuring Hiraeth's safety. Or he could explore a little. If he encountered anyone, well, he could turn heel and run back the way he came, with no consequences. The fact that he was loath to return to that hideous broken body, when he could enjoy this perfect body of light in a paradise, he elected not to acknowledge. With the decision made, Trevelyan said to Tyst stiffly, "Will you accompany me on my travels?"

Tyst bowed as before and replied "It would belie my purpose if I were to refuse" he said once again cryptically, but this time Trevelyan thought he saw a hint of fear in his eyes. If he could feel fear.

Chapter Eighteen

The day was bright and warm, even with no sun. It was strange to be walking on such a glorious day with no familiar sun above to mark the passing of time. Tyst and Trevelyan had been walking for some time now, with Tyst answering what questions Trevelyan could think of as they went. So far, Trevelyan had learned that since his first arrival in Hiraeth, a dark, and powerful presence had made itself known in the western mountains across the far side of Hiraeth. The black mountains had birthed amongst them fiery volcanoes that spewed magma across the lower grasslands, turning them to charcoal and ash. The few wanderers that crossed those burned and blackened plains were never heard from again. Tyst had witnessed these dark developments as they occurred, all stemming from some bane, somewhere deep below the black mountain range. The mountains themselves, said Tyst, were born of a mighty calamity, aeons before, that struck Hiraeth from the heavens above. This caused the mountains to be riven from the ground in a torturous blast. A mighty chasm had been wrought from the bedrock alongside the black mountains. This had drifted away, as the continental mantle had split from the sheer force of the blast, and now occupied the North East. Since this disaster, some called the "wrath of the gods", a darkness has surfaced that was not there before. Something unnatural and malevolent that works against the natural order of life. The mountains were a forbidding place after the blast, but the rising dark had only made itself known since Trevelyan's arrival. This suggested some link between him, and it. Trevelyan had to pose his questions thoughtfully if he wanted to glean as much information from Tyst as he could. He guessed they had been walking for around an hour before anything of interest appeared in the distance. The trees continued to line the way on both sides of the ever widening copse, but as they walked, Trevelyan could see that they were on a promontory, butting into the sea. Several miles ahead, they would join the mainland. Between them and the mainland, lay a tower, looming in the distance and growing ever larger as they approached.

"Tyst, what is that tower ahead of us? Will there be people there?" asked Trevelyan, hoping to avoid any contact with the denizens of Wayfarers Isle, in fear of attack.

"That is Nestor's watch'. Built to prohibit the Wayfarers advance." Said Tyst. "Abandoned many centuries ago and uninhabited now, except for the woodland creatures that made it their home." Trevelyan felt acute relief and continued his questions as they approached the tower.

"Can you tell me more about the darkness that lies beneath the western mountains?" Trevelyan asked, trying to evaluate his options.

"As I have said, the blast wrought the chasm and the black mountains into being. In the centuries that followed, these blasted lands yielded no life or promise of such. They were abandoned by all who survived the calamity, and so they remained. A being of great power emerged beneath the mountains. Through a theurgy unknown before, he caused the mountains to erupt in fire, brimstone, and poison fumes. The 'blight," as it is called, has been creeping across the lands of the west, corrupting all that crosses its path. I alone know of this entity that calls itself "Diras" as none have seen it and lived to tell. He seduces and corrupts the souls of all living beings and twists them into creatures of his own design. He then sends them out to snare others and bring them to him so that he might build an army of darkness with which to march upon the bright lands and enslave those that he encounters. His realm he calls 'Dinas Diras.' With it, he intends to defile all of Hiraeth for reasons that are as yet unknown to me." Tyst lapsed into silence as they walked, but Trevelyan was aghast! He stumbled, and reached out to Tyst to steady himself, only to find nothing but air as he fell to the soft ground and sprawled unceremoniously on the floor. For all his appearance, Tyst was incorporeal to the touch. He had seemed to Trevelyan to be as solid and material as everything else in this strange world, but he was not. His shock winded him, and he took a moment before attempting to stand up. Tyst lent on his staff as he had before, awaiting the Wayfarers will. It took a moment or two for Trevelyan to gather his wits about him. When he gained his feet again, Trevelyan reached out to Tyst, who stood unmoving, still leaning on his staff. Humour shone in his eyes as Trevelyan swept his hand through the midriff of Tyst, connecting with nothing but air.

"I don't understand," said Trevelyan wistfully." How is it you are not solid?"

"I am as present as I am required to be," Said Tyst with a hint of a grin on his face. Trevelyan let it go for now. There were too many other questions that needed answering.

He now recalled reading Seymour's journal, and his description of his moment of loss of control. His hurling of power down on Hiraeth from the realm of Infinity. Perhaps the damage he wrought with his supernatural blast caused Morgan's death? It certainly seemed powerful enough if it could create the vast upheaval that Tyst described. It was strong enough to separate the continental plate that surrounded the point of impact, causing the chasm and the land attached to it to drift eastward across the sea. Surely such a calamity would cause damage to rebound on the one who had created the land from their own consciousness. He wondered if Seymour had considered such an outcome. He assumed he would. Having reclaimed his senses, he urged Tyst to continue on their passage toward the tower, which was growing ever larger as they approached. Somehow, his arrival in Hiraeth had begun some kind of chain reaction that caused this Diras to achieve the ruin of the land. Destruction crowded his thoughts as he considered his position. He himself was a threat to Hiraeth's existence, and somehow, his arrival had caused another set of circumstances to unfold that would achieve the same ends. As Trevelyan considered these vagaries in silence, Tyst walked alongside him without a care in the world. He wore a crooked smile that refused to be interpreted. Trevelyan broke the silence by asking Tyst, "Why do you accompany me, Tyst, if my presence here is such a threat in itself. Regardless of what else it has provoked?" He spoke out of a need to fill the silence that allowed his fears free rein, more than genuine curiosity.

"I fear you do not yet fully understand the portents of your arrival, Wayfarer," he sighed. "In the entire history of Hiraeth, from the dawn of its earliest light, there has not been a more singular event that could warrant my attention in pursuit of my purpose than your presence here. Including the wrath of heaven that birthed the blight that now festers beneath the western mountains. Assuredly, these events may be the undoing of Hiraeth. Until the threat has diminished, my purpose is to accompany you as a witness to what will transpire. I am aware of the myriad of other events that occur across Hiraeth, as is my interdict. But until a greater threat reveals itself, you are my priority, Wayfarer. I hope that, by your understanding of the nature of your questions and the answers you receive, you may forestall your fate and that of Hiraeth."

"So, you believe that there is hope?" Trevelyan grasped on to the chance of a reprieve.

"There is always hope, Wayfarer," Tyst replied with a smile.

They had almost reached Nestor's watch now, and Trevelyan could make out the remains of the walls that extended from either side of the debris. It must have been quite a sight in its time, and no doubt it could have served its purpose admirably. But now it only served as a home to a family of rabbit like creatures, that scattered as the two travellers approached. The same size as rabbits and similar in appearance except for the large bat-like ears on either side of their heads. Trevelyan and Tyst stepped between the ruins and picked their way through the rubble on the other side. A vast and spellbinding landscape of hills and trees emerged for as far as the eye could see. In all directions. Far off, birds flew above the forest that lay in the distance, and the road dissolved into a vista of splendour and beauty. Trevelyan stopped to take in the spectacular view. It was incredible. The difference between Trevelyan's world and Hiraeth could be seen, felt, and heard. Here, there were no sounds other than the sounds of nature. No mass population or modern technology means clearer air and brighter skies. Only the sound of the breeze passing through the trees and the distant call of birds carried on the air. Just fertile land and natural beauty. Quite literally a world away from civilisation. As Trevelyan looked around, the expanse of Wayfarers Isle sprawled out before him. He realised he had given no thought to what he was going to do next. He had travelled several miles now in Tyst's company, passing the time with questions and answers, until Trevelyan had a pretty good understanding of his straights. He had come to this world wholly unprepared. For both what he had been told of his prophesied arrival and the chain of events it had set in motion. He thought he understood the dangers well enough. Although he could not escape the feeling that any dangers he either posed or faced were not real in the sense that he would have to suffer the consequences of any actions he took while he was here. This was a dream world. Not even HIS dream world. It was Morgan's dream, using the power she borrowed from Seymour coupled with her own. What was the worst that could happen? If he fulfilled his prophesied apocalypse. If Hiraeth was destroyed. If Diras conquered and enslaved the land and the people here, what was it to him? He had a life back in the real world, even if that life was one of horror and trauma. He could turn his back on all of this and suffer no loss.

Except... As long as he was here, he could be complete. A reprieve from his pain, disfigurement, and disabilities. It was, without a doubt the most beautiful of places he had ever seen. And it was all his. His secret garden of delight. An idyllic playground of possibilities for a broken man. But none of that helped him decide on what to do next. He took a deep breath and decided it was time to test the waters.

"Where is the nearest settlement, town or village, Tyst?" Tyst cast his eyes toward the forest and said, "Mid Ward and Nestor's Keep lay ten leagues hence beyond the trees. A settlement of four villages surrounds the keep. To the east lies the Eastern Ward, a township on the coast with a harbour, but a journey nearly twice the distance. What is your will, Wayfarer?" Trevelyan took a moment before exclaiming, "What the hell? Nestor's Keep it is."

And with that, he took his first step toward whatever fate awaited him.

Chapter Nineteen

Between the mountains to the east and the ocean to the west was the largest forest Trevelyan had ever seen. Scattered trees lined the way ahead until they merged into a mass of green leaves and treetops that gathered themselves into a forest. If they intended to make for Nestor's watch, then they must traverse this forest to reach the grass plains on the other side. As they approached the dense forest, the warm air seemed to cool noticeably as they left the blue skies behind and entered the green canopy above them. There were birds and small forest creatures that reminded Trevelyan of the creatures back in the real world. Only the colours were different, or the sizes and slightly altered features of the squirrels and rabbits. Trevelyan had stopped asking questions, and the pair of travellers fell into a comfortable silence as they walked together through the dense woodland. Tyst seemed happy to walk alongside the Wayfarer, although Trevelyan got the distinct feeling that Tyst's attention was elsewhere during their long silences. The old man had a faraway look in his eyes, as though he were staring at a horizon that never appeared. When Trevelyan did hazard a question, it was forced and uninspired. He liked to hear the sound of Tyst's voice. He found it comforting and distracted him from thoughts of capture. It was much cooler under the shade of the forest, and Trevelyan shivered involuntarily. After which, Tyst guided them westward. After several miles, Trevelyan could feel the warmth of the sunless sky as the trees thinned a little. The sound of running water echoed through the last vestiges of woodland, and they soon sighted a large river running alongside the forest.

It was there that Tyst was heading, offering some warmth to his companion, which Trevelyan found touching, and soon his flesh had warmed once more. They reached the river. Although there was no sun to reflect off the deep blue bubbling water that soon turned to frothing white as it tumbled over the rocks, it shimmered anyway, creating small rainbows in the spray. As an artist, Trevelyan had keen eyes and soon noticed the small intricacies of illusion that met the eye in a world with no sun. There were no shadows, for instance. The light seemed to come from all directions at once, and although Trevelyan had noticed a slight shade under the woodland canopy, he felt it was more of an illusion. Morgan's attention to detail was quite staggering, and Trevelyan wondered if she might have made a good artist. No painting of his, no matter how talented, could hold a candle to this majestic creation of Morgan's. They followed the riverbank, between the river and the forest for some time until Trevelyan noticed a settlement appear across the river in the distance.

"Is that Mid Ward?" Trevelyan asked, already knowing the answer but needing the balm of Tyst's voice to settle his nerves as the sound of civilisation drifted across the water.

"It is in sooth Wayfarer," replied Tyst, his gaze moving away from the river and back to the trees. A moment later, Trevelyan heard breaking twigs and the crushing of fallen leaves. Someone or something approached them from the right. He swung himself around to meet the intrusion. Panic rising in his mind. A solitary man emerged out of the fecundity of the forest. He was dressed in a black doublet with silver decoration embroidered on it in lavish swirls and leaves. In stark contrast to his bronzed features. He was tall and undeniably authoritative. In his hand, he held an elaborately carved sword that rested by his side until needed. Trevelyan was shocked at the man's sudden appearance out of the trees and turned to Tyst in silent askance. Tyst stood, leaning on his staff patiently. Before Trevelyan could utter a word, another three men dressed as the first, dropped from the lower branches of the nearest trees to stand alongside the man. All three were armed with bow, axe, or sword. The first man to show himself seemed to be the leader of the other three. When all four stood before the travellers, the leader spoke.

"Hold," he said, his voice undeniable. Trevelyan was not sure if he spoke to his companions or to Trevelyan and Tyst, and so he stood still, afraid to move an inch. With his companions at his back, the leader of the men sheathed his sword and held Trevelyan in his steely gaze, never glancing at Tyst, who remained as he was. His eyes devoured the scene as it unfolded. "What business brings you hither stranger?" he demanded of Trevelyan as he crossed his arms before himself, his men poised at his side. Trevelyan froze, the man's eyes holding him avidly.

"Weerrrr..." Trevelyan glanced around at Tyst, hoping for help, but he remained, leaning on his staff, looking slightly amused. Finding no help there, he turned back to the men before him. " I mean..." his voice faltered again as he stared nonplussed at his accuser.

"I repeat, stranger. What business brings you to the Warden's Woods?" The man's voice took on a sterner tilt, and his men moved forward a little, their hands on their respective weapons.

Trevelyan instinctively put his hands up and backed away toward the river. There was no escape there. The rapids were too strong to swim away. 'Damn it, he thought to himself. He was unprepared for a confrontation and realised the precariousness of his position. For want of a better answer to this man's demands, he blurted, "We are lost." It was meant to come out more confidently, but the fear in his voice was palpable.

"Aedan, if this stranger takes another step backward toward the river, put an arrow through his eye," said the man in charge.

The tallest of the men at his back, quick as a flash, put an arrow to his bow and drew it back, ready to release. Trevelyan did not doubt that if he attempted to move an inch, this man would do as he was bid. "Please," he said unintentionally. "We didn't mean any harm" The leader looked at him in askance, but the danger left his eyes, and he put his hand out to indicate Aedan to lower his bow.

"You keep saying we," said the man. "Where are your companions? We have followed you at a distance from the fallen tower, and you have travelled alone." Trevelyan glanced at Tyst and then back at the man, not understanding.

"Why can't they see you Tyst?" Trevelyan demanded. The leaders head tilted slightly to the left as he considered Trevelyan.

"I have elected only to reveal myself to you, Wayfarer," answered Tyst flatly. "To do otherwise would invite disaster. These beings have no knowledge of my existence or purpose, and therefore my visible presence would only cause rue."

As he spoke Trevelyan realised how it must look to the armed men. "Great" he muttered to himself.

"He is clearly insane" said Aedan to his leader. "He refers to himself as 'We' and speaks to the very aether."

"Perhaps" said the leader. "That is not for us to decide, but we cannot have him wandering loose to harm himself or others." He reached into his doublet and produced a coil of rope like material that resembled some kind of silk. He turned his attention to Trevelyan, who was still motionless with his arms raised above his head, and asked. "Will you consent to accompany us to the Elders at Mid Ward or must you be subdued?"

"I consent, I consent" said Trevelyan rapidly, preferring to walk under his own steam.

"Then we will accompany you to Mid Ward where you will be questioned by the Elder Warden, before judgement is made upon your freedom," said the leader. In silence, he lifted his arm above his head and inscribed a circle in the air. The Wardens gathered around Trevelyan as they began the long walk to Mid Ward. They travelled in silence. Trevelyan, surrounded on all sides by the Wardens, while Tyst walked alongside. Remaining unseen to all except the Wayfarer. Trevelyan played along with this new development. He had no other reasonable choice. They walked at an easy pace between the river and the trees. All the while Trevelyan could feel the eyes of the Wardens watching his every step. Their distrust was clear. As they progressed alongside the river, Trevelyan saw they were heading toward a bridge that spanned the fast-moving river. After which a dusty road headed west toward the walled village that lay in the distance. He was filled with anxiety and fears that he may be captured by these men and the elders that they marched him toward. The forest fell away to his left, revealing a small, well-trodden path that led eastward. Another forest, as dense as the one he had just traversed, began alongside the path and headed eastward with it. They, however, wheeled westward toward the bridge and then Mid Ward. As they approached the bridge, Trevelyan caught sight of a tall blue tower northwest of where he walked. It was visible from the bridge, although it was many miles away, and Trevelyan wondered at its size. As they gained the bridge, the leader said, "Aedan, make haste to Mid Ward and inform the Elder Warden that we have a stranger in our midst who will require interrogation." Aedan secured his bow and made off across the bridge and onto the plains that led to the settlement. "Saeth, inform the Arch Warden at Nestor's Keep that we must have conclave this evening."

"At once" the young Warden said and set off at a brisk run southwest and was quickly out of sight.

Trevelyan was now walking between the remaining warden and the leader, still in silence. After they had crossed the bridge, they followed the path that led them toward the village. The leader addressed Trevelyan for the first time since the forest. "My name is Morthwyl. First Warden of Nestor's Keep and the Mid Ward. On your left is Derwyn. It would be unwise to withhold your name, stranger, and so I would have it whether it pleases you or no"

For the first time since his ascension Trevelyan was, in most regards, alone. "My name is Gafyn Trevelyan" he replied.

"From where have you travelled, Gafyn Trevelyan? That you are a stranger to these shores is doubtless. Your raiments are unknown to me, and your manner is less than common." He turned his gaze to Trevelyan, awaiting his answer. Trevelyan's mind raced, trying to think of a response that would not worsen his already unfortunate circumstances. "I would have your truth, or even your falsehood, but I will not suffer your silence, Gafyn Trevelyan," said the First Warden. Tyst walked alongside the men, listening intently to the exchange, his eyes avid with the possible outcomes of events.

"We are… I mean… I am lost. I don't know where I am, or where I have travelled through to get here." Said Trevelyan, hoping the First Warden would accept this as a suitable answer, but he feared not.

"Then how did you make land on these shores?" He enquired even more forcefully.

"I didn't," Trevelyan answered before he realised the trap.

"So, you would have me believe you are native to this isle. Even though your garb is unknown, and you cannot say from whence you came?"

"Yes… I mean no…" Trevelyan was caught in the First's logic. In an effort not to anger the man any further, and to buy himself a little time, he said, "I will explain all to your elders when we meet." Hoping that would appease the First long enough to try and make some kind of believable story to explain his presence. Tyst meanwhile did as he had promised and accompanied the Wayfarer on his sojourn in both silence and intrigue. He apparently approved of Trevelyan's ploy to stall for time. His eyes brightened at the prospect.

The First bit down on his anger as they walked on. But a wry smile crossed his otherwise stern features. "You would be better served to confess your crimes to me," he said loud enough for Derwyn to overhear, " as my father's temperament is less friendly than my own."

To this, Derwyn chuckled to himself. They undertook the rest of the journey in silence. The First Warden and Derwyn marched their prisoner along the dusty path toward Mid Ward and Nestor's Keep. Trevelyan took in his surroundings, looking for some kind of inspiration for a lie, to get him out of the mess he found himself in. The tower he had seen some time ago now loomed large ahead of him. It was quite magnificent. It must have reached over a hundred feet straight up into the clear, blue, sunless sky.

Trevelyan realised the irony of his dilemma. When it comes down to it, there is no reason to panic. He is safe at Bryngaer in his father's sanctum, awaiting his return to his body. This is more of a dream than a reality. He winced when he remembered his disfigured and withered frame sprawled on the sanctum floor. But it offered him a way out of his present straights. Instead of making up some lie that will by seen through, he should play the fool, and try his best to demonstrate his innocence. He felt very relieved at this realisation and relaxed a little. Within a few minutes, they approached the large, open wooded gates of the walled town. Aedan and Saeth awaited the First Warden at the entrance.

"Hail, First Warden. It is as you commanded," Aedan said. "Your father awaits, and the Arch Warden has called a conclave in the low citadel." He bowed and took a step back. Aedan's eyes found Trevelyan's, and he regarded him suspiciously. "I have prepared a space that will act as a cell for the prisoner if you wish him detained at your pleasure?" He addressed the First, but his eyes never left Trevelyan.

"Not yet." The first said as he put his hand upon Aedan's shoulder. "I would have my father's consideration of this stranger before we dishonour ourselves with imprisonment." He turned to Trevelyan as he spoke. "But I will not hesitate to do so should I have reason." He turned to his comrades and dismissed them to their pleasures. He once again took his place next to Trevelyan and urged him through the gates and into the small town square. The First ushered him to a house larger than the others. Within moments Trevelyan was in a large timber room, with wall hangings of various designs and descriptions, all bright with coloured weave. At the far end of the room sat a man not unlike Morthwyl, First Warden of Nestor's Keep and Mid Ward. He was taller, certainly much older, with sharper features than his son. But the resemblance was there. The First Warden entered the room behind

Trevelyan and murmured to his father and Elder before he retired to the rear corner, so as not to intrude on his father's questioning. The Elder sat with his back to Trevelyan. He finished what he was doing and turned to face the stranger.

"Hail Gafyn Trevelyan. Stranger to Mid Ward." He took in Trevelyan's appearance, and then his eyes found Morthwyl. "At ease, First Warden." He said to his son. He continued, "My name is Ysbail, Elder of Mid Ward and Wayfarers Isle. You have been found wandering our lands with no explanation from whence you came or your purpose here. My Wardens report you speak to the very aether and cannot account for yourself. Is that correct?" He was a tall, slight man, dressed in a long robe with red fringes that swept the floor. He looked to be in his mid-seventies, but his eyes showed keen intelligence with a hint of ruthlessness to those who would displease him. His features were sharp and lean, but his gaze was ferocious.

"Not entirely." Trevelyan retorted defensively. "Anyway, is this how strangers are treated here?" sounding more confident than he meant to. "I mean; I have done nothing wrong. Am I a prisoner now?"

"I have yet to decide that," said Ysbail, severely, but then he sighed and softened a little. "Although I regret the manner of our meeting, we have good reason to be wary. There has been troubling news brought to us from the west. A dark, and yet unknown presence gathers in the fiery mountains and of a corruption that spreads like disease through the land... and so I ask again, Gafyn Trevelyan. Can you account for your presence here, or do I have to resort to other methods of askance?"

His look told Trevelyan everything he needed to know about his predicament, and he sighed as he answered. "I am no threat, if that's what you mean." Trevelyan said. More irony. "I am lost, and I don't know where I am, or how I got here." He said, trying his best to sound believable.

Ysbail's eyebrows raised slightly in response, as he silently considered the strangely dressed man stood before him. "My Wardens reported that you spoke to some unseen other when first they questioned you. Do you travel alone, or do you have company?" Ysbail asked, clearly suspicious of this event.

"I was surprised," Trevelyan offered in answer. But Ysbail's steely face urged him on. "I am alone," he said finally.

"Your dress implies that you are not born of these shores. I would enquire from whence you originate."

Panic rose in Trevelyan's eyes, and he was sure it was noticed. "I can't remember," he blurted, trying to avoid the Arch Warden's stare.

Something seemed to change in his questioner's eyes to that answer, making Trevelyan wish he could take it back immediately. "Then we are done here," Ysbail said, his face red with anger. "First Warden, would you take this man to a place of confinement until I have decided his fate?" Ysbail then turned his back on Trevelyan. The First Warden did as he was commanded and grasped Trevelyan's arm in a vice like grip. He hurried him out of the house and through the small village square, to another smaller house, where Saeth stood at attention.

"He is to remain here. Guarded at all times until I return for him."

Saeth nodded stiffly, and pushed Trevelyan inside the hut, closed the door, and barred it from the outside. Throughout all this, Tyst had been by his side, unseen by all except Trevelyan. He found him to be a disconcerting distraction while under question. Now he was grateful for the privacy.

"What am I going to do, Tyst?" Trevelyan asked without looking at the old man. Silence was his only answer. Sighing, he tried to think of another way of framing the question that may prompt a response from Tyst. OK, he thought, how am I going to get out of this? Escape was impossible. He did not have many options, if any, and all of them seemed inadequate somehow.

Chapter Twenty

Saeth had brought food and drink for Trevelyan. While he awaited the Warden's pleasure, he ate a little of the stew, although he was not hungry, and he drank nearly all the water that was given in one gulp. He had asked Tyst if he could describe the events transpiring at the conclave. He needed time to consider a way out, and the old man's voice soothed him somewhat. Also, the more information he had, the better chance he stood. Tyst's eyes seemed to refocus elsewhere as he said, "The Arch Warden and Ysbail are discussing the events from across the sea before the other elders. Ysbail insists that this threat must be met with force. That an army should be raised and sent to meet this corruption in the field. Whereas Hafren, the Arch Warden, is more concerned with your arrival than with events across the other side of the world. He insists you are Nestor's prophecy made flesh. That it falls upon Mid Ward to carry out the sentence bestowed upon the Wardens by Nestor himself. Ysbail warns against this as a barbaric act unworthy of the Wardens of Mid Ward and Wayfarers Isle. Your guilt or innocence has yet to be proven. When asked by the Arch Warden what course of action he would suggest, Ysbail declared that he and the First Warden have elected to form an escort for you. From here to the far Citadel at the northern headlands of Wayfarer's Isle. The First and three chosen from the Wardens will deliver you henceforth for the consideration of the Nestorian monks. The First Warden will consult with the head of the Sentinel Guard and the Magister of the Citadel regarding news from the west and what shall be done."

Tyst turned to face Trevelyan. His face seemed grave.

"There is one among the Elders descended from the long line of Nestor. Although not an Elder himself, he has the respect and, more importantly, the ear of Hafren. He serves as counsel between the Citadel and the Conclave. He insists on accompanying the escort and will deliver you personally to the Magister with his recommendations. His name is Rhydian, he is the last living descendent of Nestor the seer, and believes it is his duty to conclude his forefathers' service." Tyst's focus wandered again. Trevelyan felt he was being given a warning. "After much deliberation," Tyst continued, "it has been decided that the fate of Hiraeth cannot be decided by the Wardens alone. Ysbail and the First have seen clearly the true course of action that must be undertaken. Rhydian will serve as your keeper on the journey, so that he may learn what he can of you and present you to his order for judgement. As I speak, the conclave has finished, and the First Warden is preparing for the journey. He sends word to present you in the town square, ready for departure."

While Trevelyan listened with rising apprehension, Tyst lapsed into silence once more. He wondered if he had done the right thing by ascending to Hiraeth. Regardless of the wonders of the land and his renewed appearance. It occurred to him then, that he knew of no other way to get back to Bryngaer, and his presumably sleeping body on the floor of the sanctum. This gave him cause for alarm. If they were to travel north away from the portal, how would he ever get back? What would become of him both here in Hiraeth and his body back in Bryngaer? Stopping short of panic, he calmly tried to form this question for Tyst.

"Tyst, how can I get back to where I came from? Is there another portal? Or another way of returning home?" His voice shook a little as this new peril dawned on him.

"There are many thresholds hidden throughout Hiraeth," replied Tyst. "Most are situated near monoliths, that I may be summoned. There are many more across the land that are unknown to me." He considered for a moment before saying, "A power as great as yours may dismiss you from Hiraeth by force of will. Unless your will is stronger... Is it your wish to abandon us, Wayfarer?"

Trevelyan grimaced at Tyst's choice of word... 'Abandon?' Surely if he removed himself from Hiraeth, he would take the threat of annihilation with him? But before he had a chance to question Tyst further, the door opened, and Saeth spoke to him for the first time.

"The First Warden has requested your attendance in the town square. You are to change your raiment and accompany me in haste," he said, thrusting a pile of rough spun clothes to Trevelyan. He then stood in the doorway with his arms folded in a clear demonstration of authority. Trevelyan did as he was bid, silently all the time, thinking about how he might get back home. He donned the woollen trousers and jerkin. Not knowing how to fasten the cloak, he unceremoniously threw it over his shoulder, pausing to whisper swiftly to Tyst.

"Will you come with me? You could disappear until I call your name again?" Tyst nodded and was gone.

Gathering his resolve, he strode out the door to meet Saeth's icy stare. Moments later, he found himself in the town square, facing a small crowd of people. The First Warden sat on horseback along with Aedan, Derwyn, and another well-dressed man. Saeth soon rode into the square with a fresh horse for Trevelyan, and all fell silent as Hafren, the Arch warden, addressed the company.

"Having held conclave, we, the elders and wardens of Mid Ward, have decided that we are not sufficient to determine the import of this stranger's arrival during a time of corruption and burgeoning war! Together, we have elected to send the stranger to the far Citadel for further scrutiny. He will be accompanied by the First and three other Wardens. Rhydian of Nestor will journey also at his own personal request to attempt to fathom his ancestor's interpretation and the meaning of the stranger. Aderyn monk will also travel to the far Citadel to seek the wisdom of his order and bring it back to the Wards. The journey is several days long, and so Brigid and Gwenith will accompany you as well. They will cook and prepare camp as maidens of Mid Ward." Hafren cast them a sideways glance before continuing. "And learn their place. They will remain at the far Citadel until such time as their penance has been accounted for. All hail the Ward!"

"All hail the Ward!" the gathering said in one voice. With this, the Arch Warden was returned to his litter and taken back to his hut. All the while locking eyes with Trevelyan as he passed him slowly. The First Warden saw Trevelyan's panic-stricken face and asked, "Do you acquiesce, Gafyn Trevelyan?"

"Do I have a choice?" Trevelyan retorted with more anger than he meant to admit.

"No," said the First Warden smiling briefly.

The two young maidens were clad similarly to the rest of the company. They busied themselves loading provisions and bedding on the horses they would ride, throwing shy glances at Trevelyan and giggling to each other. When all the company was ready to leave, they filed out of the single gate of Mid Ward. Following the path back to the bridge, Trevelyan had crossed earlier in the day with the Wardens. The First and Derwyn led the party, followed by the two maidens. Rhydian and Aderyn were next, before Trevelyan and Saeth brought up the rear. As they travelled toward the bridge, the tower Trevelyan saw on his way to Mid Ward was getting a little nearer. They crossed the bridge and turned north. The tower became more visible now, lying on the far bank of the river several leagues away. Saeth seemed content to remain in silence as they rode, and so Trevelyan took in his surroundings. The watchtower was a squat stone keep at its base, with the tower reaching hundreds of feet skyward. Made from a bluish stone, it was capped with a white marble observation platform. Above it all burned a bright orange flame. Twenty feet into the sky like a beacon. With the river on his left and the woods to his right, Trevelyan picked his way through the scattered trees while his horse did most of the navigating. He had never ridden before and was surprised at how easy he found it. They were only moving at walking pace, as the road was rocky. When it opened into lush grassland after half a league, the First Warden picked up the pace, and Trevelyan's horse fell into a cantor alongside Saeth. Trevelyan found it hard going at this speed. He had to adjust himself and his timing in order to continue without extreme duress. As they moved northward, the horizon seemed to grow as they neared it, leaving Trevelyan confused. Before long, it became clear. An almighty cliff face spanned Wayfarers Isle from east to west. Visible from this distance, their size must have been enormous. It reminded him of his coma dreams. Perhaps they were not dreams after all. Clouds had gathered around the party as the weather changed, bringing rain and mist down on them. This weather seemed to descend out of nowhere. Settling over the party, moving with them as they progressed north. The First Warden was visibly surprised at the turn in the weather, and expressed his concern to Derwyn as they rode at the front of the company. They ambled their way toward the cliffs alongside the riverbank at a steady pace. The escarpment loomed above them as they drew nearer. Trevelyan could see a waterfall drop from the precipice, crashing toward the ground, and the roar of the water became louder as they neared. The waterfall fell onto the lowlands from the great height of the cliffs, the wind scattering the falling water on its descent. What remained formed a large pool, which split into two rivers. One heading southwest and the other running south, past the large tower and on to Mid Ward and beyond. The weather now was worsening as they neared the giant cliffs, and the First's concerns grew as the sky darkened and boiled, building to a storm.

"We must seek shelter. We cannot hope to climb the stairs in this weather," said the First as they approached the base of the cliffs. The company veered away from the waterfall. Headed to a break in the mighty cliff's stone face, where rude steps had been hewn into the rock face itself, and ascended into the mists above them. The party gathered together at the base of the cliffs next to the steps and dismounted. Huddling below the overhang and out of the increasingly hard rain. As Trevelyan looked back toward the tower and Mid Ward, he could see the blue sky beyond the clouds that hung above them. The First and the three other Wardens unpacked a bundle of well-used leather rain cloaks and handed them to the members of the party that had not thought to prepare for the rare event of a storm. The two young girls hung together while Rhydian and Aderyn moved toward Trevelyan to keep out of the rain.

"Hail Gafyn Trevelyan," Aderyn said as he approached him. "We have yet to be acquainted; I am Aderyn," he said as he bowed in a gesture of greeting. "This young fellow beside me is Rhydian. Last living descendent of Nestor the Great. Prophet and seer." Trevelyan met Aderyn's eyes and nodded. He glanced at Rhydian. He could sense the suspicion in the man's eyes as Rhydian watched him narrowly.

"Impressive, is it not?" said Aderyn, indicating the massive wall of rock that towered above them. "It is called 'The Rive.' It separates the highlands from the lowlands and has done for centuries. There are many myths concerning its origins. None that are worthy of consideration in these enlightened times." Aderyn leaned closer to Trevelyan and whispered. "The truth lies with the Citadel and will likely remain there." This was said quietly so as not to anger Rhydian, who was busy helping the Wardens prepare the horses for the long ascent up the steps of the cliff.

Trevelyan was very aware of the company's unsettled mood because of the storm and asked Aderyn why. "Storms are not usual in the lowlands of Hiraeth, and this one appears to defy the winds on which they arise, See..." He pointed to the sky above them, and Trevelyan took a moment before he understood. The storm was moving against the wind and toward them rather than being carried away to the north. And its ferocity was growing.

The First approached the group as they huddled against the cliff and raised his voice above the mounting shriek of the storm. "It appears that the storm will not pass. We must ascend the stairs, regardless. The horses are strung together ready to ascend, but they cannot bear riders as the way is too steep. Derwyn will lead the horses, and we will follow on foot. I urge caution, as the rock face will be slippery in the face of such a preternatural storm. The going will be difficult. Stay close to each other. The wind will be stronger as we ascend. Gafyn Trevelyan, you are to remain in front of me as we climb. Saeth will follow behind the others. If you are ready, we will begin." And with that, he ushered Trevelyan to the first step and fell in behind him, as did the others. Trevelyan could not help feeling that this storm contained something more than just wind and rain. It felt like a punishment as he forced his way behind the horses, steadily climbing one foot in front of the other. He felt nauseous and dizzy, but he kept on plodding forward through the stinging rain. Every now and then a gust would push him forward, while another pushed him backward, threatening to dislodge him from the steps and cast him down into the storm. He turned to hide his face from the rain and saw the others climbing steadily behind him. His eyes met Rhydian's icy stare again. But this time, he saw a hint of eagerness about him. He wore a smirk as he watched Trevelyan climb, almost as if he expected him to fall. He realised then that Rhydian had no trust in him at all. He also realised that the storm was not affecting the others in the same way it did him. His arms and face felt like they were being pricked by tiny, sharp needles. His head hurt in the same manner, but on the inside. It worsened the higher he climbed until he felt he could barely open his eyes any longer. Suddenly, as he stepped up to the next stair, the wind spun him around on one foot and almost pitched him off the rock face. If it was not for the First's swift and sure hand on his shoulder, he would be hurtling to certain death. They were over halfway by now. The First, witnessing Trevelyan's struggling efforts, gripped him firmly about the waist and half carried, half walked him up the steps. As long as the First had hold of him, the winds relented. As soon as he released him, even for a moment, the wind pulled at him with invisible hands. The First's face expressed his concern with these events and continued to keep Trevelyan secure in his vice like grip. Trevelyan looked up and ahead at the horses. They all but disappeared into the storm above. Finally, he glimpsed them cresting the precipice. As Trevelyan almost reached the cliff edge, the rock beneath his feet seemed to lurch sideways, causing him to slip on a rounded step. He tumbled backward past the First. Saeth caught him as he bowled head over heels and brought him to a sudden stop. He shouted to the First that Trevelyan was safe and motioned the others ahead. Saeth pushed Trevelyan ahead of him on the final steps as the others made the cliff edge and disappeared into the night. Trevelyan followed the steps and had almost reached the summit, when, to his surprise, he stopped short and could go no further! There was no barrier or obstruction ahead. The very air itself denied him access to the precipice. Saeth pushed him once more, but still Trevelyan could not advance. He reached out to the aether in front of him and was painfully rejected. Something prevented him from crossing the threshold of the cliff. Trevelyan's confusion reigned. Saeth had to barge his way past him, through the same space that denied Trevelyan. He turned and glared at Trevelyan's obstinacy, holding out his hand for Trevelyan to grasp. He reached for Saeth's hand, but was once again painfully rejected, and almost stepped backward off the cliff. Saeth could now see that something was very wrong, but before he could react, the First shouted a warning.

"Wolves! Aedan, ward the horses!" Saeth turned to see a host of yellow-eyed wolves appear through the storm from the woods beyond. He guessed perhaps a dozen. And they all made their way straight toward him and the stranger called Gafyn Trevelyan.

Chapter Twenty one

Moments before the leader of the pack hit Saeth square on, an arrow pierced the storm, and the wolf's eye killing it instantly. But not halting its forward motion, it crashed into Saeth, knocking him over the precipice out of Trevelyan's view. He surged forward, trying to break the invisible barrier that held him and pounded on the air. He could see clearly, almost in slow motion, what was happening. The rest of the pack had split in order to tackle the company. Keeping them from aiding the intended target Trevelyan. As his eyes swept the scene from his position below the ridge, he once again caught Rhydian's fierce grin. Even amid his own demise. The First was defending the girls from two advancing wolves. Aedan dropped his bow and secured the horses. Derwyn harried any who came near enough. Aderyn wielded his staff in all directions toward himself and Rhydian. Trevelyan was helpless and about to be devoured by yellow eyes and teeth. In an act of desperation and defiance, he refused to accept that he was about to be killed by wolves that lived in his imagination. The absurdity of it actually made him laugh out loud. He felt as though he was teetering on the edge of an inner precipice, too. A tipping point. For a fraction of an instant, he saw Rose in the yellow eyes of the nearest wolf. Sweeping toward him from a world away. Suddenly, the humour was replaced by anger and rage that seemed to come from nowhere. And just like that day with Rose, as if from nowhere, fire erupted in gouts and furious whirls of incandescent power. Trevelyan was bathed in a whirlwind of silver and red flame as his fury mounted. He could feel a cataclysm building within him that was almost unstoppable. But almost was enough. He raised himself, arms outstretched. He gathered the whirlwind to him and held it tight against his bosom. With an act of sheer will, he targeted the wolves as he hurled his fury at the invisible wall that separated him from the others on the clifftop. Seconds seemed to last an eternity. He bathed the cliff in caustic fire. While the company and horses remained untouched, the inferno vaporised the wolves and the barrier in an ear shattering blast that shook the heavens and the cliff. As the blast receded, so did Trevelyan. If not for Saeth's swift catch, he would have pitched over the edge and plummeted to the ground below without even knowing.

∞∞∞∞

Trevelyan awoke. He knew not how long after the clifftop. He heard voices. Two of the men in the party were shouting at one another, but he could not tell which of them it was. His eyes focused, and he noticed the storm had abated, almost like it had never existed to begin with. It drew his vision to a fire that was burning brightly a little way in front of him. He could feel the warm glow of heat reddening his cheeks. He did not move and remained silent as he tried to gather his wits about him. He needed to understand what had happened and why. The girls were both asleep next to each other. He could make out the three Wardens attending to the horses while they talked and threw wary glances his way. The First, Aderyn and Rhydian were behind him. He could hear them clearly now that he was more focused. The raised voices came from Rhydian and the First with Aderyn trying to calm them both. Trevelyan was not sure what they were talking about, but he was certain it was about him.

"They must be told!" shouted Rhydian to the First. "They have the right to know that the abomination is amongst us!"

Trevelyan could feel the First turn and look in his direction before he sighed and muttered. "As you will, Rhydian. But you will then content yourself until we reach Dryweryn Township. Then you may depart or remain as is your wish, but if you remain in this company, you will do so silently." With that, The First strode toward the Wardens, barking orders to share watches through the night and to remain vigilant. He then made his way toward Trevelyan and stood by the fire, considering his options. He spoke to Trevelyan without turning to face him. "Rhydian ap Nestor wishes to address the company before we continue to Dryweryn Township on the morrow. It has been a day of strange omens, and so I have allowed it. It concerns you, Gafyn Trevelyan. And the events that transpired on the The Rive. I bid you to attend or at least listen to what is said, as it may shed some light on your predicament." He paused and then murmured. "And ours." Within a short time, the First had assembled everybody around the fire, including the Wardens, and announced Rhydian's wish to address the company. The Wardens stood a little apart from the rest of the party, but close enough to hear Rhydian's words. He stood in front of Trevelyan by the fire and spoke.

"The First Warden has granted my wish to address you all in respect of what occurred on The Rive. You may have believed yourselves to be in danger, but I assure you that the only one that had need to fear the wolves of the woods was the stranger, Gafyn Trevelyan. He was the intended target. Any aggression on the part of the wolves toward the rest of the company was to stop us from harrying the pack. You all know me as Rhydian ap Nestor, the only living descendent of the great prophet himself. You may also know of the prophecy he warned against centuries ago. It is my belief that the prophecy has come to pass with the arrival of Gafyn Trevelyan. Stranger to the lands of Hiraeth. I name him Wayfarer and the Doom of the Age. To that end, I believe that you all should be aware of the danger and sacrilege of travelling with this... Abomination!"

"I know you, Rhydian ap Nestor, and I know of the prophecy." Spoke Aderyn. "But I do not see how this implicates the stranger, Gafyn Trevelyan? If I recall, during the attack, it was his display of power that saved each of us, including you. I saw the yellow eyes of the wolves and knew them to be possessed, but not by anyone here. None of us has the art required for such an act of corruption. I would ask you to provide evidence of your accusations before I would condemn a man for saving my life. In all sooth the means and extent of his power is indeed in need of question. I will report all that I have witnessed to my order as soon as we make the far citadel. Until then, I would advise restraint against any accusations or..." He held Rhydian in an icy stare. "Actions that would bring dishonour amongst us."

"Pah," retorted Rhydian. "You monks lack the rigour of belief. You rationalise and urge restraint, but in the end, you dishonour yourselves and the memory of my ancestors with your cowardice." He spat. "Another travelled with Nestor all those years ago. Another acted as his guide and counsel when he first arrived on these blessed and cursed Isles. His name was Gideon Slay. A true believer and beloved of Nestor. It was he who laid the trap at The Rive. It was he who bewitched the wolves. In defence of the land. Against this destroyer of the world you love." Rhydian turned as he spoke to face each of the company as he continued. "It was his theurgy and foresight that created the barrier that contained the Wayfarer to the lowland. In his great wisdom and learning, he created the Hazard that each and every one of us passed through with ease and have done so for centuries. Only the Wayfarer. Only the destroyer of Hiraeth... Only he would be barred from the upper land and beyond. It was Gideon Slay himself who wielded the power that split the island and created The Rive. For the sole purpose of forbidding this monster from gaining access to the mainland and practicing his dark arts of doom. I know this to be true. I have read the account of its creation. In the annals of the Citadel and through the oral teachings of the great prophet, Nestor, himself! And so, I say, slay him now! Have no mercy on this vile creature. Lest that mercy condemn your children and loved ones to burn in the apocalypse that this man brings on all our heads." Rhydian was almost shouting now as his passion and madness rose in him. "I implore you to kill the Wayfarer and fulfil the prophecy of Nestor the Great!" He grabbed the dagger from his belt and lunged at the presumably sleeping Gafyn Trevelyan. Only the swift action of the First halted his murderous attempt by wrapping his arms around Rhydian in a bear hug. He physically carried him from the company and beyond the light cast by the fire.

Trevelyan did not see how his pretence of sleep could be believable in the wake of Rhydian's outburst. But he continued to lay as he was, with his back to the rest of the company, and waited for them to disperse and continue to make camp for the night. He waited until the company had retired. Then crept off into the dark. Taking care not to rouse the attention of Derwyn and Aedan as they held watch for the night. He walked far enough away that his voice would not carry to camp and sat down on the damp grass with a sigh.

He could see the campfire burning not too far away and quietly spoke to no one. "Tyst... are you here?"

With that, Tyst materialised out of thin air before Trevelyan's eyes and resumed his usual stance, leaning on his staff. "I am here, Wayfarer," replied Tyst

"Don't call me that," Trevelyan snapped. "I've had enough of that nonsense for one night." But then relented and apologised to Tyst for his remark. "Is it true?" He asked. "Did this Slay character really set a trap to keep me from Hiraeth?"

"Rhydian ap Nestor spoke sooth." Tyst replied almost reluctantly. "Gideon Slay did indeed accompany Nestor on his travels here to this Isle. He did split the very earth with his mighty theurgies. It was both wondrous and terrible to behold," he said.

"You were there?!" Trevelyan gasped.

"Indeed, have I not declared that I am Tyst, Testament to all that transpires in Hiraeth?" he answered with a smile.

"Then is it true?" groaned Trevelyan. "Am I the Wayfarer? Am I going to destroy Hiraeth?"

Tyst raised himself upright on his staff and spoke with a kind of reverence in his voice. "It is truth, Wayfarer! You are he who was foreseen by Nestor the prophet. Cause of his dreams and madness. But you are also Gafyn Trevelyan. Stranger to the land of Hiraeth. Walker twixt the worlds! Those who design to dream can not decide your fate. For you are beyond the dreams of prophets and madmen. For good or ill, Gafyn Trevelyan, you are here. And until you return to the world from which you came, your deeds here are your own. As are your intentions. And they remain unknown to any but yourself." With this, Tyst resumed his stance and fell silent. This comforted Trevelyan somewhat, and he realised he was getting sleepy in earnest. He dismissed Tyst with thanks. He was about to return to his place by the fire, when the First stepped silently from the edge of the woods and intercepted Trevelyan on his way back to camp.

"I would counsel you to caution Gafyn Trevelyan," he said. "You have made a powerful enemy in Rhydian. I would not test him further by conversing with the unseen. We will make Dryweryn Township around midday tomorrow, and I will speak with the Elders there. In the meantime, keep your distance from Rhydian. Come... I will accompany you back to camp!" Trevelyan and the First shared the short walk back to the fire, and before they parted company, the First said. "Rhydian ap Nestor is being watched tonight away from camp. I will deal with him on the morrow. Until then, I suggest you sleep, Gafyn Trevelyan." He nodded at Trevelyan and left the fire. Trevelyan resumed his place, but sleep would not come. Instead, he tried to balance the contradictions that plagued him. He spent the rest of the night with his thoughts until the sunless sky brightened overhead.

The rain clouds drew nearer as morning broke. The company roused, and one by one they packed their belongings and awaited instruction from the First Warden. The other Wardens had packed already and awaited the First with the others. The first strode through the scattered trees on the edge of the woods and declared in a voice tight with anger. "Rhydian ap Nestor has stolen away in the dark of night. He has taken his horse and scattered the others. Derwyn and I will attempt to find them in the woods. Aedan and Saeth will remain to ward you all until we return."

Derwyn and the First melted away into the woods, leaving the company to a breakfast of berries, cheese, and bread. And a cold dip in the river for Aderyn monk. After his absolutions, Aderyn dressed and sought out Trevelyan by the fire that still burned.

"The rains have found us," Aderyn spoke in a voice that seemed to imply that he did not expect otherwise. "I estimate around ten leagues to Dryweryn Township, wet ones at that. So if we leave shortly, we should arrive by the late afternoon." He spoke directly to Trevelyan, hoping to pry him from his thoughts. "I wondered if I might ride with you, Gafyn Trevelyan? I would hear more of the man who can put Rhydian to task when all my efforts have failed." His smile attempted to disarm Trevelyan into conversation. Trevelyan glowered involuntarily. Aderyn added, "Or to ride in silence would be acceptable as well." He put his hand on Trevelyan's shoulder and whispered. "Fear not, Gafyn Trevelyan. You have friends here," he said before he joined the others to await the first.

Chapter Twenty two

In what seemed like no time, the First returned with Derwyn and the scattered horses. The company packed their horses and mount before the rain started in earnest. They formed two lines, led by the First and Derwyn. The young girls next, and then Aderyn alongside Trevelyan. With Aedan and Saeth at the rear, they set off northward along the riverbank towards Dryweryn Township. After several leagues, Trevelyan accepted that Aderyn was true to his word as he rode in silence alongside Trevelyan. Searching for something to talk about with Aderyn, Trevelyan broached the subject of Gideon Slay.

"Ah... Gafyn Trevelyan. My gratitude to you for saving my honour by way of conversation. I feared I would break my vow of silence to you within the next league." He smiled at Trevelyan. "In answer to your question, I will tell you what I have learned of Nestor's companion. It would seem Gideon Slay befriended Nestor shortly after Nestor arrived at Afon Eigion, the westernmost port on the mainland. He told Nestor his master and lord in the west sent him to him. To aid and serve Nestor in his endeavours to warn of the coming of the Wayfarer and destruction. Nestor, being poor and alone, welcomed the interests of lords and masters that sent aid to his cause, believing himself to be the true prophet of the age." Aderyn seemed lost in thought as he continued. "Slay followed Nestor east, with his master's wealth and Gideon's sorcery, until they made shore here on the Isle. For it was here, said Nestor, that the Wayfarer will arrive. Together, over the years left to Nestor, they built the keep at Mid Ward. And the east and west Wards. The towers that you beheld on your passage through the Wardens woods, and then again on the journey to The Rive. These, along with many pages of prophecy that Nestor and Gideon collated and recorded. These were gathered together to become known as "The Black Book." The rest of the company fell silent as Aderyn spoke. "Many years after their arrival, Nestor died abed wrought by madness and cruelty. Gideon Slay, however, seemed not to age during his time with Nestor and after his death transported his body north to be buried on the site of a new citadel. Built in Nestor's honour. During the journey, Gideon Slay halted the funeral procession and declared it a wish of Nestor. A Place of forbidding to arrest the Wayfarer's advance north. It was here that Gideon Slay wrought, by sorcery and theurgy, the separating of the High and Lowlands. A display of power hither too unknown to the people of the Isle. His conjuring's and magic's caused the very earth to rend and thus was born the "Rive. He then continued north to found the far Citadel and the order of Nestorian monks. Nestor was interned, and the Citadel built over his bones. Gideon Slay appointed those he saw fit to rule in his stead, and left plans for a fortification he called "Cadarn," a vast fortress using the northern mountains as part of its defences. He left instructions for an order of warrior monks to be garrisoned at Cadarn to serve as its defenders. Naught else was seen or heard from Gideon Slay, and he has since passed into legend, although some say he lives still." Aderyn sighed deeply before continuing. "Alas, it seems Rhydian ap Nestor retains some of his ancestor's madness, seeking murder where words would prevail." He looked at Trevelyan with empathy in his eyes, as if he understood Trevelyan's predicament. "I believe, Gafyn Trevelyan, in reason not superstition, and I offer myself up in your defence. I know little or less of you and your arrival here, but its meaning is not lost to me. However, I see no death when I look upon you, or the power you wrought in our defence on The Rive. Only the wolves were destroyed in your fire, and the company remains uninjured because of your intervention. Therefore, I say again...you have friends, Gafyn Trevelyan." Having related his tale, Aderyn fell silent. Trevelyan was grateful for any support he could muster and realised he did not feel so alone as he did when he began the journey. In an effort to show his appreciation, Trevelyan answered Aderyn's questions about himself. Revealing himself to be an artist in his world, and details about the real world that Aderyn seemed quite horrified to contemplate. As they spoke, the First relayed the message down through the riders that Dryweryn Township was in sight, and they would arrive shortly. Aderyn's words eased slightly Trevelyan's trepidation. He stiffened his back to ease his aching muscles and looked toward the north, where the small town on the right bank of the river sat. He pulled up the hood of his cloak to keep the rain from running down his back.

They had got no further than a league when a man emerged from the woods on their right. He was waving his hands above his head and shouting to the First and the wardens, but Trevelyan could not hear what was being said. The First spotted him immediately and returned the wave breaking rank to ride to him. After a brief exchange between the man and the First, the wardens at the head of the company changed direction and made their way toward the man. He then disappeared into the dense undergrowth of the trees while the rest of the company followed. The First passed the word down that they were being diverted from Dryweryn by a friend and they must hurry behind the First and remain silent. Trevelyan felt very uneasy at this, but held his tongue along with the rest of the company. Once behind the tree line, the man led them in silence through the dense wood until the only light to pierce the foliage was from above. They travelled this way in silence for some time until the man emerged into a small glade. The First gathered the company together and spoke with the man for a few moments before approaching the company with him. "This man is Tristan. He is to be trusted. He warns that Rhydian passed this way at first light, rousing the village and announcing the arrival of doom upon the land." His eyes met Trevelyan's squarely. "He demanded that we all be held as prisoners upon arrival, as he intends to alert the Sentinels of Cadarn to our presence here. They come to take us all as heretics and to put Gafyn Trevelyan to death. Our fate will be decided by proxy as we are proclaimed betrayers and traitors for not ending his life on The Rive." He paused for a moment before continuing "It is no longer safe for us to remain here or to make for the Citadel." Trevelyan saw in the First's eyes the gravity of the situation. "I have decided on a course of action that will ensure the safety of Gafyn Trevelyan to the best of our abilities. But the rest of you must decide for yourselves if you would follow. My intent is this. I will send one of the Wardens back to Mid Ward and the Elders with warning. I fear the reach of the Sentinels' wrath. Those who would, may return with him. Myself and the remaining wardens will escort Gafyn Trevelyan from here to Highlands Harbour. Once there, we will set sail for the port of Carreg Ddu. The Sentinels' influence does not extend too far from this isle, and we will be harder to track across the sea. From there my intention is to make for "Old Stones." News from the west is troubling indeed. A War council has been called for all the clans across Hiraeth—an event previously unattempted in our history. Doubtless, not all will attend, but I believe our best chance of survival lies there." With that, he bowed slightly to the company and he and Tristan went to water the horses and talk privately. The Wardens gathered together. Presumably to decide who will return and who will accompany the First and the remaining company west. Gwenith and Brigid followed the First, leaving Aderyn and Trevelyan together.

"Alas, it seems that our travels together end here, Gafyn Trevelyan. The First is right to seek counsel at Old Stones. You will be safer across the sea. I know these Sentinels; they are more zealots than monks. Once their enmity is roused, it is not so easily denied. I shall continue on to Dryweryn Township. There I will attempt to reason with Macsen of the Guard, leader of the Sentinels. If reason fails, perhaps falsehood may prevail. I may be able to convince him of an alternative path of your departure." Aderyn straightened himself and looked Trevelyan squarely in the eyes. "I consider myself fortunate to have shared your story if even only for a short time. Go in peace Gafyn Trevelyan." And with a bow, he made his way to Tristan and the First before leaving the copse and heading toward Dryweryn.

Trevelyan wished he could question Tyst, but that would have to wait until he was sure he was alone. The First and Tristan once again summoned the company to counsel. The First looked about the company and said, "Aderyn has elected to appeal to Macsen of the Sentinel Guard. I argued against this, but he would not relent. That was his decision to make. Now I must hear yours... With the exception of Gafyn Trevelyan." Once again, his steely eyes met Trevelyan's, but only for a second. "For he is under my protection and that of my wardens." He looked squarely at the girls now. "Brigid, Gwenith. Under any other circumstances I would offer you no choice but to return with the Warden to the safety of Mid Ward... But you both have rare skills and courage, and I may have need of both. I will also ask you to ward two others that have yet to join the company. They are twin girls younger than yourselves. Daughters to Tristan. You were sent to the Citadel as penance for your desire to become wardens instead of maidens. I would grant your wish if it remains. I will arm you both sufficient to defend yourselves should the need arrive. If you decide to depart home, I hold your honour intact and I thank you for your company. But should you decide to accompany me, you will obey my every command. Without exception or hesitation." He paused to give the girls time to think. But none was needed.

"We will serve," they said in harmony.

"Then it is done." He bowed to the girls and turned to Tristan. "We will ready ourselves, go fetch the twins. Be swift Tristan, I have an uneasy feeling." Tristan bowed and hurriedly sprinted into the trees and out of sight. The First turned to the other wardens. "Have you reached your decision?"

"We have!" they echoed together.

"Was it unanimous?" asked the First.

"It was!" came the reply.

"Then the one to return to Mid Ward will prepare his horse. I shall be with you shortly with a message to bear for my father and him alone. The other two make ready for leaving. We have time to eat but no fire. I shall care for the horses." He bowed to all three and turned to Trevelyan. "Gafyn Trevelyan, after I have spoken to Saeth before he departs for home and I have tended the horses, I would like to break bread with you. It seems we are about to begin a long journey and I would have us understand each other better. And our situation." It sounded like a question. Trevelyan just nodded, but this seemed to satisfy the First. He turned and made his way toward Saeth, now mounted and ready to depart. Trevelyan awaited the First, watching the two girls from the corner of his eye so as not to draw attention to himself. For the First to ask two young girls of no more than seventeen to accompany him on what was a perilous task seemed unlike his rigid moral code. He must remember to ask the First when they, how did he put it—break bread? He was still musing to himself when the First approached him with some fruit, bread, and cheese. He sat next to Trevelyan on the floor and shared the food between them. Trevelyan was not particularly hungry, although he probably should have been. He ate anyway, wondering if his body back at Bryngaer was doing ok when his thoughts were interrupted by the First as he spoke.

"I know not how to learn the truth of you, Wayfarer." It was the first time he had referred to him by that name. "Gafyn Trevelyan." He seemed to weigh the names against each other. "In sooth, I know not even how to name you. Rhydian would have me believe I have committed treason, and I am a heretic and betrayer. He has convinced the citadel and the sentinels of this well enough for them to dispatch Macsen and his armed guard. I believe that they would indeed do you harm if they were to find us. I cannot guarantee the safety of my wardens, or the girls, accused such as we are. I know of Nestor and his prophesy. I also know Macsen and his army of fanatics. Therefore, I have decided to flee these Isles and seek council amongst those who prepare for the coming of war and propose a defence against it. I also know people." And here he turned to Trevelyan, making sure he had his full attention. "I knew Saeth would be the one to return to the Wards, just as I knew it would be a unanimous decision. I also know the reasons why. Saeth has a young wife and newborn child." He stopped talking for a moment and sighed heavily. "I believe that your fate, and that of Hiraeth, is not yet written. And so, I name you, Gafyn Trevelyan, stranger and friend to Hiraeth."

Suddenly, there was a crashing just beyond the treeline. People running and running fast. The First and the wardens were on their feet and armed within a heartbeat. Awaiting whatever or whomever came bursting into the copse. Two girls, younger than Brigit and Gwenith, appeared bedraggled and inconsolable.

"What has happened? Where is your father? And where is your brother, Caerwyn?" The First demanded.

"Dead," the blonde-haired girl sobbed.

Immediately, the First demanded. "Were you followed?"

"No, I don't think so," the other twin said.

Chapter Twenty three

The First and the Wardens readied themselves for an imminent attack from the Sentinels. After several minutes, it became apparent that the girls had not been followed. Saeth and Derwyn ventured further into the woods toward Dryweryn Township to see if there were to be any incursions from the Sentinels. But there was no sign of danger. They held their positions, awaiting any advance by Macsen looking for the company or the frightened girls, who now sobbed desperately. The First asked again "What happened to your father?" Bronwyn stopped her sobbing long enough to explain what they saw.

"Macsen of the Guard captured a monk as he entered Dryweryn Township. He began questioning him as to your whereabouts." Bronwyn broke down, sobbing once more.

Her twin sister, Olwyn, took up the tale. "The monk denied you were nearby. He told Macsen that Rhydian was mistaken in his tale of the Wayfarer's arrival. That the stranger accompanying the Wardens was a madman found wandering the wardens' woods. He was released beyond The Rive. Aderyn claimed he himself saw the stranger wander into the wolf's wood toward the eastern shore, raving as he went. He said the First and his wardens had returned to Mid Ward and that he travelled alone to Dryweryn, intending to break his fast before making his way to the Citadel to report all that he had seen." Olwyn sobbed again and took several minutes to gather herself and continue. "My father arrived at our hiding place and told us to be ready to leave. He left us to find Caerwyn. He said if he was not back by the time it took to pack and ready ourselves, we were to leave swiftly and silently, and that we were to find you in the copse." She began to sob again.

Bronwyn continued in her stead. "We were ready to leave when we heard Macsen shouting at the monk and ordering his men to seize him. His guards held the monk down. Macsen declared to the Township that this is what happens to those who betray the Citadel and its teachings. He told the monk that if his eyes could not see the truth. If his hands could not metre punishment. Then they belonged to the Citadel." Here, they both took to sobbing. "He... He plucked his eyes out. And cut off his hands!" She wailed, "Father tried to intervene. He cursed Macsen for his cruelty and arrogance." She broke down and could not continue.

It was Olwyn who finished with "Macsen told my father that Bronwyn and I were to be taken to the Citadel in service to the Magister. Without even so much as a word, took his sword and ran my father through before the eyes of the entire Township!" Her eyes were wide with terror. "He then commanded his men to search the Township for us. So we left at a run for the woods. I'm sure we were neither seen nor followed, but... we did not see Caerwyn." She began to cry too, and the First knew he would get no more from them now. They had just seen their father die in defence of a man he hardly knew. And what of Aderyn? Did he still live? The First spoke quietly to Saeth who nodded, leapt on his horse, and was away through the forest in a heartbeat. He ordered the Wardens to gather the horses and for the company to mount up as they were leaving immediately. His plan was to turn back south for a league or two. They would remain out of sight and then head west for the whispering woods. Then north west. To the largest of the two snow-capped mountains that ran from the sea. One either side of the Isle. Forming the valley where lay the walled fortress of Cadarn. Home of the Sentinel Guard. They would stay west of the mountain and attempt the lower pass to the harbour. Solemn as a funeral, they started their way south through the dense woods. The First leading the way and Aedan at the rear, Derwyn moved between the two relaying messages as the rest of the party fell in line between them. For several leagues, they travelled in silence.

The First stopped at the forest border and whispered to the company. "We will move quickly. Two a breast. In short intervals until we gain the whispering woods. Once under cover, wait for the rest before going any further. Those woods are less travelled than most, and for good reason." The party formed up in pairs, with Derwyn and Brigit first. Then Bronwyn and Olwyn joined in their grief. Next were Trevelyan and Gwenith, followed by Aedan and the First. They sprinted on horseback the distance between the two woods, and, once beneath the dense foliage and out of sight, they gathered to await the First and Aedan. The light was beginning to drain from the sky. Twilight settled above the company as they gathered under the trees of Coed Sibrwd. Whispering wood in the common tongue. The waterfall at The Rive was within earshot as they turned north and picked their way between the dense trees of the forest. The twin girls were still traumatised by what they had witnessed in Dryweryn, but their sobs had subsided to a grief-stricken silence as they rode together.

Trevelyan was starkly aware that he had begun a chain of events that threatened to spin out of control. This was not what he expected, by far. While still in awe of what his mother and father had created, he could not escape the remorse he felt for the death of Tristan. Not so much for the man but for the two twin girls. And Aderyn's punishment—he could argue that each of us is responsible for our own fate. That Aderyn chose to confront the sentinels. But deep within, he knew it was his ascension that was responsible for everything that had happened. And will happen. His very presence was a threat to the people who lived here. Especially those that aligned with him for whatever reason. He felt accountable for them all. He needed to return to Bryngaer, but he did not know how. Tyst could not help. Trevelyan needed to keep him a secret from the rest of the party. So far, he had been going along with it all because he did not really know what else to do. He decided back in Mid Ward that any actions on his part would probably end badly for those around him. If not himself. He wondered if he managed to somehow get himself killed here, would he simply return to his body on the floor of the sanctum back home? The thought that he would die here and not return to his body was too terrifying to contemplate. He is in a secret room that no one knows about in a large mansion. How long had he been there? Time was difficult to predict. He had been in Hiraeth for nearly two days now. How long that was in the REAL world, he could only guess. He would have to find time to consult Tyst if he could ensure he would not be disturbed. His reverie was broken by the perception of a voice somewhere behind him. It sounded like a woman's voice, soft like velvet, but with a loamy edge that reminded Trevelyan of the scent of moss on stone after a summer rain. He instinctively turned but saw only Aedan bringing up the rear. Then the voice was gone. But Trevelyan could sense that it was still near.

As the light receded, the First moved between Derwyn and Aedan, and with a nod, they moved further away into the woods, away from the rest of the company. The First called a halt to the company's progress in a small clearing within the dense foliage. Here, he decided they should make camp. They could light no fire and must remain quiet. The strain of the last day was evident on the face of the First. His task was to deliver the Wayfarer to the Citadel along with Gwenith and Brigid. Aderyn was only along for the company, and then he would return to Mid Ward with the other Wardens. Now he had lost a friend in Tristan and was humbled by Aderyn's sacrifice for the safety of the company. Not only that, he now had to find his way across the sea in order to preserve the lives of his companions. Not to mention the burden of protecting the Wayfarer. The very man prophesied to bring about the doom of all he loved. As the others prepared their bedding and formed a tight circle within which to sleep, the Wardens secured the perimeter. Arranging watches between them through the night. The warden's loyalty toward the First was without question. Trevelyan believed they would give their lives at his command if he asked it of them. He also decided that he would slip away in the night sometime to talk with Tyst. He could not continue to remain passive. Of that, he was sure. After he heard of Tristan's death. And Aderyn's punishment. He realised that if he was to be the cause of these tragedies, then he should have a part in events that proceed them. He was not powerless. But he did not understand the power he had or how to wield it. He sensed that any outpouring of power from him had some kind of rebound effect on those that surrounded him. He was suddenly very aware of his actions and their consequences. But, at the same time, he could not refuse to act. Torn between this contradiction, he elected to sleep a little and hoped that when he woke, he could steal away for a short while and consult Tyst. He closed his eyes and withdrew from the sound of the others. Before sleep took him, he thought he heard the voice call to him. Not as Gafyn Trevelyan. As Wayfarer. Portent of doom. Before he drifted away, he wondered. Can you dream within a dream?

∞∞∞∞

He could. He dreamed of Rose again. Here in Hiraeth. They were deep underground, within a massive cavern. Rose was ablaze some distance ahead of him, pointing into the cavernous darkness just beyond the light of her immolation. He felt the company behind him more than he saw or heard them. There seemed to be some kind of urgency in Rose. Her face was contorted, but not in pain. In pure anguish. He awoke to darkness. He lay still so as not to draw attention to himself and listened carefully for sounds of his companions. All was silence. He let his eyes adjust to the dark and slowly cast his gaze around the camp. He could see the four girls sleeping together for warmth and the First and Aedan keeping watch. He waited until the wardens changed watches, then a little longer, until he felt confident enough to leave camp and consult with Tyst about what he should do next. He left his bedding to appear as though he was still sleeping within and stole away into the trees until he was sure he was out of hearing range of the camp. He found a fallen branch large enough to take his weight and sat down upon it. He knew he would not have long before he was discovered or daylight would break and the First would discover his absence. He decided on his questions and spoke out loud to the stillness between the trees, "Tyst, are you here?"

"I am here Wayfarer," said Tyst as he materialised from the darkness in front of Trevelyan, leaning on his staff.

"I don't have much time, Tyst. I am hoping you may answer a question or two." Trevelyan said without greeting the old man. Tyst continued to lean on his staff without answer. 'Of course,' thought Trevelyan. It was not a direct question. "Tyst. Is there another way for me to get home other than the threshold I used to enter? Somewhere nearby? I mean" he asked without hope.

"There is no other threshold on this Isle Wayfarer," Tyst replied almost cheerfully. Trevelyan groaned inwardly. He knew going back down The Rive and past Mid Ward would be a grave mistake. The Sentinels would surely take him on the road. His only hope was forward, not backward. His next question had been as clear as crystal, although he suspected the answer would not be so easy. "Are the others in the company in danger because of me? I mean, if the sentinels take us, will they be harmed like Aderyn was?" His own question made him wince.

"Most assuredly, Wayfarer. They have been denounced as traitors and heretics. The Magister of the Citadel has ordered your capture, return to the Citadel, and death to any who travel with you. The Sentinel Guard follows orders without question or conscience. Believing as they do that, they serve a greater purpose than mercy."

Trevelyan sighed heavily, his face in his hands. "Is there nothing you can do to help, Tyst?" he said, not realising he had asked out loud.

"Alas, I cannot Wayfarer. Though I see your anguish. But there is another here who would give you counsel if you would allow?" he said with a glint in his eyes.

"Another... what do you mean?" Trevelyan said, not comprehending.

"There are others such as me. Those that inhabit Hiraeth unseen by its denizens and have done since the creation. Our purpose differs from one to another, but our service remains true." Tyst waited for Trevelyan's answer.

Trevelyan was unsure whether to accept. He was in enough trouble already. He had no wish to complicate matters further, but he needed some kind of plan if he was going to take an active part. Perhaps this unexpected help could be the answer. He could not turn it down. "I am grateful for any help. If you trust them, Tyst, then let them speak."

With a nod, Tyst turned to his right and bowed long and low. To Trevelyan's surprise, a figure materialised out of the woods and walk toward him and Tyst. A woman. A very tall woman. She emerged from the dense foliage. At first, it appeared as if she had somehow merged with the forest. Trevelyan thought she was wearing a gown of greens. All different shades and textures. But as she approached, he realised that this was no gown. She was clothed in the remnants of the forest. Bark, moss, and leaves all merged into one. Upon her head, she wore a festoon of ferns and flowers. Woven together. Between her deep green eyes, a shining pale green light. Almost like some kind of emerald. Her skin was green also, but it seemed to change hue the longer he looked upon her. As she moved, Trevelyan could hear the rustling of leaves and bracken. She approached Trevelyan slowly but deliberately. She bowed deeply to him. Both her hands came up and touched the light between her eyes, and then she extended her arms to her sides in supplication. Trevelyan returned her greeting in the same manner.

"Wayfarer be welcome here," she said. Her voice the sound of the wind and the shaking of leaves on a tree. The voice he heard call to him when he first entered the woods.

"I am Anwedd, Guardian of the Green Ray. Custodian of all things that grow in nature. I bear both a warning and a gift. Which would you have first?"

Trevelyan stared in ignorance at her for a moment, trying to decide. Awkwardly, he said. "A gift?" He meant it as a question, but Anwedd nodded in abeyance and continued.

"You are the Wayfarer. Walker tween the worlds. Yours is the power of creation. But this power is latent within you. There are those who have counselled against my aid. Preferring to have you impotent, that you do not awaken your power, thus sparing Hiraeth from your desecration. But it is my fear that to do so would allow the bane that grows in the west to corrupt all. While sparing Hiraeth from destruction, we would permit an altogether worse fate. Therefore, have I elected to grant this boon in the name of hope. To see all that Hiraeth has become perverted by corruption... The natural order of life twisted into a mockery of nature. This I cannot permit. The very purpose of my creation opposes it. To bereave you of your puissance would be the true doom of Hiraeth. While you wield the power to oppose corruption, there is hope." As she finished speaking, she raised her hands to her forehead, plucked the shining emerald light from between her eyes, and offered it to Trevelyan. "This is my offering to you, Wayfarer. When there is a need for power and you cannot find it within yourself, hold this in your right hand and repeat my name. This will allow you to access your full power. This gift may be used only three times. Each time, your power will grow until you have consumed the gift entirely. My hope is that you will, by then, have attained the wisdom required to access it at will, as is your right." When she had finished speaking, she extended her hand with a closed fist to Trevelyan, who in turn extended his to receive it. As she opened her hand, Trevelyan saw only an acorn. His eyes met Anwedd's in question, and she smiled at him in answer and bid him to take it. Trevelyan reached out for the innocuous item, and as his fingers touched the small acorn, he could feel some tide within himself swell and rise like a storm at sea. He thanked her for her gift, put it in his jerkin pocket, and clamped his fist around it. As soon as he held it tight, he could feel the hope Anwedd had for the fate of Trevelyan and that of Hiraeth. "And now, my warning, Wayfarer." Her tone changed, and instead of the rustling of leaves and the wind among the trees, an element of danger crept into the sound. As though a deadly storm was imminent. "There are those here in Hiraeth that oppose you. That will urge you to power. Trusting to you to fulfil the prophecy of doom." Her eyes flashed from emerald green to crimson fire. "This you must resist, Gafyn Trevelyan and Wayfarer. Power born of anger or despair can only achieve ruin. The power you touched on The Rive against the Hazard and the wolves gives me hope. For in that display, your power was directed at the dangers you were presented with and not the company with which you travelled. All were spared your wrath. This discernment is the seed of hope." Her eyes returned to the soft green of the trees, and Trevelyan saw a hint of pity there. "Your path will be strewn with calamities, Wayfarer. Hold true and let not the taint of corruption stain your heart." With this, Anwedd stepped back and bowed once again. Trevelyan bowed in return, and Anwedd slowly melted away into the trees and foliage until she completely disappeared, leaving Trevelyan and Tyst alone in the woods. Trevelyan could hear the company rousing from slumber not too far away amongst the trees, and thanked Tyst for his presence. He made his way back to camp in time to blend in with the waking party as they gathered their belongings. He thrust his hand into his jerkin and gripped the acorn. He had the beginnings of a plan of action at last, but he would keep it to himself for the time being.

Chapter twenty four

Trevelyan kept his plan to himself. The First would never agree to it, and so Trevelyan decided it was best to not inform him until it was time. The First rode point alone, while Brigid and Gwenith rode with Bronwyn and Olwyn. There was a sombre mood shared among the company. They weaved their way between the trees, unseen. Moving northward toward the great snow-peaked mountains. Trevelyan considered his straights as he rode. He could no longer continue to let others make decisions and take risks on his behalf. He felt as though he had Tristan and Aderyn's blood on his hands. It was his presence in Hiraeth that caused all this trouble, regardless of whether he had accepted his role as Wayfarer or not. He knew he could not continue to let others pay for his transgressions. The First announced that they would enter to the pass before dusk and that they would make camp below ground and out of sight. Cadarn lay to the east, and so the First pushed west and away from any patrols that might happen by. During the journey, Trevelyan caught up with the four girls and offered his condolences to Bronwyn and Olwyn for their loss. They did not appear to blame him and were courteous, if not friendly. He left them to their grief and moved to talk to Brigid and Gwenith instead. He did not feel like engaging in conversation with anybody, but it helped keep his fears at bay. Furthermore, he had little to no contact with either of the girls until now. After all that had happened since leaving Mid Ward, he felt he should at least attempt to get to know his companions. After a little small talk, Trevelyan asked the reason for their exile to the Citadel in the first place. It surprised him to find that both girls had been secretly training to become wardens. Brigid seemed a little defensive in her answer. "There is no reason women could not join the wardens," she said. "Other than it had never been attempted before." She explained, "the women of Mid Ward were happy to be dutiful daughters and wives. Never once dreaming that they too could become wardens and protectors of the lowlands. We will be the first female wardens." This was stated with a fierce pride that Trevelyan respected.

Gwenith continued, "The elders were unprepared for two girls to endeavour to join the wardens. Instead, they decided that we were to receive instruction from the monks of the Citadel. Until such foolishness had passed." She dropped her voice several decibels, imitating Hafren's voice.

"Women should be homemakers and carers for their husbands and families. Not ranging around the countryside on horseback armed and armoured." This made both girls laugh loudly. Trevelyan joined in their laughter. It felt good. It seemed so long since he had laughed, and he was grateful to them both. They admitted they were glad of the detour, and the chance to prove their worth to the First Warden. It seemed to Trevelyan, at least, that the First had made the right decision to keep the girls at hand instead of returning them with Saeth to Mid Ward.

After talking to the girls, Trevelyan caught up with the First as he led the company northward. The First seemed distracted until Trevelyan caught up with him and fell in beside him. "I see you have become a better rider since leaving the Ward." said the First without looking at Trevelyan. "We will reach the entrance to the pass soon. There, we will set the horses loose to return to the lowlands, and we will continue below ground on foot."

"Are you sure the pass is safe?" asked Trevelyan.

"The pass will be guarded, but we will move below, unseen. The hidden entrance to the caves below the mountain are known to but a few." He replied, thoughtfully. "I used to come with my father to trade at the harbour for goods that were reserved for the Citadel. Not the lowlanders. We would use the caves to pass unseen and return to Mid Ward with wine and grain and salt beef. It remains our best chance of gaining Highlands Harbour without being detected." He paused for a moment. His face showed his grief. "Tristan had arranged passage for his daughters on board a ship called Morrigan. He had expected the Sentinels arrival and had guessed the Magister's goal. It seems these twins are special, although I have yet to learn why," he said. "It is my hope that I can barter passage for the rest of us, too." He fell silent for a moment before continuing. "My advice, Gafyn Trevelyan, is this... As a stranger to these lands, you will draw attention. It will not be long before someone informs the sentinels of our presence. I ask of you to remain discreet and not to draw any unwanted attention. If we can board ship shortly before departure, I am confident that we will escape the sentinels before they know we were there. They may send some guards to follow, but we will have at least three days' start once we reach Garreg Dru. As long as we remain discreet, we should make 'Old Stones' without discovery."

Although the First seemed confident of his plan, Trevelyan could tell that until they were underway across the sea, the First's responsibility rested heavily upon him. In a change of subject, the First asked Trevelyan about his home and how he came to arrive in Hiraeth. Trevelyan did not wish to go into detail about his life back in Bryngaer. Or how his parents created the world he was now a prisoner in. These things were not easily explained. So he told the First that his arrival was an accident. That should he find a way home, he would take it and end the threat he posed to Hiraeth, the Citadel, and everyone else. Then, perhaps, Hiraeth could go on as it had before his arrival. The First asked if the threat from the west was connected to his arrival in Hiraeth. But Trevelyan had no answer for him. He had wondered about that himself. Besides, he had no intention of compounding the First's fears with his own.

The other wardens had spread out from the company in order to scope the landscape and avoid detection from prying eyes. But as they neared their destination, they joined the company and reported to the First. The way was clear. If they were to quicken their pace after leaving the sanctuary of the woods, they would arrive at the entrance within a league or two. Derwyn was tasked with passing the news to the rest of the company. They held for a moment or two before leaving the border of the forest and let the horses gallop across the open plain. All the while, the Wardens scoured the horizon for any signs of witnesses. The mountains grew larger as they drew nearer, and the weather seemed to chill around them. They were riding gradually uphill, and the temperature was dropping as the day wore on. Within a short time, they had arrived at their destination. A small outcrop of rocks jutting awkwardly from the ground. The First instructed the company to take only what was required to reach the harbour. Anything else would be buried beneath the rocks. The horses were unbridled and sent running south towards home. The company ate a light meal as the First and the wardens set watches until they were ready to descend below ground. Derwyn and Aedan had collected enough bracken and materials to fashion torches. These were bound in rags doused in oil. Within a few moments, the company was ready. The First indicated a small gap between the rocks that was barely big enough to fit a man through. He disappeared down the gap and shouted the rest to follow.

Chapter Twenty five

It was getting dark when Saeth arrived at the border of the woods and Dryweryn Township. He waited beneath the foliage, watching the town square. There was no sign of Macsen of the Guard and his men. Only two Sentinels that carried Tristan's body away to a charnel pit ready to be burned. Saeth knew then that Macsen and his guards had moved on, these two were left behind to finish Aderyn off and burn the bodies. Saeth did not have much time if he hoped to save Aderyn. Perhaps he had died already of his injuries? The two guards returned and took Aderyn's legs to drag him to the pit when he let out a low groan. He was still alive! Saeth left his position beneath the trees and circumnavigated the town until he was a short distance from the pit. He could see better from here, and although Tristan was quite clearly dead, Aderyn still clung to life. But for how much longer. Saeth could see the extent of Aderyn's injuries from where he was hiding. His eyes were gone. Instead, there were two gaping maws on either side of his face. His hands were burned and bloody stumps. Cauterised by Macsen to prolong his pain and suffering. It was obvious to Saeth that he would not last much longer. Of the inhabitants of Dryweryn there was no sign. Saeth waited for the two guards to unceremoniously drop Aderyn's moaning and limp body next to Tristan's. They made no attempt to show Aderyn any mercy by ending his suffering there and then. Only amusing themselves at the sound of his suffering.

"This one will not live to see the morn." Said the largest of the two. "I say we go find some wine and maybe a wench." He motioned towards Tristan and said, "The dead one had a couple of pretty daughters hiding somewhere around here. Gifted they say. What say we interrogate 'em? Just to be sure, this rebellion dies with him."

The other guard took his meaning and grinned like a devil. "Just to be sure, like you said." He patted the large man on the back as they went in search of their entertainment.

Saeth watched from the shadows until they were out of sight and silently made his way to Aderyn, who lay draped halfway over Tristan's corpse. He grabbed Aderyn's legs and dragged him back towards the trees, eliciting a weak cry from the maimed and dying monk. Once out of sight of the Township, Saeth draped Aderyn over his horse and mounted up swiftly. He raced away through the trees. South toward The Rive and Mid Ward. Aderyn had passed out from the pain. Saeth could still see his chest heaving and knew that he would live if he received care to his wounds within the hour. Tristan, it seemed had the right of it when he sent his daughters to the First. Even in death, he had spared them the perverse pleasures of the guards. After several leagues to the southeast, Saeth stopped and dismounted. They had left the trees behind some time ago. Saeth could hear the sea beyond the black, rugged landscape of large, sharp, scattered obsidian rocks that lay between the woods and the ocean. They were out of sight of the treeline and out of the wind, behind the shelter of the rocks. He carefully lifted Aderyn from his horse and laid him on the bedding he had prepared. Saeth made a fire and slowly made Aderyn drink some water before leaving him to forage for certain herbs and leaves that grew nearby. These would make both a poultice and a salve for Aderyn's grievous wounds. He returned within a few minutes with the ingredients he required, only to find a blonde-haired youth in his late teens dressed in the colours of Dryweryn Township sitting next to Aderyn near the fire. He was washing Aderyn's wounded face of the blood and gore around where his eyes should have been. Saeth dropped what he was carrying and, within half a heartbeat, unsheathed his sword and challenged the stranger.

"Hold boy! Were you followed?" Saeth had already identified the youth by his features. This was surely Caerwyn, Tristan's missing son. The youth lifted his tear-stained face to Saeth and shook his head in silence. As Saeth returned his sword to its scabbard and collected the dropped items, Caerwyn spoke to no one in particular.

"I saw them cut him down. My father. He only asked for mercy for a tortured monk, and they…they just slew him where he stood…without warning or challenge. He had not enough time to arm himself, and they just…" His voice trailed off into silence. Saeth felt his grief, even though he did not know the youth's father. He had died an honourable, if deplorable, death. He left the boy to his silence and prepared the dressings for Aderyn's wounds. When he was ready, he gave the boy some food and water, and bid him attend to the fire while he dressed Aderyn's stumps with salve and clean bandages. He also made a thick cloth blindfold to hold the dressings in place over Aderyn's face. When the monk was as comfortable as possible, Saeth forced him to eat a little, and take some more water before leaving him to sleep. He made his way to Caerwyn and sat beside him at the fire.

"If the monk lives through the night, my mission requires me to make for Mid Ward and the Elders. I must give warning about Macsen and the Sentinels and what has befallen the First and the rest of the company." Before Caerwyn could ask of the twin's fate, Saeth reassured him. "Your sisters met with the First before I left to find the monk. He intends to get them all to Highlands Harbour through a concealed entrance to the pass. They will travel below ground and therefore out of sight. From there they will gain passage to Garreg Ddu and then 'Old Stones' for all the clans have been called to counsel by Goronhyr Gwillt the Arch Druid. After I have got the monk to safety and delivered the Firsts warning, my intent is to make for the west Ward and passage to Garreg Ddu. There I will unite with the other Wardens. If it is your wish, you may accompany me in the hope of reconciliation with your sisters". Caerwyn nodded his acquiescence and the two made camp for the night.

∞∞∞∞

The following morning, Saeth roused Caerwyn from his sleep and attended to Aderyn. He changed his dressings and cleaned the stumps where his hands had once been. He then changed the dressings beneath the blindfold and replaced it when he had finished. Saeth asked Aderyn if he felt he could travel, to which Aderyn nodded and rose to his feet. Saeth and Caerwyn helped him to mount his horse and within a few minutes they were ready to depart. Saeth elected to stay close to the coast as they picked their way south toward The Rive. If they could remain undetected, they could navigate the stairs slowly to the lowlands. From there, it was a short distance to Mid Ward and succour for Aderyn, counsel for Saeth, and a decision for Caerwyn. Until then, they travelled in silence, all the while searching the horizon for signs of the Sentinel Guard. After reaching the Steps of the Rive they slowly descended, with Saeth leading, and Caerwyn bringing up the rear and the horses. Aderyn, secured on horseback by a rope between the two men, made slow progress, and within half a day they attained the lowlands and Mid Ward was in view.

Chapter Twenty six

The light from above illuminated only a small path, that disappeared beneath the mountain and into pitch darkness. The First lit his makeshift torch and led the way. The girls all bunched together in front of Trevelyan, while the Wardens brought up the rear. The passageway was narrow and weaved in all directions around the massive stone roots of the mountain. Water trickled everywhere and echoed through the passageway, which was dimly lit by the torches. Trevelyan could feel the weight of the mountain on his shoulders. Threatening to crush him in an instant. He tried to distract his thoughts from what lay above him by going through his plan once they gained the fresh air on the other side of the pass. Specifically, how he could extricate himself from the company in order to put his plan into action. He could no longer afford to put other people in danger on his behalf. So far, he has gone with the flow, making no decisions since he ascended to Hiraeth. He had learned to fear the consequences of his actions long ago. Rose had taught him that. All that achieved was death for Tristan and punishment for Aderyn. He needed another answer. He needed to isolate himself so he could think things through with the help of Tyst. The company travelled in silence. Every sound amplified by the echoes under the mountain. Time had lost its meaning in the dark passageway. Only the shuffling in front and behind him could reassure him that he was not alone. The way was slow due to the narrowness of the passage and the obstacles it bypassed. They must have travelled several leagues by now. As they entered a small cavity in the rock, the First halted and waited for the company to gather together. "We are beyond the halfway point now. Take food and rest while you can. What lies on the other side of the pass, I know not? If we are unhindered, we should reach Highlands Harbour within three leagues of the pass. Aedan and I will go ahead and make our observations, but we will not leave cover until darkness has fallen. Do not leave this place until we return." He glanced toward Derwyn. "Keep them safe." To which Derwyn nodded in silence. The company relieved themselves of their packs and began to share the fruit, bread, and cheese they had left. After they had eaten and rested for a while, Trevelyan felt more sure of his plan. He would make a break for it at the first opportunity. He would miss the companionship of this motley company, but he could not risk their lives further. His eyes slowly moved around the company from one to the other, trying to store their faces in his memory should he ever get out of here. His eyes settled on Olwyn and Bronwyn as they held hands in the flickering light. It could be the shadows playing tricks, but he was sure they looked afraid. Very afraid! He was about to ask if they were alright when Olwyn whispered a word beneath her breath. Trevelyan could not be sure, but he thought he heard her say "Bear." A moment later, she stood up and searched the cavern for Derwyn. As soon as her eyes found his, she said aloud. "Bear!"

Bronwyn suddenly shrieked. "A Bear... coming up behind us." As she spoke, she pointed the way they had come. Derwyn took his sword and started back down the passage. He instructed the company to remain absolutely silent. His back disappeared around the first bend, and he suddenly reappeared, scrambling as fast as he could through the passageway.

"A bear has followed us into the pass. The way was narrow, but it has persisted and is nearly upon us. If it gains the cavern, we are lost! Gather what you can and follow the path taken by the First. I will gain you some time." Saying that he sheathed his sword and took up his shield returning to the entrance to the cavity and wedging his shield between the narrow passage walls." "If it gets this far, I can hold it while you make your escape. Move. Quickly! Now!" He wedged the shield in a position that would halt the bear's progress for a while. But if it was as determined as it seemed to be, it would make short work of the wooden shield. Leaving nothing between the company and it except Derwyn. And his sword. The company gathered their packs and scurried through the passage after the First and Aedan. Trevelyan ushered the girls ahead of him and handed them a lit torch. Derwyn crouched behind his wedged shield awaiting the bear. Trevelyan could smell it before he heard it beyond the nearest bend in the path. It came into view slowly as it lumbered through the passage, squeezing itself between the walls. It looked crazed and half starved. Which would explain the efforts it was making to get to them. If it gained the cavern, Derwyn would be lost and the rest of the company in danger. Trevelyan could see its eyes. Avid with the promise of a meal. It was almost upon Derwyn and his shield, but Trevelyan could not leave. Could not let Derwyn die. Once the bear had reached Derwyn's shield, it clawed and ravaged the wood and steel with its claws and teeth. It could smell Derwyn beyond its reach, and its hunger unleashed its fury on anything between it and its meal. Derwyn was thrusting his sword either side of the shield, but the walls of the passage restricted his movements, causing nothing but glancing blows on the bear. The sound of splintering wood echoed throughout the cavern as the shield began to deteriorate. Mere feet stood between Derwyn and the crazed bear as it brought its mighty paw down on what remained of the shield and crushed it into shards. Trevelyan left his position next to the exit of the cave and grabbed Derwyn by his tunic, dragging him across the floor of the cave moments before the bear's head emerged into the cavity. Trevelyan helped Derwyn to his feet and pulled him to the exit. The bear, in its fury, lunged into the cave and caught itself between two outcrops of rock that jutted out of the wall at right angles. They would crumble at any moment, but right now it stopped the bears advance. Trevelyan shouted "Run!" to Derwyn, who had no choice if he did not want to bar Trevelyan's exit from the cave and the bear. They followed the passage in almost total darkness. Only the reflection of the torch given to the girls by Trevelyan, gave any light up ahead. If the bear broke through into the cave, it would be on them in a heartbeat. Fearing to turn around, Trevelyan ran as fast as the terrain would allow on the heels of Derwyn. Out of pure instinct, he turned his head as he ran to see if he was being pursued. The light fell upon the bear's mighty fangs in a slobbering mouth, only seconds away from Trevelyan's back. He almost stumbled as he took in the bear's proximity and raised a hand behind him as if it could ward him from death! Without making a conscious decision to do so, he called fire from his outstretched arm. Just in time to see the bear almost upon him, its mouth open in a killing lunge. He felt time stand still as if it were his last moment and mentally made a pushing gesture in his mind toward the bear. In an instant, the bear roared in pain as fire engulfed it. Its fur accelerating the inferno, casting shadows. Immediately, it fell in a fireball. Roaring in agony. Lighting the passage for Derwyn and Trevelyan to make their escape. The smell of burning hair and flesh followed them down the passage toward the dying light at the end of the tunnel. Night was falling as the company approached the exit of the caves that led to the other side of the mountain. The First held the company back in the caves until the light had dissipated altogether and darkness reigned. Derwyn and Aedan explored beyond the cave entrance for signs of the Sentinel Guards.

The company rested for a while before the Wardens returned and reported that the pass was clear. Cadarn lay to the east. They would stay close to the mountain, avoiding the plains that led to the Citadel, as the Sentinels were surely on the lookout by now. There were several leagues between the pass and the harbour. Once again, they must travel in silence. If Trevelyan did not execute his plan now, he would be drawn further away from his goal. But how to escape the company without alerting the Wardens or the First eluded him. The company readied itself in silence, discarding unwanted items at the northern entrance to the pass. They took with them only what they needed for the last leg of their journey. The First held palaver with the other Wardens while the rest of the company waited, ready to move westward and to the harbour. The First stopped mid sentence... The thunder of horses! The sound grew steadily closer from the east, and voices could be heard carried on by the wind. They were coming this way. "Conceal yourselves," the First warned, trying to be as quiet as possible as the company took refuge behind the rocks that littered the base of the mountain. No sooner had they hid than the first of the horses appeared, followed by another three Sentinel Guards carrying lit torches. They remained on horseback, but two of them drew up close to the mountain, peering into the darkness that swallowed the light from their torches. The company remained deathly still and held their breath. The riders passed slowly, searching for the company or any other travellers upon the pass. If Trevelyan were to extricate himself from the rest of the company, now would be the time to do it, he thought to himself. As they passed the company moving further westward, the First signalled the company to retreat back into the hidden cave and darkness. One by one, they returned to the cave, and the girls huddled together. The First sounded solemn as he addressed the company. "We must remain here until the riders return the way they came and pass us once again. I fear they are searching for us and are aware we may make for the harbour. These caves are unknown to most, and our chances of being discovered are slim at best while we remain here. If the gods are good, we may still be able to reach the harbour before daylight returns. If not, we must make the best of it, as there are no hidden paths to take but the plains. Darkness is our shield. Our chances of success are greatly exaggerated if we can depart here before the light. I suggest that you sleep if you are able. The Wardens and I will watch for the riders return. Be ready to move at a moment's notice, as time is now against us." With that, he instructed Aedan and Derwyn to find places above the cave from which to watch for the riders return. The First left the cave to search for a path that would provide as much cover as possible before reaching the plains. Leaving Trevelyan and the girls alone to await instruction. This would be his chance. If he hoped to leave undetected, at least for a short while, this would be the ideal opportunity. He had already decided that he could not leave without explanation, and thanks to the First, the Wardens, and the girls for their acceptance of him and their unfortunate predicament caused by him. He gave the Wardens and the First time enough to be otherwise occupied before he made his way to the girls huddling together for warmth. He leaned toward Brigid and whispered to her.

"Tell the First that I cannot allow anyone else to die or be punished on my behalf. I will provide a distraction for you all to make for the harbour. I don't know if I will ever see any of you again, but I cannot thank you enough for all that you have done and been through on my behalf. I must put an end to all of this before things get worse and someone else is killed." Without waiting for any reply, he nodded to the girls and slunk out into the night.

Chapter Twenty seven

The descent from the top of The Rive was slow and laborious. Saeth led the way with the horses tied one to the other in single file, followed by Caerwyn at the rear. Aderyn lay draped and bound on the horse, directly behind Saeth. Between the two trailed a rope; in the unlikely event that Aderyn should fall from his horse and topple off the steps, Saeth would act as an anchor. Saeth feared for Aderyn's survival. He was barely alive, and his wounds had festered. He urged the horses on briskly, impatient to reach the lowlands. Within half a day, they had gained Mid Ward, and Aderyn was quickly taken to the healers. Saeth, with Caerwyn in tow, rushed to Ysbail with the First's warning of the coming Sentinels. Saeth described events after leaving Mid Ward several days ago and what had occurred in Dryweryn.

"What of my son, Saeth?" Ysbail asked anxiously, "Does he live?"

"He does, my lord," answered Saeth. "He makes for Highlands Harbour through the hidden pass. Aedan and Derwyn accompany him, along with the Wayfarer and two young girls. Twin daughters of Tristan, slain in defence of Aderyn by Macsen of the Guard. He has ordained Brigid and Gwenith as prospect wardens upon their request. It was Tristan who warned us of the Macsen's presence in Dryweryn, therefore sparing our lives. Aderyn took it upon himself to confront Macsen, hoping to reason with him. The First advised against this, but Aderyn would not heed him. When we heard of Tristan's death and Aderyn's punishment, the First instructed me to aid Aderyn if I could, but to hasten here with warning. He intends to gain passage to Garreg Ddu and then to 'Old Stones' where there is to be a great gathering of the clans. Goronhyr Gwillt has demanded conclave. A dark power has arisen in the west; he believes is a threat to all Hiraeth. The First intends to present Gafyn Trevelyan to the conclave." When he had spoken, Saeth bowed to Ysbail and asked, "What do you command of me, my lord?"

"You must depart Saeth, and quickly. Few have seen you arrive, and fewer must see you leave. Will your ward leave with you? If he remains, we will do our best to conceal him, but I fear for us all if he is discovered," muttered Ysbail.

"I would not linger and endanger you further." Said Caerwyn abruptly. Breaking his habit of sullen silence. "If Saeth is to leave, I would leave with him. I have nothing left upon this Isle." Saeth nodded his approval.

"Then it is settled. Where will you go?" Ysbail asked.

"West Ward and passage to Garreg Ddu. From there to 'Old Stones' where I will unite with the other Wardens," Saeth said.

"Take what you need from the keep before you leave but leave swiftly. When you unite with my son, tell him..." He paused as if struggling, "Tell him I wish him well".

"It will be done, my lord." Saeth replied as he bowed. "And the priest, Aderyn? Will he live?" asked Saeth.

"My healers say that he should have died during the journey here. The very fact he did not breeds hope. His wounds will be treated, and he has been given relief from his pain, but his survival is dependent upon his will. Were it me in his place, perhaps it would be better to..." Here he trailed off. Saeth nodded once more and bowed before Ysbail. Turning, he took Caerwyn by the arm and ushered him out into the cold night air. They left Ysbail behind to make his preparations for the arrival of the sentinels.

Saeth led the way through the Ward, between the dwellings and meeting halls, to the large stone built keep within the centre of the Ward. "Behold. Nestor's Keep. The first structure built on the Isle by Nestor the prophet." Saeth sneered. "In my opinion, the only thing of benefit he did. In times of peril, the entire Ward can hold fast within for a year or two, fully provisioned. The walls cannot be climbed, and the only entrance protected by several murder holes." "Will it be necessary when the Sentinels arrive?" asked Caerwyn.

"No." Saeth replied with a wry smile. "Should the Arch Warden feel the Ward is under threat, both he and the remaining wardens are more than capable of defending themselves and the ward. He may appear an old man, but he can still best the First Warden in a contest of arms." They were within the keep's walls now, and Saeth headed straight to the armoury.

"Take what you need, Caerwyn, but be swift. We will travel on foot, so only what you can easily carry. I have a wife and child to visit before we leave. I will also get food and water. Meet me at the keep entrance." With that, Saeth disappeared beneath one of the arches, leaving Caerwyn to peruse the weapons and various armour at his disposal. He chose boiled leather, light chain armour, and a light but sturdy sword. He slipped a dagger beneath his belt and picked a bow and quiver full of arrows before heading back the way he came. Leaving the cold stone behind and emerging into the daylight once more. Caerwyn donned his armour and adjusted his belt to accommodate the sword and sheath. He slung the bow and quiver across his shoulder. When Saeth joined him outside the keep, he was ready and eager to get underway. Saeth shared the rations and water between them and inspected Caerwyn's choice of weapons and armour. Suitably impressed, he slapped Caerwyn on the back and said, "If your father could see you now, he would be proud indeed." Instantly regretting his words the moment they left his lips. Caerwyn gave a grim smile and nodded his thanks.

"Have you crossed the borders of the Isle before Caerwyn, son of Tristan?" asked Saeth, in an effort to get the boy talking. He had said few words since he joined with the Warden outside Dryweryn Township, and Saeth did not wish to leave him to brood.

"Before our meeting, I had seldom left the borders of home." He replied, sounding a little sullen, but then took a deep breath and sighed. "Now I find there are no borders I would not cross." He offered the Warden a timid smile and bowed to him. He straightened himself and held Saeth's gaze. "I thank you, Warden, for your kindness and service. If on our journey I can repay that which I owe, I shall do so with humility."

Saeth let out a hearty laugh before replying. "Fear not, boy, I shall see to it that you do." He clapped Caerwyn on the back once more, and they made their way to the western gate. Saeth wondered to himself if the boy knew how to swim. They would find out soon enough.

Chapter Twenty eight

After leaving the girls in the cave, Trevelyan headed straight on to the plain. When he felt the stone and gravel disappear beneath his feet, replaced by soil and grass, he turned left and eastward, toward Cadarn and the Citadel. It did not matter now if he was seized along the road by the Sentinel Guard. In fact, it would make things easier for him, as he did not know where he should be going. So, he continued eastward in plain view, in the hope of capture. Before he summoned Tyst, he once again wanted to give himself a little time in which to prepare the questions he would ask. The irony of what he was attempting was not lost on him and carried more than a risk to himself. People had died protecting him from the sentinels and the Citadel. Here he was marching straight toward them with no real idea of what he was to do when he got there. He supposed that the sentinels were not under instruction to slay him where he stands. If the Magister and the Citadel had been awaiting his arrival for centuries, he supposed they would want to at least behold this abomination before torture and death. Since he had ascended to Hiraeth, Trevelyan had not had any time to think about his position here. Things had moved from one event to another without his participation, other than going with the flow. He had almost forgotten about his burned and broken body back at Bryngaer and the life there that awaited him. He had tried on several occasions to decide whether the land and the life that were in Hiraeth were real in any sense of the word. Was he lying on the sanctum floor, drooling, in some kind of fantastic coma? Were these events and predicaments no more than some kind of projection from his traumatised mind? Things here felt more real than the things in the real world he left behind. Here he was complete and undamaged. Here he was Gafyn Trevelyan…Wayfarer. Back in the real world, he was Gafyn Trevelyan, a burned and broken freak. Perhaps he was naive, thinking that he could walk around this new Eden, enjoying the sights and sounds and acting like a damn tourist. He had no idea that there would be consequences to his actions here as in the real world! All the consequences of his thoughtless actions had led him to being all but destroyed. At a time when he should have been living life to the full, enjoying his newfound wealth. That he should end up in another world created by his parents, and make the same mistakes he had before, seemed almost to amount to some kind of cosmic stupidity. It was time to take at least some control of the events surrounding him when people were suffering in his name. The way he saw it, one of two things would likely be the outcome of his plan. Either he would be captured and killed. Or he would confront his captors and end them with power. The outcome did not really matter to him at this moment in time. Just as long as this pursuit ended, and his companions could continue with the lives they lived before they ever encountered the Wayfarer and his legacy. If indeed he were to be taken and sacrificed on the altar of the Citadel then he would awaken hungry and parched in his blackened husk of a body but otherwise unchanged, But then… would he?

If he died here in Hiraeth, would he return to his physical body? Perhaps not. Perhaps he would end up comatose or otherwise lost to himself. It did not matter. It had to end. Trevelyan could not stand the responsibility for the lives of others. He barely felt responsible for his own life. He was caught in self conflict. A broken life back in Bryngaer or a life of accountability here in Hiraeth. If he stayed here, he would accumulate more death on his hands. The deaths of others who worked to protect him, save him, or otherwise try to help. Tristan, Aderyn… lives altered immeasurably because of him. When he first ascended to Hiraeth, he imagined a playground for himself full of wonders and miracles. Somewhere he could escape from his other life of deformity and pain. To walk in his parents' creation like some tourist in a heavenly garden. The reality was somewhat sobering in the beginning. The realisation that others had suffered the consequences of his arrival was enough to bring him to his senses. He must return to Bryngaer. Leave all this behind. Close the journals, lock the sanctum, and never open either again. Be content to know that his refusal to ascend was enough to keep people safe from those who would harm him. If he could end the cycle of death and punishment caused by the Sentinels before he returned to the real world, then all the better.

Before he could summon Tyst to answer his erudite questions, he heard the sounds of horses behind him. Without turning to face them, his first instinct was to run. To hide, but that would avail him nothing more than to prolong the threat over himself and the rest of the company. At least if he allowed himself to be captured, it should earn the First and the Wardens enough time to reach the harbour and freedom. He was quite sure that he would be taken to the Citadel for questioning by the Magister and therefore deflect any attempt to catch the others. Tyst would have to wait. Along with his questions. Within moments, the first of the riders rushed passed him and turned to block his path. The man on horseback faced him squarely, with a sly smirk growing as he studied his quarry. He was bald, but not old. His face was hard, lined with cruelty and spite. The rest of the guards had surrounded him within moments, and he stood his ground. He never took his eyes off the man before him. Instinctively, he knew that he was standing before Macsen of the Guard. The man who had slain Tristan and maimed Aderyn so terribly. One look at the man's steely gaze told Trevelyan this was not a man to anger. He also felt quite sure that as long as he offered no resistance, he would not be harmed. At least until he reached the Citadel. "Where are your traitorous companions, Wayfarer?" spoke Macsen, his voice deep and dark. He was smiling at Trevelyan, but there was no humour in it. That smile told Trevelyan all he needed to know about Macsen of the Guard. He had his man.

"They drove me away before we reached The Rive. They returned to Mid Ward, but would not allow me to remain with them. I had caused them more than enough sorrow," Trevelyan said, unabashed by Macsen's glare. "I have come to face the judgement of the Citadel alone."

Macsen's eyes showed his surprise, but only for a single moment. His smile had never left his face, but now that smile turned into an all-out grin as his eyes narrowed, and he barked, "Seize this wretch," to his men. Trevelyan was taken, and his hands bound. A blindfold was tied around his head, and he was forced to march between the Sentinels as they made their way to the Citadel.

Chapter Twenty nine

The First and the Wardens arrived back at the cave, having scouted as far along the ridge of the pass as would allow. The girls were, as the First left them, huddled together for warmth. The two twins were visibly upset as Olwyn announced the Wayfarers departure and his reasons for doing so. The First had seen him leave the safety of the cave and wander down the pass and onto the grassy plains that led to the Citadel. He had already guessed his purpose, but it was too late to stop him. Not long after he had gained the plains, the First saw the guards on his trail and knew they would intercept him before he reached the Citadel. Unwilling to let Trevelyan seek his own death at the hands of the Magister for the sake of the company, the First elected Aedan to follow in pursuit and observe the outcome of this madness. He reasoned that either the Wayfarer would dispatch the enemy with power and would therefore need assistance in finding the company before they depart. Or would be himself overcome and put to death for the crime of being a stranger in a strange land. Either way, the First would need to know Trevelyan's fate before he addressed the gathering of the clans at Old Stones. In the meantime, the rest of the company would proceed to Highlands Harbour and meet the man with whom Tristan had entrusted his daughter's escape. The First was no stranger to Highlands Harbour and had friends on whom he could depend if things got rough.

Aedan departed swiftly and was lost in the twilight within moments. The First and Derwyn urged the weary girls on to their feet and out of the cave, following the ridge as far as possible westward and to the harbour. With the highlands under the Sentinels control, the harbour was sparsely guarded, which the First found slightly unsettling. But with no other course to follow, he held his resolve and picked their way through the foothills of the mountains until they reached the road that led to the harbour just over the next rise. He and Derwyn removed their leather armour and concealed their swords beneath their tunics so as not to draw any unwanted attention on their way to the port. The man they were to meet was named Caradog, Captain of The Morrigan. A cargo ship bound for 'Ynys Ysbryd' more commonly known as the Haunted Isle. When meeting Caradog, the First was instructed by Tristan to hand him a small white stone along with the cost of passage he had given the First. This was a prearranged signal that would prove that they were indeed sent by Tristan and should be treated with secrecy. They passed through the town like ghosts, moving silently toward the dock. Once the First had identified the ship, they waited at a safe distance. The First watched the comings and goings aboard the ship. Once he was satisfied they were in no danger, he made his approach. Derwyn and the girls waited on the dock while the First sought out the old harbourmaster. For a small donation, he acquired the information he was looking for before he boarded the ship and requested parlance with the captain. He was greeted by a large, muscular, and battle hardened man introduced to him as 'Captain Caradog, seadog, and sailor'. The First and the captain retired to the captain's quarters in privacy. The First shook hands with the captain, and they spoke pleasantries for a minute or two before the captain asked outright, "Are you my forbidden cargo, and if so, where are the twins?"

"They are safe." replied the First without elaborating, but never breaking eye contact with the captain. The captain shrugged as though he couldn't care less and proffered his hand out for payment. The First handed him the small bag and, with it, the small white stone Tristan had given him. The captain received the bag but discarded the stone to the deck before opening the bag and inspecting the contents. All seemed to be in order, and the captain smiled and said,

"Then let us depart these shores, I am eager to get underway. Fetch these girls, and I will stow you below deck," he announced, stuffing the bag roughly in his pocket. The First nodded silently and departed the ship to rejoin the others. They were as the First had left them, tired and hungry, waiting along the harbour but out of sight. To Derwyn, he said. "There is treachery afoot here. The man I met was captain perhaps, but not of the seas. He had the hands and demeanour of a soldier, not a sailor. I have known enough of both to know the difference." He paused for a moment, considering his next move. "I have knowledge of another, smaller vessel departing now and bound west. I will not risk the 'Morrigan' although I have paid passage. I will barter passage across the sea on this other vessel. The girls will cook and clean, and we will deckhand until we gain Garreg Ddu. Are you willing?" Derwyn snapped himself to attention and nodded in silent acquiescence. While the man who claimed to be 'Captain Caradog sea dog and sailor' awaited his quarries arrival, the First, Derwyn, and the girls were leaving port aboard a small barque westward bound.

Chapter Thirty

Trevelyan marched many leagues, surrounded by the Sentinel Guard with Macsen at its helm. He was kept at a running pace between the horses without respite or rest. Trevelyan was almost at the point of collapse when the horses began to slow to a canter and finally stopped. He was brought to a halt outside a large domed building surrounded by various trees in blossom. Beautiful in contrast to the stark white stone of the Citadel. Macsen dismounted, took hold of Trevelyan's arm, and roughly dragged him, gasping and panting from exhaustion, through the large entrance to the Citadel. Trevelyan paid no heed to his surroundings as he was manhandled through various chambers and dragged into the antechamber that made up the central dais of the Citadel. He was thrown to the ground within the centre of this chamber and ended up on his back, staring up at the large domed ceiling held up by various arches.

Macsen bowed low to an unseen witness to this abasement and announced, "Behold, Magister! Here lies the threat of doom and destruction that has harried Hiraeth since the days of Nestor and his prophecy." He sneered. "Here lies the great Wayfarer, prostrate at your feet, harmless as a child!" The derision in his countenance said more than the words he spoke as he cut Trevelyan's bonds. A chuckle was heard in the shadows of the great hall. Followed by another and then another that turned into spiteful laughter that echoed throughout the chamber. The owner of that laughter emerged from the silhouettes. Trevelyan twisted his face toward the sound of laughter only to be greeted by a short, enormously fat man dressed in golden robes and adorned with jewellery, rings on every finger, and chains of office gathered about his voluminous neck.

"I thank you, Macsen; you have outdone yourself yet again, my most faithful servant; your rewards will be great. The Citadel applauds your worthiness." He said, his voice deep and rheumy. "Food and rare wine await you and your guards in the feasting rooms. Women also await those who have gifted me this boon. Use them to sate your lusts and avarice, and leave this cur to me." He licked his lips as he spoke quietly, but his voice echoed throughout the chamber, resounding back down upon Trevelyan from the domed roof above.

Macsen bowed deeply once more. "I am ever your servant, my Magister." And with that, he left Trevelyan sprawled on the floor still gasping for breath at the feet of this corpulent little man. The Magister delivered a small kick to Trevelyan's midriff as he circled him, chortling to himself. "Ah... at last we meet Gafyn Trevelyan. Or should I call you Wayfarer...hmmm." The amusement in his voice was unmissable as he mocked the man that lay before him. Trevelyan remained silent and held the Magister's superior gaze, still breathless but more alert. "Now that you have gained your wish to appear before me, I ask you... what now?" The disdain in his voice angered Trevelyan, but still he remained silent. The Magister was right, though, he had fulfilled his plan but had no idea what to do next. "I think you are somewhat out of your depth, Wayfarer. Can you feel your fate as it crowds around you?" All the time the Magister taunted Trevelyan, he walked in a circle around him, forcing Trevelyan to shift his position in order to see the fat, bulging man sneering down at him. "All of your choices have brought you here. Defenceless and alone." He chuckled again. "And yet my lord and master's manipulations have hardly even begun!" Now the chuckle broke out into a bubbling laughter that chilled Trevelyan's blood. "You find yourself in a most untenable position, do you not?" He turned to hold Trevelyan's gaze, and his beady eyes narrowed in that fat face, turning his countenance into something subliminally more threatening. "Your silence will not save you".

Trevelyan slowly raised himself to his feet and faced the Magister squarely, causing him to stop circling Trevelyan and to stand still and face him in return. Neither of them spoke for a moment as they sized each other up. The Magister looked around the age of fifty or so, but his manner proved the lie of his appearance. He held himself as a much taller, younger, and slimmer man than the one who now faced Trevelyan. But the smirk that lined his face was unchanged. "Come now, Gafyn," as he spoke he watched Trevelyan's face for some kind of recognition of the danger he was in. "Let us discuss this matter as men of honour. I know more about you than you may guess. For instance, I know that you allowed yourself to be reduced to naught but blackened, twisted flesh at the hands of a mewling whore." He raised his eyebrows as he spoke, relishing Trevelyan's obvious shock and incomprehension. "Yes, Wayfarer, yes. I know all about you and your withered arm and disfigured flesh." He almost spat the words as he spoke them. "I know of your fate in your home world and your reasons for entering Hiraeth. I mean...look at you! A complete and, may I add, somewhat handsome man here. The mighty Wayfarer... a man to be feared! Although I cannot see why." He sneered again, "But back there, you are nothing more than a pain addled wretch too cowardly to end your life and spare those who gaze upon you the discomfort of your face." The maliciousness in his voice was unmistakable.

Trevelyan had remained silent in the midst of the ridicule poured upon him by this fat pustule of a man. Now he had regained his purpose and found he was being drawn into a confrontation. "Fuck you." He spat in retaliation. "Either fight me or shut the fuck up." Instinctively, he stuck his hand in his pocket and held the acorn given him by Anwedd tightly against his leg. His confidence in the face of his adversary was not lost on the Magister. Trevelyan noticed a flash of fear in those beady, cunning eyes, but only for a moment, and then it passed, replaced once again by his mocking derision.

"Fight you!... Oh no, Wayfarer. I am not here to fight you! If I wished for your demise, do you really believe you would have gained The Rive before I brought my hand down against you and your companions? No Wayfarer. I have spared your life and those you travelled with so that I may offer you a bargain." As he spoke, Trevelyan could feel a thousand calamities crowding around him.

"Bargain...what bargain?" He asked, nonplussed.

"I offer you your life. And those of your companions who, even as we speak, are aboard ship in Highlands Harbour waiting to set sail across the sea." He stopped speaking to let the weight of his words sink in. "I have replaced the captain and crew of the ship with men faithful to the Citadel." He chuckled to himself once more. "One word from me and they will have their throats slit in the dead of night and be thrown overboard to feed the fish." He met Trevelyan's eyes to ensure that he understood his position. "Including the two twin girls that joined your company at Dryweryn. I had hoped to interrogate them myself as I hear rumours that they possess 'Nwyfre'." Trevelyan did not understand the reference made by the Magister but chose to ignore it for now. "It is sooth that Nestor saw far in his prophecy, but my lord and master Diras sees further still," he sneered. "The Hazard I set at The Rive centuries ago was but a trifle compared to the delights that would await you should you refuse my bargain." He paused for a moment to let Trevelyan process this statement. The look of shock on Trevelyan's face filled the Magister with mirth, and his amusement echoed around the dais of the Citadel, resounding louder until its echoes faded. "Yes Wayfarer...It was I who accompanied Nestor on his journey east. It was I that helped him found the keep, and the watchtowers on the lower land, and it was I that smothered him in his sleep as he grew old and decrepit. I alone commanded the building of this Citadel and created the Sentinel Guards to serve me. It was I who waited centuries for your arrival. So that I may complete my purpose in service to my lord and master."

"Gideon Slay. You are Gideon Slay!" Trevelyan blurted, trying to understand what was happening.

"Indeed, Wayfarer, I am at that. I am surprised that the unseen one who travels with you did not alert you to my presence." Once again, he allowed the news of his awareness of Tyst to settle on Trevelyan. "Even now he stands beside you, silent and unseen...Helpless to intercede. As ignorant and impotent as you! Has it not occurred to you, Wayfarer, that he attends you in hope that you will complete your destiny and destroy all that has been created here? Only you can release him from his long service by ending Hiraeth... Show yourself, beggar!... Deny your blasphemy in the presence of your equal!"

Trevelyan looked helplessly around the dais, searching for a sign of his companion. "Tyst?" He asked aloud. With this, Tyst materialised next to Trevelyan, adopting his usual stance of leaning on his staff but spoke directly to the Magister in dark monotones.

"If I am to be summoned, it will not be by you, worm!" Tyst said. This made the Magister chuckle all over again.

"You name yourself Testament and so cannot deny the truth of my words...Hmmmm?" He licked his lips again, almost in anticipation of the long moments that lay ahead. Tyst remained as he was in silence. Neither confirming nor denying the Magisters accusation. "And so, Wayfarer, to my bargain...I will spare your life and the lives of your companions on one condition." He paused here, relishing Trevelyan's apprehension. "That you leave Hiraeth now and vow never to return." His tone of voice suggested it was a simple choice, but his carnivorous eyes told another story as he licked at his lips feverishly.

Trevelyan was speechless. It was more than he could have hoped for. He expected some kind of sacrifice of his friends, himself, or some other equally damning cost, but this! "How do I know that you will keep your end of the bargain should I accept?" He said as confidently as he could, trying to hide his relief.

"The beggar beside you knows the truth of it." Returned the Magister looking directly at Tyst. He turned his gaze on Trevelyan and licked his lips once more for good measure. "What say you to my terms?...Hmmmm."

Trevelyan turned to Tyst. The question written across Trevelyan's face meant that no asking was necessary. Tyst nodded in answer, but his eyes never left the Magister. Before he agreed, Trevelyan asked, "If I agree, how can I leave now? The threshold is on the far end of Hiraeth, at least two days' travel.

"That is not of your concern, Wayfarer. I ask again...Do you agree to my terms?" replied the Magister his face almost quivering in anticipation. Danger crowded around Trevelyan as he tried to guess the trap that he felt was close at hand but could not reason. As if in answer to his growing apprehension, the Magister barked," My patience grows thin." All signs of mirth gone. Trevelyan's head spun. Could he trust the Magister to hold true to his word? His choices seemed damned from the outset but in the end he blurted. "I agree!"

At this Gideon Slay seemed to almost grow in stature, his obese frame swelling with self pride. "Then it is done!" he shouted elatedly, and Trevelyan's heart lurched. "My lord and master saw far indeed and in sooth. For here within this very chamber is a threshold that will relay you to your home world. If you are willing or no, I insist we begin"

As though time were a factor, the Magister all but bundled Trevelyan beneath the largest of the four arches holding up the dome and bid him to remain still. Before the Magister could begin whatever he had in mind, Trevelyan turned to Tyst. With so many questions about Gideon Slays admission that Tyst wishes him to bring an end to Hiraeth, his last question to Tyst was, "Will he keep his word, Tyst? Will the First and the others be safe aboard ship?"

Tyst straightened himself upon his staff and replied. "Gideon Slay has achieved his end, Wayfarer. The company will be safe." He fell into silence once more without offering his companion a farewell. Instead, Tyst held Trevelyan with a gaze that seemed full of contradictions, but his mouth let a small, cryptic smile creep through his aged mien, and he was gone from sight.

The Magister Gideon Slay stood before Trevelyan and said, "The power you hold eludes you, does it not?" Even now, in his victory, the mocking tone returned to his voice. "Fear not, wretch. Although I do not have theurgy equal to your own, I do have the means to access yours briefly." Something in his eyes and the frantic licking of his lips alarmed Trevelyan. Perhaps this is where his bargain would betray him, but now, of course, it is too late. Gideon Slay stepped forward, raised his bloated, fat forefinger, and touched Trevelyan's forehead lightly. Instantly, he was lost in a blaze of white light. He fell into the same ocean of nothing that awaited him back in the ward at the Hospital when he first awoke after the fire. But there were differences...instead of the nothingness, there were clouds and skies and... buildings? Was he back home? He did not recognise any of the streets or houses that he saw. Suddenly he was arching downward at a terrific speed. His incorporeal body passed through the roof of the house below and stopped dead above a sleeping woman in her bed. Her eyes suddenly opened, and a scream began to build in her throat. And then, just as suddenly, he was whisked away. Drawing her with him still screaming. Blackness followed, until he caught sight of Gideon Slay laughing beneath the Arch of the Citadel. He saw the woman being drawn behind him, roughly deposited on the ground beneath the Magisters feet. His face a crown of victory and glory. This was the trap. Slay had used Trevelyan's power to draw another from the real world here to Hiraeth. Trevelyan tried to aid the woman, but he could feel the pull of the threshold as it took him from the Citadel back into nothing. Before he translated completely, he gripped the acorn tightly in his grasp. He repeated Anwedd's name and felt the surge of fire within. He launched a devastating blaze of theurgy and fire at the Magister. Alighting his robes and melting his corpulent flesh. Before Trevelyan was gone, he saw the smile burn off Gideon's Slays face. Along with the rest of him. He saw the Citadel domed roof topple down on Gideon Slay and the woman. Then he was gone. Moments felt like days. Until, slowly, he became aware of the hard floor beneath his body. And the pain that crept in through the holes in his tortured psyche from the burned and twisted body he now possessed again.

∞∞∞∞

Miranda Brookes stood in the rain staring into the charity shop window she passed twice a day six days a week on her way from home to work and back. The same painting sat on the same stand in the same place never being bought or moved in all the time she has lived here. Six months was not that long admittedly, but she never failed to notice it. No matter how many people were on the street or how late she was, it always caught her eye. To the point of angering her inside the way only small details in life can anger you and for no fathomable reason. She had even considered a different route that would take her longer, to avoid walking past it and its inevitable call to her senses, but that was ridiculous. It was another ten minutes onto her journey and she was not going to be intimidated by a painting on a stand in a shop window. She even considered buying the damn thing even though it's subject matter was of no real interest to her. Still, it called to her. It was a watercolour painting of a sweeping landscape. The head of a vast hanging valley overlooked the lower lands and a large freshwater lake surrounded on both sides by glorious green mountains. Royal oak trees with large green leaves turned to the deep blue cloudless skies above. The painter had some talent without question but it was not that which drew her attention. It was that particular perspective. She was almost certain she had seen that very same scene many times from her earliest childhood but for the life of her she cannot remember where. To the left of the lower lands before the lake springs into view, she KNEW that a small bubbling river ran behind the headland. It ran out of sight before reaching the shimmering lake that mirrored the cloudless sky above in azure. She knew that the lake ended in the distance with a rocky outcrop that created a gushing waterfall into the river below. It was not the instinct of her overactive imagination. It was a fact. She had the inclination to buy the damn painting for some paltry sum and research the artist and location. It was that important to her for some reason, but at the same time it scared her more than a little and she could not say why! And so she continued to pass it by with her uneasy mental salute. Suffering the agony of it for a brief second, but today, here in the rain she could not pass it by. As she approached the shop on her commute, she had given up trying to avoid it and decided she would stop and take a long hard look at it in the hope it would be some kind of catharsis. Hoping to find some kind of flaw in its depiction of her memories, but on examination it confirmed her fears and worse. It was definitely a place she had visited many times. Even the sound of the rain when she looked at the painting turned into the sound of the babbling brook running down the valley unseen. She glanced at the periphery of the painting looking for a signature but found only a faint worn out scribble that was unintelligible.

The painting cost less than the taxi she had to hail to get the damn thing home without spoiling in the rain. She felt proud of herself for dealing with the situation, and even if she never cast her eyes on it again, at least she will not have to go through the anxiety it caused her to walk past it. When she arrived indoors and changed her wet clothes to dry, she took the picture and leant it against the bedroom wall. Face in so she did not have to see it. Was this what her sponsor had meant when she said that Miranda needed to start taking effective control of the small things that caused her stress or anxiety? So that in time she could build up to the bigger things? She would remember to ask her at the next meeting. After having an evening meal and reading for an hour or two she retired to bed and set her alarm for the following morning. As she closed her eyes she conjured before her the vista in the painting and walked barefoot down the valley toward the lake

∞∞∞∞∞

She had awoken early and to her surprise realised it was her day off work. That posed as many problems as it solved. At least at work she had a way of dampening her anxieties with repetition and solitude. Here, with a full day yawing before her needing to be filled, her anxieties would run riot crowding her thoughts. She dressed quickly and took a look outside the window to the busy streets below. Too many people and too much noise. She opened the window a little to let some air in. She watched the people busying themselves with all the pointless nonsense of modern living. She watched and wondered why we subject ourselves to all this charade. If we stopped for a moment and thought about the big picture, would we realise the truth? That all the stress and strain that we put ourselves through to get to the end of the day so that we can sit back and say we are doing great would silently kill us? She was no different than everybody else. Caught in the same spiral of self deception.

Thinking it will matter at the last minute, of the last hour, of the last day. When you have no time left, the biggest regret of all is the time you wasted. She wondered what time she would regret when it was her last minute. She sighed and turned from the window and pulled her tracksuit bottoms on and her gown around her as she got back into bed. No one to get up for. No kids, no pets, no partner, and today... no job. She already knew she was not leaving her bed until she had work on Monday. She glanced at the painting leaning against the wall and declared "And you can sod off too".

She had been clean and sober for over a year now. Learning how to deal with the depression and anxieties that plagued her daily and led to her long years of self-medicating with anything she could get her hands on. She had learned long ago that this creates more anxiety and depression along with a costly addiction. It took a long, long time for her to break this cycle. She used her qualifications to secure a job as an assistant librarian in the local university. That was a year ago. Although she has not fallen off the wagon, she has damn near thrown herself under the wheels a few times. With no help from illicit drugs, she must rely on her prescribed medications. Which, although she takes religiously, she still must deal with herself and her reactions to the life that goes on around her. She has to find a way of keeping herself busy to refrain from losing herself in her thoughts and emotions. Work was usually an effective way to beat the gnawing feeling inside her head, but on days like these, she felt very vulnerable. A slave to her own mind. Most people, when they hit the brick wall and breakdown have someone to help pick them up again. Family or friends or both. She had run from her parents at the earliest opportunity and had not stopped running from them since, in her mind if not her life. She had learned she was adopted at the same time she noticed the cruelty some people have inside them. Her salvation had been waved at her like a flag of victory since she could remember. How lucky she was that they had come along and taken pity on her. And the pity did not last long. There was never any love or nurture. Only a constant barrage of beatings and neglect. Until at age twelve, when her so-called father started to take an interest in her changing appearance. Her mother had noticed too, and the beatings got worse. It was not long after that she decided that if she stayed, she would become more of a victim than she was now. That was if her mother did not beat her to death first in a fit of jealous rage. This was her struggle now. No drugs to kill the pain or dull the senses. She still had to deal with her life and her head and keep up the impression that she is well balanced and in control. But she had gotten the feeling recently that the balance was slowly shifting. She was not at any crisis point. It was just her mind and its daily struggle to bring her down by going places she dreaded to visit. She had no control over it. She drew her gown around herself and returned to bed. She was not tired, but she felt less vulnerable like this. She did not want to participate in the weekend's events outside of her door and elected to stay in bed where it was safe and sound. She realised what kind of a figure she must present. A woman of her age should be out and about. Dinning with friends. Dating men, not locking herself away from the world until she was back in work. But the simple truth was that she did not fit in the outside world. She had no point of reference with which to form any kind of attachment. She knew if she were to disappear from this room today, never to return, there would be no one to mourn her. No one to remember her. She had no family other than the parents she had escaped. She had formed no friendships or relationships with other people through choice. She often felt anxiety when in the company of other people. She never knew what to say or how to act, forever feeling awkward and longing for her own company. She often wondered if one could get through a lifetime forming no attachments to others, only to die alone with no one to weep for you. She concluded it happens all the time. The people like her that can slip between the cracks of society and be forgotten about must exist in every corner of the world. The sad fact is that the broken had no place in modern society. No place in life! Those that sequestered themselves away from the others in an act of self-preservation are not welcome within the realms of the well-adjusted. She had chosen a job that she could undertake alone, keeping her out of reach of the general population and the distress they imposed. Sometimes she wondered if she were to slip away in her sleep would she be missed? Would the world be better off without her in it? Would it even notice? She had left the curtains drawn and decided to try to sleep some of the day away. She would deal with the night when it arrived.

    She settled back and drew the cover over her, in an effort to distance herself from everything outside of her head. She had been doing this from an early age, providing an escape from the trauma of childhood and her parents.

She would cover her head and play her internal film show she had produced, directed and starred in. She conjured up the image of the painting in her head, instead of the image she used as a child, because it seemed so real to her it would make it easier to escape into. She could recall every little detail of it. Even though she had only glimpsed it. She even recalled the small faded signature that was scribbled on the bottom right-hand corner. As she built those valleys and the lake beyond in her mind's eye, she could not help but wonder about the artist and his vision. She was drifting along those valleys when she felt a shift in her environment, like a blip in her film. She was no longer drifting horizontally now, but she was ascending… rapidly. The ground fell away in an instant and she was falling upwards. Dragged by some kind of riptide within her mind. And she was no longer alone! There was somebody with her! A Man! She could make out a face as she hurtled upward. He seemed to move in the opposite direction, but for a moment, they were face to face. She opened her eyes and screamed at the man before her, and then he was gone. Replaced by an ivory white dome and an impossibly fat man grinning like a fox about to shred the throat of his quarry. And then… Fire! Not just fire, but fury and desperation. The fat man's grin turned into a scream as he was engulfed with flame and wrath. She saw his flesh melt as his robes erupted ablaze. The fire did not stop there. It hit the dome of the chamber she found herself sprawled within and brought it down upon both the remains of the fat man and herself. Her last recollection is of the face of a man in torment. Trevelyan's face. And then nothing.

HERE ENDS PART ONE OF THE MAGICAL DIARIES.
Volume one

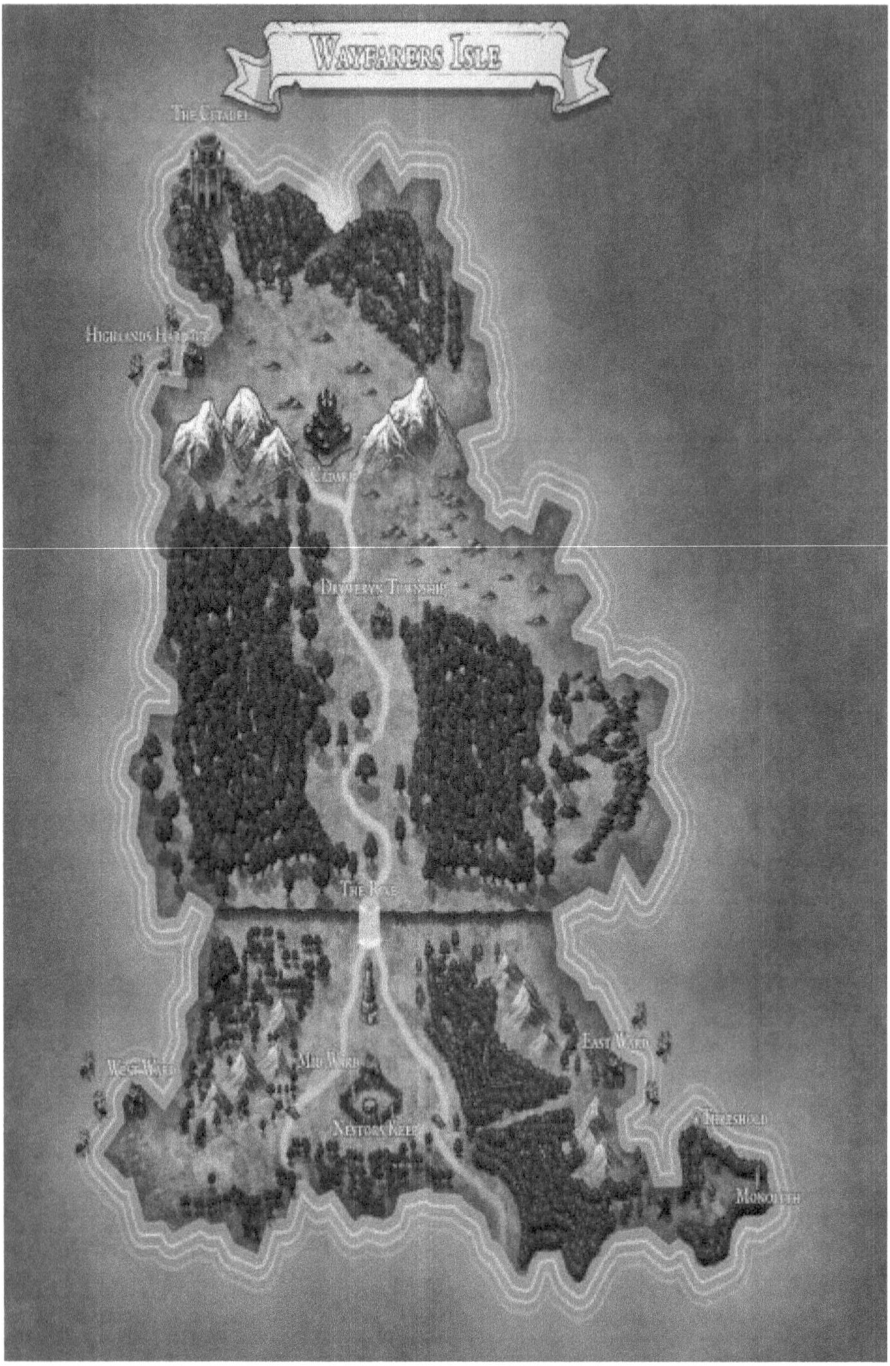
Wayfarers Isle
The Citadel
East Ward
Nestors Keep
Mid Ward

Don't miss out!

Visit the website below and you can sign up to receive emails whenever G.S Tabberner publishes a new book. There's no charge and no obligation.

https://books2read.com/r/B-A-ODWZ-ZNLMC

BOOKS 2 READ

Connecting independent readers to independent writers.

Milton Keynes UK
Ingram Content Group UK Ltd.
UKHW010633100124
435791UK00001B/75